HER SAVAGE SAVIOR

Yes, he was handsome, but there was no way Tara was going to believe this wild stranger was exactly what he seemed. Even if he had rescued her, taken her back to his cave and was trying to tend to her sprained ankle. Tara was sure he must be part of some clever hoax. "If you try *anything*, you'll be crying quicker than you can yodel, or yell, or whatever the hell Tarzan does."

He reached for her. "Don't . . ." She tried to pull away, but one hand locked around her calf while his deft fingers went to work on her throbbing ankle.

"You wouldn't happen to be a doctor doing a little acting on the side?" No response. "Maybe a cardiologist by day, and a Tarzan impersonator by night?" She was babbling, she knew, but she needed a distraction from the tingles racing up her leg from his touch. "I could really use a good cardiologist about now." She pressed a hand to her thundering heart, hoping to slow its beat. She tried to see past him, but he was too large, too close.

She fell back onto the fur rug and stared at the ceiling of the cave. The fire in her ankle blazed hotter, sending a blast of heat pulsing along her nerve endings. Her body trembled. It was an odd sensation, being tended to, handled by such a beautiful—if a bit feral—man.

Before she could dwell on the notion, he turned away and reached for a large club. A scene straight out of Stephen King's *Misery* flashed in her mind.

Whack! He brought the weapon down on a thin strip of wood, not her tender ankle, and her sudden panic eased.

"So you're a carpenter by day?"

Other *Love Spell* books by Kimberly Raye:
ONLY IN MY DREAMS

Something Wild

Kimberly Raye

LOVE SPELL BOOKS ◆ NEW YORK CITY

LOVE SPELL®

August 1998

Published by

Dorchester Publishing Co., Inc.
276 Fifth Avenue
New York, NY 10001

ISBN 0-505-52272-1

The name "Love Spell" and its logo are trademarks of Dorchester Publishing Co., Inc.

Printed in the United States of America.

Something Wild

Prologue

She came to him at night.

Always at night, when darkness fell and sleep drifted over the Great Smokies in a shroud of impenetrable mystery. When there was no more daylight to threaten his existence, to strip away the hearsay that surrounded him and turned him from a myth, a legend, into nothing more than the man he was.

Zane nestled into the bearskin and closed his eyes, his mind lulled by the buzz of night creatures, the whisper of the wind and the knowledge that he was safe. Hidden. Alone. It was always a time of peace for him, those first few moments when the sun gave way to the moon.

Until the shadows grew deeper and loneliness came to call.

The isolation circled him then, a vulture ready

to swoop down and pick his bones clean. And it would. He knew that fact just as surely as he knew that death waited for him beyond the mountains. His heart thundered. His breath came in quick, frantic gasps. Fear settled in his stomach, fed by the emptiness yawning deep inside him.

And then she was there, leaning over him. Pale, golden hair cascaded around her, shrouding her face so that she seemed little more than a shadow to keep him company. But she was more. Real.

The scent of her—fresh mountain water and wild daisies—filled his nostrils. Her breath, soft and shallow, slid into his ears. Her warm, lush body fit against his. Their hearts beat in perfect synchronization and they touched. Chest to breasts. Belly to belly. Man to woman.

For a few precious moments, she shattered the silence that was his life, the loneliness that defined his existence, and her very essence filled the hollowness inside of him.

"Love me," she whispered, her voice a sweet balm that soothed his hurt, his fear. He couldn't refuse her, couldn't turn away. She was the air that filled his lungs, the life that pumped through his veins, the only relief for that hot, hungry part of him that needed so desperately to possess her—

"No!"

Her image shattered and he bolted upright. He drank in the dark interior of the cave, and disappointment gnawed at his gut. Gone. She was gone!

"That is a good thing. Very good." The voice, so wise and familiar, thundered through his head, and he turned to see the raven perched in the open

mouth of the cave. Moonlight outlined the fierce black bird, making it seem bigger, stronger, the way he'd been so long ago. When he'd been alive. A man.

"You sent her away, Grandfather." The accusation roared in Zane's head, and he directed it full-force at his grandfather's spirit animal. *"You made her leave!"*

"She doesn't belong here. This is your place. Your life. Yours and yours alone. That is the way of things. The best way."

"Why does she come then? Who is she?" Zane begged.

The answers came as fiercely as the gust of frigid wind that marked the beginning of winter. The beginning of pain and sorrow and survival.

"She is death, and she comes to steal your soul."

Then the raven disappeared and darkness closed in. Pitch-black and absolute. But the night brought no safety, the solitude no comfort. Not since Zane had first dreamed of her.

Now sleep eluded him, and peace hovered just beyond his reach. He roused himself and left the cave to roam the mountainside like a lost animal sensing a coming storm. Restless. Anxious.

Alone. So very, very alone.

Chapter One

"Let me get this straight." Tara Martin paused, one hand on the latest fix for her ever growing appliance addiction—a cappuccino maker that whipped and foamed at the speed of light—and stared over the bar that separated her ultramodern kitchen from her classic starving-journalist living room. "You want me to go traipsing through the Smoky Mountains after King Kong?"

"It's Big foot, and forget I even asked." Lisa, a petite blonde with a short pixie hair-cut and vivid green eyes, plopped down on Tara's secondhand sofa. "It's a stupid idea anyway. I mean, you're busy." She reached for a box of tissues that sat on the crate that served as Tara's coffee table. "I shouldn't have come over here in the first place. You've got better things to do on a Friday night than listen to me cry on your shoulder."

Tara poured two cappuccinos and headed into the living room. "Yeah, the men are just beating down the door."

"Okay, so you haven't got anything better to do, but that's your own fault." Lisa shot an accusing look at the high-powered laptop sitting on the warped dining room table. "I doubt another Watergate will break and you'll miss it just because you took a few hours off for a date. But then who am I to give love advice?" Lisa hiccuped and took the mug Tara offered her. "When my own love life is going down the toilet right before my eyes."

"Don't you think you're overreacting a little?"

"I'm not overreacting; I'm desperate." Lisa wiped her puffy eyes and blew her nose. "But even so I know it isn't fair for me to expect you to give up your respectable job at the *San Diego Sun* to take off for two weeks to cover a tabloid trash story so that I can marry the man of my dreams."

"I thought you hated Ethan."

"That was last week, and it was just a little disagreement. He didn't really flirt with that waitress." Lisa sniffled and sipped her cappuccino. "He wants me; he said so. We're talking the big C." She started crying again, her tears plunking into her mug like fat raindrops. "I—I can't believe this. A man finally asks me to marry him, *the* man, and I can't because I have to work. Life really sucks."

"Ask your editor for a few days off."

"If I do, Fritz will hand over the story to Mitzi. She's been after my byline for two years now." She shook her head frantically, plunked her mug on the coffee table and blew her nose again. "That tramp will do anything to get a front page story. She even slept with Milton in the mail room just to get first look at the letters our readers send in about prospective stories."

"I didn't realize tabloid journalism was so dog-eat-dog."

"It's brutal. There are reporters out there who would cut off their arms for a chance to cover an alien landing in Montana, or that purported vampire running the string of tanning salons down in Texas, or that house in Syracuse allegedly being haunted by the ghost of Lassie."

"Lassie's ghost?" Tara widened her eyes in mock excitement. "Hey, I'd cut off my arms *and* legs for a chance at that one."

"Okay, so it's not the *Times*, but tabloid stories are big business, and it's better than writing obituaries, which is what I did in grad school. The *Squealer* pays the rent and keeps me in Dior suits. At least it did," she said, her bottom lip quivering. She grabbed Tara's hands. "Please, please, *please* do this for me. Just cover this one assignment while I elope to Vegas."

"Wouldn't you and Ethan like to take a few weeks and plan a real wedding? Flowers, bridesmaids, a cake . . ."

Lisa shook her head. "It's now or never. It's taken him three years to pop the question. If he has to wait, he's liable to change his mind."

"That's exactly why you should wait."

"Look who's talking, Miss I-married-the-first-bozo-who-asked-me-right-after-high-school."

"And it was the biggest mistake of my life. I was

only eighteen. I should have been out having fun, dating, *living*." Instead, she'd married a Neanderthal who thought a woman's sole purpose in life was to cook his dinner, clean his house and birth a litter of children. Bye-bye college and a career.

"Ethan isn't Merle," Lisa said as if reading Tara's thoughts. "He respects women and he really loves me, and he wants to be with me. Forever. Tonight, *if* you promise to cover for me."

"You know I'd love to go hunting for Tarzan—"

"It's Bigfoot, not Tarzan—I wouldn't wish that on you, not after Merle."

"I'm better at real news."

"This is real news, or it could be. Dozens of sightings have occurred in the Bear Creek area." Lisa wiggled her eyebrows. "I don't know about you, but it smells like an exclusive to me."

"You're just trying to bribe me."

"Is it working?"

"Not a chance. Besides, I've got the city council meeting to cover on Thursday; then there's the mayor's annual food drive on Saturday, and the police chief is giving a press conference on his new antidrug program. My next two weeks are completely booked."

Lisa's green eyes filled with fresh tears. "You're right. What kind of selfish, hateful person am I even to think you—a single, unattached woman with no family, not even a dog—could just take off and abandon everything? And all so that her best friend can live happily ever after." She sighed, a pitiful sound that—obvious ploy though it was—

tugged at Tara's conscience. "I might as well face it. I'm destined to be an old maid."

"A guilt trip is not going to work."

"Just put me out to pasture now."

"I'm not listening to this."

"Better yet, shoot me. That's what they do to old horses right before they ship the remains off to the glue factory—"

"All right." Tara might not agree with the idea of a happily-ever-after for herself, but who was she to deprive her best friend? "Call Fritz and tell him I'll take your assignment."

"You're the absolute best." Lisa squealed, throwing her arms around Tara's neck.

"I still think you and Ethan should wait."

"I'll note it for the record. Thank you, thank you, *thank you.*" When she leaned back and saw Tara's sour expression, she added, "It *could* turn out to be a real story, and if not, well, tabloid stories are actually fun. Think of it as an adventure. A vacation. You hop a plane, relax in a hotel room for a couple of weeks, order room service every night, watch cable TV, lounge by the pool, loll in the steam room—all expenses paid."

"Well, I haven't taken a vacation since I started with the *Sun,*" Tara conceded.

"See there? You're due, girlfriend. You've earned this trip. Let someone else cover that old stuffy city council meeting. You head to Tennessee and enjoy yourself, and make sure you check out all these names while you're there." She whipped out a list at least three pages long. "These

16

are people who've actually seen the Beast of Bear Mountain."

The Beast? Tara reached for a Hershey's kiss, and ignored the sinking feeling in her stomach. Okay, so it wasn't a Pulitzer-class assignment, and both her prizewinning parents would roll over in their graves at the prospect of their only child disgracing the family's journalistic credibility.

Then again, it wasn't as if she stood a chance of landing the award, not covering local human interest stories and Who's Who in the boring world of city government. Not with a mayor who kept his nose cleaner than Tara used to keep Merle's kitchen floor.

Think vacation, she told herself, attempting a smile. "Who needs good, solid, socially important issues when I can scarf down room service, laze by the pool, and traipse around after Godzilla?"

"That's the Beast."

"King Kong, Tarzan, Godzilla, the Beast . . . what's the difference?" She smiled. "They're all just myths. Everybody knows that."

"You owe me for this one, Lisa." Tara stepped off the bus at the foot of Bear Mountain, a towering mammoth in the heart of the Great Smokies, and stared at the broken-down building—little more than a one-room shack really—that housed the office of the town's sole motel. "Big-time," she muttered.

She straightened her full skirt, plucked her perspiration-damp blouse from her chest and blew at a loose tendril of hair that hung over one eye—all thanks to the *Squealer* and the unair-conditioned bus they'd commissioned to meet her at the airport in Knoxville. She scanned her surroundings, from the nearly impenetrable forest of trees, to the eyesore that called itself a motel. "We must have taken a wrong turn. This can't be right," she told the bus driver. "The itinerary said I'd be staying at the Marriott."

The driver, a fortyish man by the name of Jack Coates who chewed tobacco and drank black coffee—often at the same time—followed her off the bus and dropped her bags on the ground.

He let loose a stream of tobacco juice, then said, "Damn straight, little lady," and pointed to a rickety sign nailed to the far corner of the structure. THE MARY OTT MOTEL. He gestured to the row of similar units that stretched back into the trees. "Biggest motel this side of Bear Mountain. A whopping twenty rooms, if you count that one back yonder. 'Course, Cecil ain't quite finished the roof yet, but if you got a hankerin' to get back to nature, that's your room."

"I don't suppose there's a pool?" Or room service, or a steam bath, or anything else she'd been looking forward to.

"Nope, but Mary's got herself a pond just beyond them trees there. Good for skinny-dippin' or fishin', whichever you got an itch to try. Dug the thing herself about five years ago. Said the motel needed an added attraction. She and Cecil, her brother, started this place pretty near ten years ago. Made a decent livin' with the tourists and all, till them highway people come along and built

Route 10 over on the other side of the mountain.
It connects with the Blue Ridge Parkway that runs
clean through three states and links all these
mountain chains. Now everything bypasses Bear
Creek. Things been pretty tight for Mary and old
Cecil ever since." He let another stream of tobacco
juice fly and smiled. "Danged if she ain't gonna be
tickled from here to Texas to see you."

Her gaze swept the outside of the structure,
from the peeling canary yellow paint to one broken window, to the steady *drip-drop* of water coming from a leak in the porch roof. "Someone
actually lives here?"

"Sure 'nough, little lady. Hey, you want to get
my picture for that newspaper of yours?" He
puffed out his chest and struck a pose next to the
bus. "This is my I'm-a-damn-fine-lookin'-man
pose."

"Perfect." She pasted on her best smile and
grabbed the camera hanging around her neck. Go
through the motions, write a fluff piece about a
town's overactive imagination and her work
would be done. "Sure. So, have you actually seen
. . . *it?*"

"The Beast?" At her nod, he shook his head.
"Not myself, mind you. But Mabel Mercury, Mary's
nearest neighbor about ten miles down the road—"

"Ten miles?"

"Maybe twelve," he went on. "Anyhow, she spotted him a couple of times. Says he's as tall as one
of her Daddy's red spruce trees, and just as strong.
Picked up her watering trough one night and

threw it twenty feet before scooping up some of her livestock and carting them off. Probably for his dinner."

"Okay," she said, trying to get a mental profile. "What we're dealing with is tall and strong, with one hell of an appetite."

"True, and it ain't no *it*. It's a him."

"You know that for a fact?"

"Well, stories differ, mind you, but the one thing they all have in common is that *he* is awful rich, if you get my meaning." Jack winked at her.

"I'm afraid I'm not following you."

"He's got enough family jewels to start his own dynasty."

"Oh." She tried to ignore the sudden heat that swamped her cheeks. *Professional*, she told herself. *Ask questions, be cool and detached.* "Any other defining qualities?"

"Some say he's got hair all over, like a bear, only he ain't a bear."

"How do you know?"

" 'Cause folks around here know bears, and he ain't one. He runs with 'em, all right, but he ain't one. He's different. Meaner. Stronger. Just ask Mary and Cecil. They seen him. And the man they had out here from that newspaper over in Nashville. He saw him, too."

"Really?" She clicked off several more shots while Jack huffed and puffed and smiled and spit, and all the while the hair on the back of her neck stood on end as if someone watched her.

She glanced up at the bus window where Jack's twenty-something-year-old son—the only other passenger on the four-hour ride from the airport—stared back at her with a starstruck gaze and a lopsided smile. It wasn't every day the folks in Bear Creek met a real "highfalutin reporter," to quote Jack, Sr.

"How about you?" she asked Jack, Jr. "Have you seen the Beast?"

"Me?" He turned beet red, as if she'd just asked him out on a date. "Well, uh," he stammered. "Not really. I mean, I, uh, thought I saw something one time when I was out huntin'. Coulda been just an old bear—they's plenty around these parts—but I, uh, cain't say as I could tell for sure."

"Hush up now, boy. You're distracting the lady. How about this?" Jack, Sr. propped one leg up on the bus step and tried to look intimidating. "This is my get-the-hell-out-of-my-way pose."

She was definitely out of her element, she decided, clicking off another round of pictures. Muggers, gangbangers, murderers—she'd encountered them all before she'd been moved from the daily crime scene column to the political daily report. She'd done story after story about the crime rate in San Diego. She'd even covered a few police sting operations and seen San Diego's strange and deranged up close and personal. But she'd never, ever faced down the cast from *Deliverance*.

Jack wore faded work pants and mud-stained boots. A fat belly hung over the waistband of his pants and stretched his soiled white T-shirt until it was practically transparent. She could see the dark hair covering his chest. His shoulders. His back . . .

"Jack, are you sure you haven't had some sightings of your own?" *Like when you look in the mirror?* He was certainly hairy enough to be Bigfoot. But a Bigfoot who drove a renovated yellow school bus and taxied fishermen around a small Tennessee town? That was too much of a stretch, even for the *Squealer*.

"I ain't never seen the Beast, and he ain't never seen me. Lucky for him, otherwise I woulda put a load of buckshot in his backside." He motioned to Jack, Jr. who promptly produced one of the biggest shotguns Tara had ever seen. "How's this?" Jack, Sr. propped the gun on his shoulder and scowled. "This is my I've-got-a-gun-and-I-know-how-to-use-it pose."

She stifled the urge to laugh and took a few more pictures. "Do you name all your poses, Jack?"

" 'Course I do. A fella's got to know what image he's after. Image is everything, ain't that right, Jack, Jr.? Speaking of image"—he glanced at his watch—"I need to get going, otherwise my wife's gonna be steamin' mad. And if there's one thing I try never to do, it's make my Margie mad."

"It's terrible for his image," Jack, Jr. chimed in. "And his back. He ends up sleeping on the couch."

Tara smiled. Jack was a little rough around the edges, and there was a definite possibility that his family tree didn't split. Still, she couldn't help but like him. For all his disgusting habits, he still trembled in his boots at the prospect of angering his wife.

"Mary's probably out checking traps," Jack told

her after he climbed back into the bus and handed his gun over to Jack, Jr. "Dinner's included in the room rate. Nothing like fresh squirrel or spiced possum to fill your belly and give you sweet dreams." He leaned on the horn for several long seconds. Silence followed. "Yep, looks like Mary and Cecil's out somewhere. Trapping or fishing or some such." He slid behind the wheel. "They'll be back before dark. Have Mary give me a holler when you're ready to head back into town." He revved the engine and started to close the door.

Tara's hand shot out, her fingers closing around the edge of the door a fraction before it clamped shut. "Mr. Coates—I mean, Jack. You can't just leave me out here." *Alone.* The thought streaked through her, and she found herself staring longingly at Jack, Jr., who was practically drooling against the bus window.

Panic tiptoed up her spine, but she kicked it back down. Okay, so he was drooling, but maybe it wasn't his fault. He could have a medical condition that caused the drooling and the ogling.

Or maybe he's been in prison or a mental institution and hasn't seen a woman in years. Or maybe he's related to Hannibal the Cannibal and you look like dinner.

The bus rocked and groaned as Jack prepared to take off and leave Tara out there in the middle of nowhere. By herself. Her gaze swiveled back to Jack, Jr. What kind of person would she be if she held a bona fide illness against someone? "Maybe Jack, Jr. could stay and keep me company?"

"Hot dog!" Jack, Jr. was on his feet, a grin splitting his face as he staggered toward the front of the bus. "It'd be my pleasure, little lady—"

"Forget it, boy." Jack's arm shot out to block his way. "Your ma expects us both for dinner, and you know how she gets if we're late. Sorry, ma'am."

"Dadblame it, Pa . . ." Jack, Jr.'s words faded into the smack of the door closing, the creak of the bus and Tara's frantic, futile "Wait!"

Fear skittered through her as she watched the bus disappear down the dirt road. The yellow blur finally faded into the dusky shadows of the trees, and Tara found herself completely alone.

She forced a deep breath. Okay, so she was out in the middle of nowhere. Tired. Hungry. *Alone.* The last thought made her jerk back around. She forced her feet to carry her onto the front porch. Wood squeaked and groaned as she reached the front door. She tried the door. Locked.

She knocked and called out, "Is anyone here?" Nothing. Not that she'd expected anyone, not after Jack had sat on the horn long enough to wake the dead.

Mary and Cecil were probably out checking traps, just as he'd said. They'd be back soon. Before dark.

Probably.

Hopefully.

She smoothed her hands over her arms to chase away the sudden chill that prickled her flesh, and walked to the edge of the porch. Shafts of fading sunlight worked their way down through branches, to send shadows skittering over the ground.

Before dark.

Not that she was afraid of the dark. It was just that the darkness made her feel more alone. Isolated.

She shook away the thought, slipped off her heels and sat down on the porch steps. Mary and Cecil would be back soon. Until then, she would simply make do by herself. She plucked at the silk blouse sticking to her sweaty skin. It was so hot and humid, all thanks to the rainstorm that had swept the area not more than an hour ago. So why was her skin prickling?

It was the fear. It was a familiar sensation. The feeling of being lost, as if the end of the world had finally come and she was the last person left. Forgotten. A feeling she knew all too well.

"Relax," she told herself, focusing on the sound of her own voice. It gave her some comfort, the way it had so long ago, when she'd been a child on her own at home while her parents, both headlining journalists, jetted around in search of story after story.

Not that she'd ever been completely by herself. She'd always had an adult on hand, a nanny, a butler, even the gardener's wife once. But there'd never been anyone really *there* for her. Someone to rock her at night when she had a nightmare, to listen when she had a problem at school. Someone who cared.

Emotionally, she'd been on her own for as long as she could remember. Alone. Lonely. That was why she'd fallen for a loser like Merle. She'd been so in love with the idea of sharing her life with someone that she'd been blind to what a controlling, manipulative bastard he'd been.

He hadn't wanted a wife, a partner, a soul mate. No, he'd wanted a puppet, and like a lovesick fool she'd obliged him. She'd dressed the way Merle had wanted her to, watched the TV shows he liked, cooked and ate the foods he loved—anything to keep him by her side. If he wanted her hair short, she chopped it off. If he wanted her eyes blue, she bought colored contacts. If he wanted fresh-baked bread rather than store-bought, she slaved over a hot oven all day. She'd bowed to his every whim, and he'd left her anyway for another woman.

She hadn't been thin enough, pretty enough, or her loins fruitful enough to give him the children he'd wanted. She'd dieted and exercised herself right into the hospital during the three months following their split—eager to correct the things she could. Finally she'd healed, both physically and emotionally. She'd come to see Merle for what he was—a jerk. He'd tossed out a few sweet words and she'd willingly given up everything for him— from her favorite red dress that he considered too risqué to her beloved chocolate, from her dreams of being a journalist to her freedom. For Merle and his promise to "love, honor and cherish till death do us part," she'd given up her sense of self.

"Never again," she said for the umpteenth time.

She pushed all thoughts of Merle out of her mind and concentrated on her next course of action. She would wait for Mary and Cecil and check into this sorry excuse for a motel. Then first thing tomorrow, she would start following up on this ridiculous story. The sooner she went through the motions and killed the rumor, the sooner she could hop a plane back to San Diego, to her air-conditioned apartment, her high-powered cappuccino maker, her whirlpool bath.

She squared her shoulders, refusing to give in to the disappointment that spread through her. So this wasn't going to be the vacation she'd thought. So what? She would still make the best of it. She'd never been to the mountains, and they really were beautiful, so huge and majestic. And the local wildlife . . . She'd seen several deer, squirrels, rabbits and a dozen different kinds of birds.

Her gaze fixed on one in particular perched in a nearby tree. The animal flexed its blue-black wings and let loose a shrill *cawwwwww*. The sound echoed in her ears, and a strange sensation skittered up her arms, as if the bird watched her, spoke to her.

She shook away the insane notion. "Okay, so the wildlife is as creepy as the rest of this place. . . ." Her words faded into the creak of floorboards directly behind her. "Thank God," she said, climbing to her feet. "I thought you were never coming back—" The words stalled in her throat as she turned. Her head jerked up, her mouth dropped open and a scream split the air.

Bigfoot.

Chapter Two

Bigfoot?

The scream died as her frantic gaze swept the man in front of her, from his black shoulder-length hair and beard, to his worn brown shirt and faded denim jeans. He was big. Huge. Hairy. But he was still just a man.

As if he could have been anything else, she thought disgustedly. She was losing it. Five minutes out in Timbuktu and she was starting to imagine all kinds of things. There were no such things as Bigfoots, or King Kongs or Godzillas or Tarzans or two-headed alien babies—or anything else reported in the tabloids. It was all just hype, make-believe to sell papers. She knew that, so why did she keep getting the feeling otherwise?

Atmosphere, she told herself, glancing around

at the trees, the falling-down motel and the missing link who was grinning back at her.

"Landsakes, Cecil," came a female voice as rusty as the old water bucket sitting next to the door. "Leave the poor woman be. Sorry, miss. You'll have to pardon my brother." The woman, her shoulder-length black hair pulled up in pigtails, wore blue-jean overalls and a red plaid shirt buttoned up to the neck. She slapped the brute on the arm. "He forgot we was expectin' comp'ny. Tell her you're sorry."

"Sorry," he mumbled.

"No harm," Tara managed, shoving her irrational fears aside. She was a reporter; this was a story, however ludicrous. *Be a professional,* she told herself. *Remember your objective.* "I'm Tara Martin." She thrust her hand out in front of her.

"You the lady from that tabloid paper?"

" 'Course she is, you big oaf." The woman pushed in between them and pumped Tara's hand. "National tabloid. Over three and a half million readers, ain't that right?"

Tara nodded and pulled her fingers free. "How do you know the paper's distribution?"

"I'm a loyal reader, and I'm pleased to make your acquaintance. Mary Ott, at your service, ma'am." She pointed to the man. "And this here's my brother, Cecil. Say something to the nice reporter, Cecil."

"You really a reporter?"

"I sure am—Oh!" Something soft and furry skittered across Tara's foot and she pitched forward.

29

The missing link caught her by the arms and righted her.

"Dammit, Cecil. If I told you one time, I told you a thousand and one, boy. Keep them squirrels in their cages, unless you're anxious for a repeat of what happened to Lula Bell."

"Lula Bell?" Tara straightened her skirt and took a deep breath as a family of squirrels skittered to and fro across the porch, and scratched their way across the tips of her new Gucci shoes.

"One of Cecil's squirrels. He's got a whole batch of 'em. Got a name for every one. Loves the hell out of those babies, till I get a hold of 'em with my meat cleaver, that is. Then it's every squirrel for hisself, ain't that right, Cecil?" Mary laughed and poked at her brother.

"Now, now," she said, when he stared down at his boots as if he might cry. "You know God put those little critters on this earth to keep our bellies full.

"Cecil here knows that," she went on. "But I tell you, it still brings tears to his eyes to let go of one of 'em. Mopes around here for days. Which brings me back to Lula Bell. When that Alabama man from the *Montgomery News* come out here two weeks ago and flattened Lula Bell with his fancy black four-by-four it near killed my poor baby brother." She clapped Cecil on the shoulder. "Guess it's one thing to lose a pet as God intended—for good eatin'—and quite another to watch the poor thing splattered all over the parking lot."

Tara swallowed and resisted the urge to snatch

up her bags and hightail it back down the mountain. She forced a deep breath. She was strong, she told herself. She didn't run away, and she didn't cower, even now when faced with the staff from Motel Hell.

"Traumatized him, it did," Mary went on as she directed Cecil to pick up Tara's luggage. "Poor thing," she said as her brother started off toward one of the units. "Why, I hadn't seen him near that upset since they canceled 'Happy Days.'"

The clouds seemed to part and a ray of brilliant sunshine shone down. "You have a TV out here?" TV meant electricity, and electricity meant she could plug in the foot massager she'd bought herself last Christmas. She wiggled her aching toes in anticipation, until Mary shook her head.

"Not since the heavy snow last December. It was a hard winter, and summer came like an inferno. Melted all that ice, and sent a flood the likes of which woulda scared the bejesus out of Noah himself. Nearly washed away ever' building out here. Took out power lines and even carried Lula Bee—"

"Another squirrel?"

"My milch cow. Carried her clear down to the next county. A miracle she survived. Anyhow, the power company ain't been out here to fix the lines yet. But I aim to get 'em out real soon, what with all the attention we been gettin' lately."

"So there's no electricity?"

"We got us a generator, but I wouldn't go plugging in anything important. That thing gets to churning, the power surges, and bam, everything goes haywire. Every blasted electrical appliance ruined."

There went her foot massager. Her laptop. Her portable fax machine. Her blow-dryer. Her lighted makeup mirror. Her iron. She blinked back a sudden onslaught of tears. She was just tired. She could do this. She wanted to do this. Training, she told herself, for when she finally landed a major story in some war-torn country where she'd have to sleep outdoors and fight off mosquitoes the size of pigeons. She took a deep breath and held onto that last thought. This would be a piece of cake compared to what awaited her in serious prime-time reporting.

"You like possum stew? The man from the *Nashville News* was out here last week and he loved it. But he was small potatoes compared to you. You all cover every state in the US of A, and we want folks everywhere to hear about our Beast."

"That's why I'm here." She shrugged and indicated her camera.

"Well, come on in, honey." Mary motioned her into the front unit that served as the motel office. "We'll get you registered; then you can join me and Cecil for dinner."

"I'd really like to get to bed early. Traveling's very tiring," she explained.

"Tomorrow then. I serve my guests breakfast at seven A.M. sharp."

"You have other guests?"

"Not at the moment, but I expect business'll be picking up directly, what with the Beast bein' seen around these parts. Folks are mighty curious, you know."

"So you've actually seen this alleged Bigfoot?" Tara asked as she signed her name on the guest register.

"With my own two eyes." As if she read Tara's skepticism, she added, "And I ain't the only one. Cecil's seen him, and there's a half dozen others. Mostly neighbors. Mabel Mercury, Hep Samson, Wilma Ruth Gentry and Sue Becker."

"I'd like to talk to everybody."

"I'll take you into town right after breakfast. The morrow being Sunday and all, we should catch everybody directly after church."

"And I'd like to get some pictures of one of the sighting areas."

"Right after we get back from town. When's this story gonna run?"

"Provided there is a story," Tara said, "it'll be the feature in the first weekly issue next month."

Mary's loud chuckle filled the dusky shadows and made Tara's skin crawl. "You don't believe we got us a genuine Bigfoot up here, do you, missy?"

"Let's just say I'm reserving judgment until further investigation."

"I love you big-city types," Mary said, patting Tara's hand as she turned to lead her out of the office. "You go on and reserve judgment, honey. But mark my words, he's here, all right. Just you wait and see. You and your three and a half million readers."

* * *

"I'm in hell," she said into her tape recorder later that night. Thank God she had the tiny machine, considering every electrical appliance she'd brought was made useless by the erratic generator.

Not that she was into material possessions. Just appliances. She'd been denied so long while married to Merle, with his overbearing attitude and his piddling excuse for a weekly allowance. No dishwasher. No electric coffeemaker. No blowdryer. No hot rollers. Nothing to pamper herself and make life easier. Once she'd finally gotten back on her feet after the split, she'd splurged. Now whatever she wanted, whatever her budget permitted, she bought. Her money, her decision.

This deprivation *was* her decision, she reminded herself. She'd come on this assignment willingly, albeit with a little persuasive help from Lisa. Still, it had been her choice, and for better or for worse, she was going to see it through. After all, her foot massager and her waffle maker and her nail dryer would be there when she went home.

"Definitely hell," she added, "but a little heat's not going to kill me. I'm tough." She concentrated on the sound of her own voice, eager to hear something save the constant, pressing silence of the stuffy motel room. Oh, sure, there was the chug of the generator just outside her window, the buzz of insects drifting through the open window, the continuous drip of the showerhead, and the *ticktick* of her portable alarm clock. But nothing real. Nothing human.

"Let's see, Cecil looks like an extra from a 'Grizzly Adams' episode, and Mary's definitely a young Granny clone from the 'Beverly Hillbillies.' But in all fairness, looks aside, beneath their mountain personas may beat the hearts of caring, considerate individuals." She remembered Cecil's strange affection for the squirrels and Mary's fierce enthusiasm, and added, "Nix that idea. I'm stuck in an episode of 'Hee Haw' meets 'The Twilight Zone.' Weird."

And suspicious. Mary seemed so sure of the Beast's existence, not to mention the fact that she seemed to know almost as much about the *Squealer* as Tara herself. Strange.

Then again, the entire place was strange, and Tara had promised herself not to pass judgment until she had more facts.

"Then there's the food," she went on, pushing her suspicions aside. "Thank God I saved the peanuts off the plane; otherwise I would have been eating something brown and runny that Mary called possum stew. It might have been possum, all right, but I wouldn't bet my money on it. Not me. This cookie's a hard sell. No proof, no buy. That goes not only for the food, but this entire assignment. Bigfoot? Hah!"

Bigfoot? Hmmm, she thought hours later as she lay, sleepless, staring up at the ceiling and listening to the moans and groans of the trees outside her window. Mary had said that if she kept her ears perked just so, she could actually hear the Beast. Or his victims.

Right! This was crazy. Could it be that several hours at Motel Hell had her starting to buy into all this stuff? No way. The fact of the matter was that there was very little chance the Beast was actually some sort of Bigfoot creature. More likely a bear, an overgrown coyote, or even a gorilla. The last wasn't common to this region, but anything was possible. She'd said that very thing to Mary, who'd shot her down by telling her the sheriff had called a wildlife expert out here who couldn't identify the tracks. Not that that meant anything. Maybe this expert didn't know his bears from his gorillas. People made mistakes. It was human nature.

The trouble was, Tara kept feeling like she was the one making a mistake. Particularly when she heard the faraway sound. It was a cry. A lost, lonely cry that slid into her ears and speared her heart.

She sat up in bed and leaned closer to the open window. The sound drifted on the wind and prickled her nerve endings. She closed her eyes and tried to swallow the lump in her throat. Was it fear or . . . sympathy?

Crazy! A few hours with Mary and Cecil and she'd started to let her imagination go wild.

She wasn't afraid and she wasn't sympathetic, not when she had nothing to fear or sympathize with in the first place.

Yet.

The word streaked through her head before she could stop it. Okay, so maybe later. But later was later, and now was now. As far as she was concerned, the strange sound was probably nothing more than an animal. *Probably,* she told herself as she punched her pillow and forced her eyes closed, though she knew sleep was highly unlikely. She wasn't too comfortable when it came to strange beds. To truly relax, she needed to be smack-dab in the middle of her comfort zone, her apartment, with the familiar sights and sounds of home surrounding her. The whir of her air purifier, the soft music from her nightstand radio, the TV casting dancing shadows across her down comforter. She thought briefly about taking the over-the-counter sleep medication, Sleepy Time, she'd purchased at the airport pharmacy, then quickly discarded the notion. She wanted her wits about her with the missing link Cecil running around.

A bear or a mountain lion or a coyote or some such, Tara assured herself again as the inhuman cry echoed through her mind. And tomorrow she would prove it. She would talk to everyone, take some pictures and maybe even call Fritz back at the *Squealer.* He could put her in touch with a legitimate wildlife expert who would disprove the Bigfoot theory quicker than Mary could recite the distribution for every major paper in North America.

Yes, it was just an animal. Definitely an animal.

He sniffed the air. The scent of her carried on the breeze, coaxing him from the safety of his lair. She was close. So close. He could smell her, feel her, taste her. . . . His senses were fine-tuned, heightened because of who he was. The gift of his grandfather's people. His heritage. His curse.

Pale hair fanned out over his chest, trailed down his belly to stroke and coax and . . .

Zane cried out again, desperate to push the vision from his thoughts, yet it remained. As crystal clear as a bubbling stream, as inviting, as mesmerizing.

No! He had to ignore her silent call and heed the warning Kanati—the Great Spirit—had given him.

But the words of doom paled in comparison to the craving that clawed at his belly. He needed . . . *something.* If only he knew what. But it was as foreign to him as the image that haunted his dream. A woman, her every detail branded in his brain. The color of her hair, her eyes. The soft feel of her skin. As if he'd touched and been touched by her before.

It was impossible. He couldn't remember having seen a woman up close, save the strange images that haunted his nightmares, so blurry and distorted he couldn't quite make sense of them. He saw visions of people, vague outlines, but no distinct features.

Yet this woman stirred something fierce and consuming within him. A hunger that couldn't be appeased with food. A thirst that water couldn't quench. A desperation that drove him out into the night. He sought the comfort of the books he kept hidden in a hollowed-out tree trunk. Desperate fingers roved over the tattered pages as he mouthed the familiar words. . . .

Words that had comforted in the past.

Words from his past, though he knew not where they came from. They were ingrained in his mind, with no beginning, no end. Simply there.

" 'Swift as a shadow, short as any dream, brief as the lightning in the collied night . . .' " His own voice rang out, offering the only repose from the silence that ruled his life.

But it wasn't enough, not this time, to ease what haunted him, and he abandoned the books to roam the mountainside until he collapsed in exhaustion beside an icy stream.

As always, he sensed the buck long before the male deer knew of his presence. He smelled the strong aroma, heard the soft grunts, and recognized the animal's anxious sharpening of his antlers on a nearby tree. It was early in the season, still two moons away, but already the buck was on the trail of his mate.

The male deer finally sensed him and struck a threatening pose, ready to fight for his mate, for his right.

Their eyes met. *I mean you no harm, friend. You or your doe. No harm.*

The animal blinked, then relaxed and resumed its scratching and sniffing. Water rippled where the doe sipped at the stream, as if unaware of the male who followed. The buck moved closer. The doe continued to drink.

He didn't wait to see what would happen. It was a sight he'd witnessed many times since he'd come to the mountains so long ago. The mating ritual. Where male and female put aside their differences for those few moments to ensure the continuity of their species. Deer and bear. Coyote and cougar.

But he was none of the above. Different, yet the same.

Physically, he looked nothing like the animals he lived among. Yet inside dwelled a kindred spirit. Wild. Primitive. Hungry. He felt the same fierce desire as the buck. The same drive to find and touch one of his own. To mate.

His heart pounded in response to the thought, and he touched his chest. Questing fingertips met hard, hairy muscle. His breathing grew shallow, and a fierce heat swamped his groin. He moved his hand down, fingers trailing over his belly to the jutting flesh between his legs. He was so hot. So hard.

So alone.

The woman's vision pushed inside his head, always ready to take control when he least expected it. To taunt him. To make his body burn, his blood race. To make him want.

"Touch me," she said softly. "Touch me. Take me—"

No! He pushed into the forest, but not before the longing inside him grew, expanded. The sound that ripped from his throat echoed with frustration and anger and, most of all, fear, because now he understood what the strange feelings inside him meant.

They were for her, and they assured his death.

Chapter Three

"He's a giant, I tell you. Eight feet tall, with arms and legs big enough to wrap around the trunks of two full-grown virgin hardwood trees."

Tara stood on the corner of Main and Bear streets in the heart of downtown Bear Creek, Tennessee, surrounded by a crowd of eager interviewees who all had two cents to add to the legend of the Beast of Bear Mountain.

"As bloodthirsty as an old grizzly. Heard tell he ripped a buck, a seven-pointer, clear in two with his bare hands and teeth."

"Well, I heard he carted off a whole henhouse of chickens. Heard he ate 'em like popcorn, one after the other, feathers and all."

"That's nothing. I heard him with my own two ears. Wails louder than a coyote at night. An awful noise that sinks clear into your bones and sets your nerves on edge. Like a wounded animal."

Or a lonely one.

The thought sparked in Tara's mind and she flipped off her microcassette recorder. Her skin prickled, despite the warm weather. Since she'd come into town with Mary and Cecil an hour ago to stock up for the day's trip into the mountains, she'd heard at least a dozen stories about the Beast—an evidently brutal half man, half monster—from the citizens of Bear Creek.

Despite their wild claims, the townspeople were hardly the crazies Tara had anticipated after spending the night with Mary and Cecil. Most of the folks were nice, friendly, maybe a bit old-fashioned, but then this was a desperately small mountain town. Still, everyone made her feel welcome, shaking her hand and smiling before telling their own wild story.

Wilma Ruth, in particular, had embraced her like a long-lost daughter before launching into her tale. It was the first one that rang with any truth.

Tara herself had heard the awful wail last night. She'd sensed the heartbreak, felt it echo through her body to settle in the center of her chest.

It could turn out to be a real story. Lisa's words replayed in her head. Okay, she wasn't stupid enough to keep pretending that there wasn't *something* up on Bear Mountain. But a monster? Lisa's preliminary research claimed over two hundred Bigfoot sightings over the past two years in the Appalachian mountain chain stretching from the Blue Ridge Mountains through the Smokies, and not one of them had panned out. There had been a logical explanation for each. An overly hairy hunter. Kids playing pranks. A bear. Yes, this was black bear country. Undoubtedly that was what the Beast of Bear Mountain would turn out to be. Just a bear. A large, brutal bear who cried in the middle of the night.

"I never saw him myself," Wilma Ruth went on, "just heard him. But a friend of mine, Myrtle Myers over in Stanton, said her daughter was out camping up on Bear Mountain with a couple of friends. One of them wandered off. They heard all this screaming and yelling and the girl comes running back, babbling about some monster who'd attacked her from behind. Said she was just standing there searching for firewood and she turned around. There he was, as big as Goliath and as nasty as an old grizzly."

"What happened?"

"The gal took off running. Said he chased her for a ways, but finally gave up. Seems to me if he's all that folks say, he could of caught that scrap of a young'un, tossed her over his shoulder and carted her off before she could blink an eye. Guess he wasn't hungry at the time, not that he could have sated his appetite with Julie. The child's nothing but skin and bones, like that there Kate Moss all the girls are so anxious to look like. Pitiful, if you ask me and the other women in this town. That's why we boycotted that awful *Cosmopolitan*."

She was liking Wilma Ruth more and more.

"A man needs something to keep him warm

when he climbs into bed at night," Wilma went on. *Amen, sister.* "He don't want to think he's sleeping with the scarecrow out in his pasture." She patted Tara's arms. "Glad to see ain't everybody out to starve themselves. Such a pretty thing, you are. A real handful."

"Uh, thanks." Tara squelched the desire to glance down at her slightly wide thighs. It *was* a good thing she'd left her Kate Moss body back in that hospital. She was a handful, and proud of it. Healthy. Happy.

Okay, so one out of two wasn't bad. The latter she was working on. Just one good story. A real story and she'd be on her way to Pulitzer Prize–winning happiness.

"What did you say the scarecrow—I mean, the girl's name was?"

"Julie. Julie Abernathy." Wilma shook her head. "But don't bother going after her. She's away at college in Nashville. Won't be back for a good six weeks. Probably wastin' away, in sore need of her mama's good cooking."

"I'd really appreciate it if you could give me her parents' number. I'd like to get in touch with them. Ask a few questions. Maybe they could give me her number at school."

"Sure thing, sugar."

"You tell her about that photographer fella?" An old man, his back bent, hobbled from a nearby doorway.

"Photographer?" Tara raised her eyebrows at Wilma Ruth.

"I was just getting to it, Cooney. This here's Cooney Rainer."

Tara's gaze flew to the sign a few feet away. COONEY RAINER'S CHEROKEE MUSEUM. "You own this place?"

"Lock, stock and barrel, little lady." He tapped his cane near Tara's feet. "Come on inside and have a look."

"I really don't have time—"

"On the house, little lady." Gnarled fingers gripped her arm and pulled her away from Wilma Ruth and the crowd of interviewees. " 'Sides, you want to hear about that fella what up and disappeared, don't you?"

Tara's gaze flew to Wilma and the woman nodded. "It's true. One minute he was thumbin' his way down the highway. And the next—poof. He just vanished."

"When did this happen?" Tara asked as she followed the old man inside the museum, setting her newly purchased camping equipment by the front door.

"A couple months back. He was from one of those papers like yours, but from up north. Real city fella, that one, with this spiky-looking yella hair, a couple of earrings in his ear and his nose, and a big tattoo right here." Cooney rubbed his chest and reached for his spectacles. "You want the official tour, little lady?" He unhooked a velvet rope and led Tara down a hallway. "Or seein' as you're in a hurry and all, I could give you the condensed version."

"Condensed is good. So what happened to the

photographer?" Her gaze went to the first display, a spread of authentic Indian clothing.

"Fella's still missing. The authorities put up a bunch of flyers from here through the surrounding six counties, but he ain't turned up, and nobody knows a thing." Cooney puffed out his chest. "This here's an authentic chief's robe and leggings passed down from my great-granddaddy's daddy."

Tara's gaze snagged on several details of the clothing, from the fringed beadwork to the hand-painted design. "You're Cherokee?"

"One hundred percent." He rubbed his balding head. "Had a hatful of coal black hair at one time, but that was in my younger days. Ask any of the folks around here. I was born and raised in Bear Creek like my daddy and granddaddy before me. This here's a real bow and arrow set." He pointed to another display. "And here's a peace pipe and a pair of moccasins."

"I didn't know Bear Creek was known for its Cherokee heritage. My research didn't mention anything."

"There's quite a few Indians still around these parts. At one time, the Smokies were home to thousands of Cherokee; then the Trail of Tears moved most of them west." He pointed to a very evocative painting. "A few stayed behind and settled in North Carolina. The Eastern band of the Cherokee. They settled on the Qualla Boundary, a sizable amount of land adjacent to the Great Smoky Mountains National Park. Some strays clung to these parts, however, my ancestors among 'em. Why, there even used to be a real-life medicine man who lived up on Bear Mountain and talked to the animals."

"Medicine man?"

"You know, a shaman, a witch doctor, a healer. Could do anything with that pouch of herbs of his." He pointed to a display case. "That there's a real deerskin herb pouch. My daddy's. That old medicine man give it to 'im right before the man passed on."

"How long ago?"

"A lot of years back, when I was just a young pup. Had himself a young'un what shared his talent for talking to the animals, but she up and moved on to college in Chicago and never came back to these parts. Now if you want to see real Indians, particularly a medicine man, you got to drive on over to North Carolina. There's all sorts of stuff, including a museum that makes this look like small potatoes, and a theater where you can watch authentic ceremonial dances. And one heck of a gift shop."

Cooney, himself, had quite a nice little gift shop, where Tara picked up a few pamphlets on the Cherokee, a mock peace pipe and a half dozen chocolate-chip cookies shaped like tomahawks—Mrs. Rainer's contribution to her husband's establishment.

"Oh, here's something else for you." Cooney followed her outside and handed her a flyer. "This is the fella that came up missing. Folks say he got eaten, but I think the monster probably just strung him up and skinned him."

47

Her stomach rolled. "What?"

"That's just my theory, mind you. This fella lived on beer and cigarettes and smelled like the inside of an ashtray. Nobody in their right mind would take a bite out of him when they could have themselves some good venison."

"I think I've got everything," Mary announced as she walked out of the general store, her arms full of two huge grocery sacks.

"So a man really disappeared?" Tara turned questioning eyes on the motel owner.

Mary shot Cooney a withering look. "That's nonsense, Cooney Rainer, and you know it. That fella just moved on to bigger and better things."

Cooney shrugged. "All I know is what I see with my own two eyes. His picture's on that there flyer, so he's missin'." He turned and made his way back inside the museum.

"You don't think this guy disappeared?" she asked Mary.

" 'Course not. Fella went on his way as right as rain. Saw him off myself from the motel."

"But his newspaper said he never made it back." She held up the flyer. "According to this, no one's seen him since he left here."

Mary stiffened. "Look, all's I know is that fella left this mountain in one piece. That's what I told the sheriff. Cecil drove him to the interstate and that was that. If that man didn't make it back to New York—"

"Seattle," Tara cut in. "It says here he's from Seattle."

"Wherever," Mary went on. "It's probably because he's one of them wandering types and just decided to hitch across America or some such. Why, I read about a fella who was documenting life across the nation. Maybe this fella got it in his head to do something like that, hitched his way out of here and got himself picked up by some serial killer or something and"—Mary drew a finger from ear to ear—"got himself killed. There's crazy folks driving the interstate."

"So you think he's dead?" A strange sense of foreboding settled in the pit of Tara's stomach.

"Maybe, or maybe he just decided to up and hightail it away from his job and family and go searchin' for himself. People do it all the time." She held up the bags. "Got everything here you asked for."

From Mary's closed expression, Tara knew pursuing the subject was useless. And as much as Tara hated to admit it, Mary was right. People up and abandoned their lives all the time, no rhyme or reason. This beer-drinking, cigarette-smoking ashtray could very well be thumbing his way across the country.

Tara stuffed the flyer into her pocket, peeked into a grocery bag and saw three boxes of chocolate cupcakes, two six-packs of diet soda and a jumbo bag of Doritos. She smiled. She might just survive this little trek into nature after all. A few more pokes into the bag and she asked, "Where's the toilet paper?"

"You ain't takin' no toilet paper up onto the mountain. Ain't you ever heard of environmental responsibility? The sheriff would haul your butt and mine in if he found a mess of dirty toilet paper."

"What am I supposed to do?"

"Moss."

"Moss?" Tara tried to tamp down the vision the word created.

"Or leaves."

"Leaves?" She swallowed.

"Whichever's handy."

"But—"

"Don't worry, missy. Folks have been using moss and leaves for years. Do you think your ancestors had a Piggly Wiggly around the corner? Hell no. They made do with what God give 'em."

"Moss and leaves."

"Exactly." Mary wrinkled her nose at the other contents of the grocery bags. "All this other stuff seems a waste to me. You ain't never had good eatin' till you've had rabbit roasted over an open fire or spit-roasted snake."

Tara did her best not to cringe. Not that she was against adventurous eating. She'd sampled her share of escargot and raw oysters and even a few delectable dishes she couldn't actually name. Nor did she want to. But there was a distinct difference between having such delicacies served on a silver platter by a waiter named Franz, and actually shooting and skinning the fare yourself.

"I think I'll stick to prepackaged foods, thanks."

"Suit yourself." Mary loaded the bags into the back of her Jeep. "How did the interviews go?"

"Very insightful."

"Glad to hear it." She rubbed her hands together. "We best be goin' if we aim to make Marshall Peak by nightfall." She motioned to Cecil, who'd just exited the store, a piece of red licorice hanging from the corner of his mouth. "Get Miss Tara's pack, Cece."

"I can carry it myself." Tara hefted the monstrous backpack the man at the sporting goods store had helped her stock. A sleeping bag, first-aid kit, enough mosquito repellent to protect a small African country, a flashlight, a pack of extra batteries for her recorder, matches, a canteen and some travel-size toiletries. Oh, and of course, a battery-powered curling iron and battery-powered single-cup coffeemaker. Ah, the wonders of technology. Just enough to get her through an overnight campout.

Maybe even a week-long campout, she thought, half-toting, half-dragging the heavy pack toward the back of the Jeep. She struggled for several minutes with the tailgate while Cecil stood behind her and gnawed his red licorice.

"I could tote that up for ya." His eyes gleamed like the pet squirrels he lavished so much affection on, and Tara felt like a nut being sized up for lunch.

"Uh, no, thanks." He wasn't cracking this nut, she thought. "I think"—grunt—"I can manage"—grunt—"There! All finished." She dusted off her hands and slid into the passenger's seat next to Mary while Cecil climbed in the backseat.

"So," Mary asked as she threw the Jeep into reverse. "Did you find out enough to know me and Cecil ain't blowing smoke up your hind end?"

"There's definitely something up on the mountain."

"Bigfoot."

"Maybe."

Mary frowned. "I thought them folks set you straight."

"The only thing I know for sure is that I'm looking for a big, hairy, sometimes hairless giant, a *male* giant," she noted, remembering Jack and half the town's claim of substantial family jewels, "with long/short, black/brown hair who looks like a man/bear/somewhere in between. He yells like Tarzan and has the table manners of the Tasmanian Devil. Hey, you know what? I think I saw this guy when I took the train to Queens last time I was in New York."

"New York?" Mary shook her head. "I doubt he's ever been off Bear Mountain."

So much for laughter to lighten the tension. "It was a joke, Mary."

"Ain't nothin' funny about the Beast. This is serious business. You'd do best to keep that in mind and get rid of that load you bought at the sporting goods store. There ain't no way you're going to make it up to the peak with that pack full of crap Jimmy sold you."

"I'll make it."

" 'Course, Cecil can always help ya."

"I'll make it on my own," she said again. After all, as Wilma Ruth had so delicately put it, she was a handful. Surely a handful could manage a pack full of life-and-death essentials a little ways up a mountain. "So where did you say we were heading? Marshall Peak?"

Mary nodded. "We'll start off at the motel and head northwest, hike a few miles until we hit the peak."

"Miles?"

Mary nodded, her lips hinting at a smile that said, despite her words of warning, she was looking forward to seeing Tara tackle several miles lugging her newly filled backpack.

"Can't we drive?"

"Terrain's too rugged. Only a motorbike could manuever that ground, and then only half as far as the peak. Hiking's better. It'll give you a chance to get some nice pictures, show folks what the mountains here have to offer."

"This is an exposé, not a travel piece," Tara pointed out. "Now how many miles are we talking about?"

"Three straight up, to be exact, afore we hit the peak. Hopefully, you'll see all you need to there and we won't have to push on. Last time I was out checking traps up there—I do that at least once a week—I saw him. If we're lucky, maybe you can get a few shots of him with that fancy camera of yours." She flashed a full-blown smile at Tara. "Wouldn't that make a nice picture for the front page of your newspaper?"

The trek to Marshall Peak was slow and painful and the worst experience of Tara's life. Just as Mary had predicted, Tara's pack was too heavy, Mary walked too fast and Cecil, a beady-eyed squirrel riding each shoulder, stared entirely too much. And worst of all, Tara got her first real lesson in getting back to nature. She promised herself that when she returned to civilization she would never take another roll of toilet paper for granted again.

She did her best to concentrate on her surroundings. The scenery really was beautiful. The land rose up above them, pushing into the smoky haze that hung like a shroud over the mountaintop. The forest was thick and green and lush, teeming with birds and raccoons and foxes. Tara even spotted a white-tailed deer. Her camera flashed at regular intervals, giving her a much-needed excuse to ease the pack off her shoulders for several blessed moments. "Wild Kingdom," eat your heart out.

Then it started to rain. No, more like pour. The heavens opened up, water gushed down and Tara found herself huddling between Mary and Cecil and the squirrels under a thin tarp. Not that it helped. She was drenched anyway by the time the rain stopped, the sky cleared and they again started walking toward the peak.

The rain turned the blue-green countryside into a steam bath. Tara dripped rainwater and sweat and found herself gasping for air more than once. She cursed Lisa, Fritz and Gucci, the latter for importing the sleek leather hiking boots she'd bought at Saks before flying out. With each step, the boots rubbed a blister the size of Mount Olympus, and it was all Tara could do not to cry out.

Finally, when she was ready to fling herself at

Cecil's feet and offer herself up as a sacrifice if he would carry her and the pack, Mary announced they'd reached their destination, a small clearing surrounded by steep, heavily forested slopes of cedar and pine and a few other types of trees Mary had mentioned.

"Sit down afore you fall down, Miss Tara. Cece and I'll get the supplies out and supper goin'."

Tara leaned back on her pack, too tired to breathe, much less lend any help. Her shoulders screamed, her legs ached, her feet begged for salvation. What had she gotten herself into? She closed her eyes. She should be at home, sitting on her couch, remote control in hand, a nice, warm pizza on the coffee table, her feet soaking in the portable footbath she'd bought last month.

Ah . . .

"Get my knife, Cecil. I'll gut the little booger and you can clean 'im."

Tara clamped her hands over her ears. She appreciated a good steak as much as the next person, but there was just something about hearing the actual precooking phase that killed any anticipation of the end product. One night, she told herself. Just one night of this, and then she'd be back at the motel and Mary would be whipping up her culinary masterpieces in the privacy of her own kitchen.

Ugh. Motel Hell was starting to sound appealing. That was definitely a bad sign.

"Eat up," Mary barked, and Tara jumped. Her eyes snapped open and she realized she'd dozed off.

"What? Where are we? What did I miss?"

"Nothing. You nodded off two hours ago, the minute we set down camp. We're just starting supper." The woman waved what looked like a teeny, tiny chicken leg.

"I—I think I'll pass." She reached into her pack, bypassed a few cans of Vienna sausages and pulled out a box of cupcakes and a can of lukewarm diet soda before settling down on the bedroll Mary had rolled out for her.

"You need your energy," Mary said, taking the seat opposite her. The fire danced, pushing back the dusky shadows quickly closing in around them. "You won't make one mile, much less the three back to the motel, by eating that stuff."

"Caffeine and sugar? Are you kidding? I'll be running circles around you guys in the morning." Tara finished a second cupcake, licked her fingers and downed the rest of her soda. She'd barely taken a bite out of her third cupcake when her eyelids started to droop. There wasn't a trash can anywhere in sight, so she wrapped the partially eaten sweet and slid it into her jacket pocket. Breakfast, she thought as she leaned back and closed her eyes.

"You ain't settlin' down to bed now, are you?"

"That was the idea."

"Don't you want to look around? I need to take a look at my bird feeder over on the other side of the gulley. I can show you where I saw the Beast last time I was up here fishing at the creek just yonder."

"I thought you were out checking traps?"

"I was. Right after I caught two of the meanest bass you ever seen. You can come along with me while Cecil packs away the supplies."

Tara hauled herself up, tried to ignore the ache in her body and reached for her camera. "I guess I could take a look. I've got a heavy flash feature on my camera, and then there's the flashlight, in case we really do see something."

"Oh, I have a feeling you'll see something, all right." Mary smiled and reached for her flashlight and rifle. "Tonight's the night. I can feel it clear to my bones."

The only thing Tara felt was tired, so tired in fact that she ignored the strange niggling at her gut. Something wasn't right. Mary was too confident. Too eager, even.

A shiver worked its way up her spine, and Tara promptly shook it away. Maybe there was something to be suspicious over, and maybe not. It was hard to tell. Mary was so . . . odd anyway that any abnormal behavior could be perfectly normal, and Tara could simply be jumping at shadows.

Suspicions aside, she did need pictures, and the last thing she wanted was to be left alone with Cecil for any length of time.

She followed Mary into a thick patch of trees, her senses tuned. The musky smell of freshly watered earth and ripe greenery filled her nostrils. Her eyes quickly adjusted to the semidarkness and she scanned her surroundings, searching for the subtle movement of a twig, the sway of a tree branch, a shadow lurking in the distance. . . .

The *cawww* of a bird sent an echoing shiver

through her body, and she glanced up to see a pair of eyes glittering from a branch overhead. A bird. The same bird she'd seen yesterday.

It couldn't be. There were probably hundreds of black birds up in these mountains, and they all made the same sound.

But they didn't all affect her this way, she thought, rubbing her arms. As if someone watched her, waited for her—

"You ever meet that Barbara Walters lady from that '20/20' show?"

Mary's question shattered Tara's thoughts and drew her attention to the woman in front of her. "Can't say that I have."

"Why, I bet she'll be hopping to have me and Cecil on her show once she gets a load of your pictures."

"I haven't gotten any pictures yet."

"And David Letterman. I always wanted to be on David Letterman. I bet that would send the folks running this way."

"Should we really be talking? I mean, won't that scare whatever it is away—"

A roar split open the night and brought Tara to a staggering halt. She jerked around to see . . .

The Beast.

Even as denial streaked through her brain, she couldn't ignore what was standing right in front of her. Covered with hair from head to toe, the Beast looked like nothing more than a sizable bear. But the minute Tara's flashlight hit the animal's face, she realized she was staring at much more. *Bigfoot.* A real-life Bigfoot. While the body resembled an animal, the face was that of a man, and it was a man's familiar eyes that stared back at her. Just as the odd thought struck her, he opened his mouth and roared again. Her speculation melted into a wave of panic. His yellow teeth caught the gleam of the flashlight, his incisors dripping blood from the mutilated rabbit he held in his claw-tipped paws.

"Ohmigod, ohmigod, ohmigod." Her head shook frantically while the Beast blocked her path and stared her down. She tried to back up, to run, but Mary stood directly behind her.

"Take a picture," Mary said in a hiss, punching her from behind. "Don't chicken out now. This is the story of a lifetime."

The story of a lifetime. The thought echoed in her head as she fought for control of her camera and snapped picture after picture.

Another bone-chilling roar and he tossed the rabbit to the ground and fled into the woods.

"I told you." Mary poked her in the arm once they were alone. "I knew it. I just sure as shootin' knew it! You got pictures, didn't you? Plenty of 'em? This is gonna be one hell of a story. Barney's Bed and Breakfast, kiss your tourist business good-bye, 'cause the Mary Ott Motel is taking over!"

"I . . . That was the Beast, wasn't it?"

"Sure as hell was. I told you. I told you!"

Tara shook her head. "There's a real Bigfoot out here."

"Sure enough."

"And I've got him on film."

"Sure do."

Tara smiled, her heart pounding, her adrenaline pumping. "Mary, do you know what this means?"

"That I'll get to meet Barbara Walters?"

"And David Letterman and Rosie O'Donnell and even Oprah."

"Oprah?" Mary leaned against a nearby tree. "I never even thought about Oprah. This is big, isn't it?"

"Really big." Tara hugged her camera and smiled. "This goes way beyond the tabloids. It'll make every major news network in the country. The world, even. We're talking Pulitzer!"

"I don't think I ever heard of him."

Tara started laughing. "It doesn't matter. I have. Boy, have I ever. Let's head back. I want to get these pictures into town and developed ASAP. And I want to call the Forestry Department. They need to get some experts out here as soon as possible to comb this area for solid evidence. The pictures are good, but they're not enough. We need to find something concrete. A real footprint. A strand of hair. Maybe a blood sample."

Tara's mind raced ninety miles an hour all the way back to camp. This was bigger than big. This was monumental, and she'd found it! She was so excited, she could barely close her eyes later that night, and when she did, sleep completely eluded her. Her mind brimmed with possibilities. She'd found a new life-form. Maybe the missing link. *Oh, boy!*

* * *

"Ssshhh, you'll wake her up." Mary's voice, little more than a whisper, slid into Tara's ears and shattered her thoughts.

"Are you sure she's out?"

"She's snorin', ain't she?"

Snoring? Hey, she didn't snore. Did she? She listened carefully and heard the steady *zzzzzzz* of her breathing. Okay, so she snored. But the air was scarce this high up and she was excited.

"Come on, Cecil. Hurry up."

Tara heard the soft pad of boots, the sound growing distant. She popped one eye open in time to see Mary and Cecil disappear into the trees. She sat up and glanced around, noting the stuffed-up bedrolls, obviously made to look, at first glance, as if Mary and Cecil were still in them.

Tara knew in an instant that her instincts had been right. Something was very wrong, and her hosts were behind it.

As quietly as possible, she climbed from her bedroll, snatched up her camera and flashlight and headed after her guides. She walked for at least ten minutes before she finally heard the muffled sound of voices.

"Make sure you get every bit of that rabbit carcass cleaned up, then douse the ground with water. That gal's gonna have this place crawlin' with experts come mornin' and I don't want them to find anything that points to us."

"It's just rabbit blood."

"And yours, too, you danged fool. You just had to go and cut yourself while you was slicing up the

61

rabbit. I told you once, I told you a thousand and one blasted times, Cecil. You got to be more careful. This was a great idea, but we can't get too careless. Otherwise, instead of drumming up business, we're going to attract a whole batch of scientists out here who can shoot these sightings to hell and back. Mystery's the key, little brother. Make people curious." She muttered a curse. "Just our luck we get ourselves a real danged reporter interested in more than a few pictures."

The reality of what she was hearing hit Tara like a punch to the gut. She doubled over, nausea rising in her throat.

Drumming up business . . .

A real reporter interested in more than pictures . . .

She fought back the sick feeling and concentrated on the puzzle pieces. They fell together, one after the other, until the truth stared her in the face. Mary's insightful knowledge about the tabloids and their circulation, her confident statements that Tara would see something, her eagerness to see the Beast on the front page of the *Squealer*.

Mary wanted to draw tourists to her decaying motel. A scam.

Disappointment gripped her all of five seconds before hope waltzed in. Okay, so she hadn't discovered the missing link; she still had a story to write, an exposé about desperate small-town motel owners who'd do anything to draw tourists to their hole-in-the-wall town, including dressing up as Bigfoot. She snapped a picture, and the *click* echoed through the night.

Looking for cover, she stumbled backward, but it was into something big and furry, and a gasp burst from her lips. It couldn't be.

"What the hell?" Mary's flashlight streaked across the path to capture Tara and the thing she'd stumbled into.

"Hell's bells," Mary muttered.

"Landsakes," Cecil added.

"Holy sh—" The words died in Tara's throat as the black bear reared up on its hind legs and let loose a roar that sent fear skittering from her head to her toes. A hungry roar.

The bear fell forward then, paws smacking the ground, nose aimed at her pocket. Remembering the half-eaten cupcake, she flung what was left of the sweet at the bear, whirled, and ran for her life.

The bear looked up, desperate for more goodies. Tara darted through the maze of trees at record speed, her thoughts consumed with visions of hungry, salivating bears.

Run! she commanded her legs when they started to cramp and her lungs burned for oxygen. *Forget that you've never had an aerobics class in your life. That the most exercise you get is walking to and from the fridge. Just run. Fast. Faster. Go, go, go!*

After what seemed like forever, she realized there was no hot breath puffing after her, no growling right in her ears, no fur brushing the backs of her legs. Obviously he hadn't given chase; perhaps he'd gone after Mary and Cecil.

The tree root came out of nowhere. Her foot hit, her ankle twisted and her legs flew out from under her. She vaulted headfirst several feet and crashed into the ground, facedown. Pain wrenched through her body, shooting white-hot streaks of fire to every nerve ending. Her vision blurred. A drum solo beat in her temples, louder, louder, echoing the frantic thud of her heart.

"Where is she?" came Mary's thick drawl, squelching the idea that the woman had wound up bear food.

Over here! a silent voice inside Tara screamed in reply.

"She ran that way," came Cecil's frantic voice. "Hurry, Sis. Find her. You have to find her—"

"Hush up. Dadblame it, Cecil," Mary grumbled, footsteps stomping through brush. "I told you to hurry up with that suit. If you ain't as slow as Christmas. Otherwise she wouldn't have had anythin' to be spyin' on. That makes twice you've screwed up now."

Twice?

"The zipper stuck."

"Sure, sure. The last time it was the rusted snaps."

"I'm sorry, Sis. Real sorry. Oh, this ain't good," Cecil said, sounding worried. "This is bad. What if the bear got her? What if she's—"

"Calm down, Cece, and start looking."

Yes!

"You head on over by the creek and I'll cover this part. If it ain't too late, we'll find her."

Too late? No. She was alive. Breathing.

"We need them pictures," Mary told him. "So get looking. When them pictures of the Beast hit the paper, it'll draw folks like flies." Boots crushed leaves, and branches shifted somewhere to her left.

"Over here," Tara tried to form the words, but her lips wouldn't cooperate. Fear lanced through her. *Maybe I struck my head, why can't I talk?*

Here! her brain screamed loud enough to set her teeth on edge. Maybe she'd just knocked the wind out of herself.

The footsteps shifted direction and panic bolted through Tara.

No! She had to roll over, to stop Mary, but every muscle seemed paralyzed. Her body felt as if she'd been tackled by the entire Dallas Cowboys defensive line. As if a few hulking linebackers still held her pinned to the ground.

"I can't find her, Sis," came Cecil's distant shout.

"Then keep a lookout for the camera, at least." The footsteps turned back, drew closer. "Maybe she dropped it. We could mail the pictures in to the *Squealer* ourselves." Mary's voice drew closer and Tara silently begged her forward.

Look over here. Yes, this way. A few more steps. Look down. Right here.

"I think I found something." The brilliant light of a flashlight trained on Tara's face from several yards away.

Tara stared into the blinding beam, gaze wide and pleading for the space of two heartbeats before the light forced her eyes closed.

"She looks dead."

"Dead?" came Cecil's frantic cry from the distance.

Dead? No! She'd stared into the light before closing her eyes. Hadn't the woman seen her reaction?

"Yeah. We're too late. She's dead, all right. . . ." A deep growl drowned Mary's words.

The flashlight hit the ground, the woman shrieked, the bear roared and Tara was left to wonder if her only hope for survival had just turned into a hungry animal's main course.

Get up, Tara told herself. *You can't let yourself be dessert. Scream for help. Beg for mercy. Something.*

She could do little more than turn her head to the side, the ground cold against her cheek as she listened to the sound of frantic voices and deep growls. The sounds quickly faded, lost in the *thud, thud* of her own heartbeat, the only assurance that she was still alive. Darkness surrounded her. The damp night air chilled her body, despite the trickle of heat that ran from her temple down her jaw. In seconds, the pain lessened, her body numbed, and she felt little except the overwhelming need to close her eyes. To sleep.

It was a long time later when she felt wetness grazing her fingers. A draft of warm air blew over her skin, and her senses came alive. She opened her eyes to find the morning sunlight spilling down around her. The wetness spread from her hand to her wrist, up her arm, and a low growl filled her ear.

The bear.

The thought barely registered before she felt the presence surround her. This was it. The end of the line. There would be no long, healthy journalistic career. No Pulitzer waiting in her future. No future, period. She was dead meat. Bear food—

A strong grip on her shoulder forced her onto her back. She blinked frantically, determined to face the bear down. If she was going to die, she wasn't going out like a coward. No quaking in her boots. Never again. She would stare death in the eye. She—

Her intentions scattered as she found herself gazing up into the most intense blue eyes she'd ever seen.

A man's eyes, despite the fact that hair covered half his face and obliterated his features. Strong hands—a *man's* hands, she quickly noted— gripped her upper arms. Broad, powerful shoulders shielded her body from the sunlight. Relief washed through her. Yes, a man. She was saved!

Then he tilted his head back, let loose a growl even more ferocious than that of the bear standing just behind him, and shot Tara's notions about salvation to hell and back.

The sound rang in her ears, sizzled across her nerve endings and raised every hair on her body, and she did the only thing a woman in her position—sprawled beneath a bloodthirsty, half-naked, real-life Tarzan—could do. She fainted dead away.

Chapter Four

She was real.

It was the one thought that rooted in his brain once he sent the black bear on her way.

Real.

His hands reached out, his fingertips trailing over the strands of golden sunshine spilling around her. Softness stroked his skin, coaxed him to touch more, to touch *her*.

He memorized the shape of her face, noting the incredible feel against his callused palms, like the petals of a flower. Smooth. Velvety. Fragrant.

His nostrils flared as he drank in her scent—sunshine and flowers and warmth. A dizzying heat rushed through his head, spiraling through his body to settle none too comfortably in his groin.

Yes, she was real this time. And unconscious,

he noted, his gaze lingering on her closed eyelids. And hurt.

The last thought served as a swift kick to the gut. He stiffened, his attention going to her right leg, the foot bent at an impossible angle beneath her. He made quick work of the laces binding her boot. As he'd seen his grandfather do so long ago with an endless number of hikers and campers too foolish to realize that even the most beautiful land could be brutal, he slid the boot off. The fabric covering her foot soon followed.

Her ankle had already swollen, the skin around her heel and the arch of her foot an ugly purplish-black.

You always know when something is broken, Zane. The bones crunch together when they move. You can feel it if you touch just so, hear it if you listen really closely.

With the same soft, easy movements he'd seen his grandfather use, Zane pressed and prodded and worked the foot slowly, gently, all the while alert to the flesh and bone beneath his hands, his ears tuned for any telltale noises.

He closed his eyes and heard nothing save the sound of her breathing. The whisper-soft draw of air filled his ears, accompanied by the steady *thud, thud* of her heart. It was the most incredible sound he'd ever heard. Oddly comforting.

Unsettling.

Stirring.

Mesmerizing, he realized as his eyes opened and he feasted on the sight of the strange creature before him. Where the dream image of her had been enough to fire his blood, the reality of her now set his entire body ablaze.

His attention slid from her face, down the column of her throat. Creamy flesh soon disappeared in a deep vee where her shirt strained at its buttons. Plump mounds pressed against the white material in a steady rise and fall that delayed his heartbeat for several long seconds. His attention dropped to his own chest, to the flat brown nipples, before shifting back to her. To *them*.

The more he looked, the more he wanted to touch. To find out for himself if they were soft and pliant or as firm as melons. As ripe . . . His fingers twitched and he reached out.

The loud *caw* of a bird exploded in his head and froze his hand in midair. Wings beat the air, and the bird streaked past him before disappearing into the forest. Zane's heart launched into a frenzied pounding as the cold fingers of reality gripped him.

Real.

He'd been warned, her coming foretold by the vision that haunted his nights, the prophecy that promised his death, and he knew what he should do. Run. Turn and seek refuge deep in the mountains, far away from this woman and what she meant to him.

Death . . .

His fingers went to the puckered ridge of flesh on his shoulder. He'd ignored his grandfather's warning once before, and he'd paid the price—a mistake that had nearly cost him his life.

This was different, he told himself. He wasn't a young child, scared witless and alone. He was a grown man.

Still alone.

But alive, a voice reminded him. *Very much alive.*

He stared down at the woman, so small and helpless.

Deadly.

Every warning instinct in him fired to life. Regardless of how she looked, he knew never to underestimate his enemy. The smallest thing could pose the greatest danger; the fairest creature, the biggest threat . . .

And she was fair.

He traced the curve of her cheek, his fingertips lingering near the edge of her full lips. Sweet breath rushed over his skin and he touched the unusual softness of her mouth, outlined it before moving on to her nose, her eyes, her eyelashes as soft as butterfly wings against skin.

Yes, very fair. Beautiful.

Did my heart love till now? Forswear it, sight!
For I ne'er saw true beauty till this night.

The words whispered through his head, as soft and gentle as her breath. As hypnotizing as her presence, as death itself.

He'd felt death's kiss, its hot breath stealing through his body, poisoning him until he'd seen the white light gleaming from the other side. As much as he'd wanted to walk toward it, to finally surrender after running for so long, he'd held his ground, gritted his teeth against the pain and endured death's slow attempt at seduction.

And he'd survived.

Just as he always would.

Determination forced his hand away from the woman, but couldn't make him turn his back. Despite the truth of her coming, he couldn't leave her to die.

Zane was not opposed to death—as it was a part of nature—but neither did he want to be death's messenger. The woman was trapped here, her ankle severely sprained. She wouldn't be able to put weight on the limb for at least several days, much less find her way off the mountain. If he left her, the bear would return. Or maybe a mountain lion. A cougar.

He closed his eyes to a new vision. Sharp fangs ripping into her velvety skin. Her sunny hair turning red with blood. Her easy breath twisting to strangled screams—

No!

He slid one arm beneath her back and one under her legs and swept her up into his arms. The bird streaked wildly overhead.

Stop! The word echoed through his mind, but he forced it aside. Instead, he focused on the faint thud of her heart, the warm feel of her body, and the sudden burning need to help her.

That was all he would do, he vowed to himself. He would aid her, as he would any vulnerable, wounded creature, as his grandfather had done time and time again for passing strangers. The medicine man had never turned away from someone in need, human or animal. He'd helped campers who'd left their trash behind, assisted hikers who'd been too stupid to wear durable shoes. He'd even helped a man who'd been dead-set on cutting down half the trees at the base of the peak. That man had broken his leg—a nasty wound where the bone had punctured his skin.

Zane could still remember the sound of the steel bird, the blades stirring the air around him and the fear deep inside. He'd hidden away as he always did when anyone came to the mountain. Watching from the safety of the trees, he'd witnessed his grandfather and several outsiders load the man into the steel bird, then watched the creature fly away.

To a hospital, his grandfather had told him. To get help.

His grandfather had helped everyone and anyone who'd needed him, and Zane could do no less. He would tend this outsider's ankle, then send her on her way.

While he might be ignoring the warning for the moment, he wasn't unaware of its significance. He knew the truth of the prophecy as surely as he knew the sun would set.

The woman didn't belong here, in the mountains. In his arms. She was like all the others. An outsider. He didn't need a vision to tell him she was dangerous to him. He felt it in the strange ache in his loins, the odd heat dancing over his skin. Dangerous, and deadly.

Not that he needed to worry. He intended to be

very careful where this outsider was concerned. Guarded and distant and quick, he told himself, picking up his steps. He would help her, then see her off his mountain, his doom-filled dreams avoided.

No matter how fair the woman, or how badly he wanted to touch her.

Or how lonely he was.

Warmth brushed against Tara's back, surrounding her, and she snuggled deeper. A sigh parted her lips.

Ahhhhhh . . . Ouch!

Her peace shattered as a red-hot pain pierced the fog of sleep gripping her senses. Tiny prickles of heat danced at her temples. She forced her heavy eyes open, took one blurry look around her and snapped them shut again.

This couldn't be happening, she thought as the fleeting glimpse of her surroundings registered in her brain. The dark interior of a cave. A solid earthen floor. The orange glow of a nearby fire. A large hound lazing on the floor. A tall, dark savage kneeling over her . . .

Wait a second. She was having a bad dream. That was it. A nightmare brought on by all the cupcakes she'd devoured last night. The junk food had finally caught up to her. Her brain had started to rot, conjuring ridiculous images of a half-naked man coming to her rescue, roaring at a bear, stealing her away to his own personal tree house—uh, make that cave.

She stared through a veil of lashes at the

stranger kneeling beside her—a figment of her cupcake-distorted imagination, of course—his attention riveted on her right foot.

No wonder her ex had forbidden junk food. He'd been a health-food fanatic, among other things, and a chocolate hater. She should have known why. He'd been as jealous, as domineering as they came. Of course he wouldn't want her dreaming about bears and fanatical motel owners and such a hunky-looking Tarzan.

Tarzan?

She'd always been into the three-piece suit types, clean-cut and professional-looking. Civilized. Safe.

This fantasy man looked anything but safe. He loomed over her, his long, dark hair streaming down around broad, powerful shoulders. A dark beard concealed half his face and crept down his throat. A necklace made of sharp claws hung from a leather strap tied around his neck. Silky black hair sprinkled a very bare chest and funneled down his abdomen to disappear into a loincloth . . . *loincloth?*

Okay, so her imagination was taking the savage theme a bit too far. Cutoff jeans would have been better, the button undone, the zipper parted just enough to reveal that tantalizing whorl of dark silky hair—*Ouch!*

Pain streaked up her leg and zapped her to the here and now. Her eyes snapped open and panic bolted through her.

This was real. The cave surrounding her, the rug

beneath her, the man looming over her. It was all *real*.

The reality of the past twenty-four hours rushed at her like a fierce gust of wind. Mary and Cecil and their Bigfoot scam. The bear and her lengthy escape. The tree root tripping her and knocking her unconscious. The bear licking her hand, ready to have her for breakfast. Tarzan coming to her rescue.

Tarzan?

Her blurry gaze zeroed in on the man again. A long-haired, wild-looking, loincloth-wearing Tarzan.

She'd fainted, and meanwhile this man, this wild man had scooped her up and spirited her away. To a cave. A secluded cave where no one would hear her scream for help.

Frantically, she struggled to get up. This guy could be a murderer, a rapist, a psychopath bent on the torture and molestation of tabloid journalists fleeing hungry bears. . . .

The thought faded into a wave of nausea that washed over her the moment she lifted her head. Pain rushed up her leg, exploded in her temples, and her vision blurred as she fought to sit up, to escape.

A strong hand on her shoulder urged her back down with little effort. Her head flopped back and her right leg blazed as the pain intensified, overriding her momentary panic. Darkness hovered, threatening to close in and block everything out.

She focused her attention on taking deep, even breaths. Soon the dizziness passed and the pain pulsing through her dulled to an ache. She became acutely aware of the probing fingertips at her ankle, the butterfly touches surprisingly gentle for a possible murderer/rapist/torturing psychopath masquerading as Tarzan.

Guilt surged through her. Maybe she was jumping to conclusions. A good journalist always reserved judgment until all the facts were known.

So what did she know?

That she'd stumbled onto one hell of a scam. "If you think I'm buying this, think again, buddy. I know you're just one of Mary and Cecil's pals, trying to con me since Cecil blew it. Well, it isn't going to work. I don't care how primitive you look, or that you saved me from being some bloodthirsty bear's breakfast. That was probably just a con, too. A trained bear. Where'd you get him? Rent-a-Bear?"

He didn't even spare her a glance. He leaned over her ankle, his profile outlined by the firelight, his expression hidden beneath his thick black beard.

"Hey, I'm talking to you." She tapped him and he jerked away. A growl rumbled in his chest and shivers danced along her skin. He was good.

"I'm impressed. You're a real pro. I bet Mary and Cecil are paying an arm and a leg for you."

She peered down and watched as he pulled some strange-looking plants from a bag and placed them in a small bowl. With a large rock he started grinding, the muscles of his arm rippling with each stab of the stone. Then he added a sprinkling of water to the mixture. After that, he turned to another small bowl and scooped up a handful of grease.

"Can't we just cut the act and call 911?" she asked when he touched the stuff to her ankle. "You're taking this a little too far—Ouch!" Pain wrenched up her leg and pierced her brain.

His fingers paused, his dark head jerked up and his gaze collided with hers. The air bolted from her lungs and her tongue tied itself into knots. He had the most incredible eyes. Like twin blue laser beams.

"I . . ." She searched for her voice. "That hurt."

He didn't say a word, just stared at her for a long, intense moment.

Suddenly her vulnerability gripped her as fiercely as the ache in her ankle. She was face-to-face with a man she didn't know. Even though it was a scam, she was still stuck here with him, her ankle in sorry shape.

Relax. He'd been hired to give her a little scare, an up-close-and-personal look at the Beast of Bear Mountain. Cecil in his Bigfoot suit had been just a ploy to make this guy seem all the more real. A *scam*. She didn't have a thing to worry about.

So why did she feel like Daniel in the lion's den? A huge T-bone waiting to be devoured by a hungry animal?

By him.

His eyes glittered, darkened, and she knew his thoughts followed the same path as hers. He knew what she was thinking, or maybe he was just thinking the same thing himself. How vulnerable she was. How easy the situation.

Boy, was he good.

She stiffened and summoned her most menacing expression. "Like I said, I'm not buying any of this, not that it matters. As long as I go back with a juicy story for Fritz and tell the world how the Beast whisked me away from a hungry bear and tended my ankle, what difference does it make if it's real or not? It's tabloid trash, and Lisa's going to owe me big-time for this. And let's get one thing straight. Just because you're supposed to be acting the macho Tarzan, don't think I'm ready to fall at your feet and play Jane." She gathered her strength and pushed herself to her elbows. Pain pulsed through her body at the slight movement, and by the time she'd managed to sit up, she was panting. Sweating. "No man"—she gasped for air— "no matter how good-looking could get me to do that again."

His beard masked his expression, but if she hadn't known better she would have sworn she saw a glimmer in his dark blue eyes. Amusement, maybe.

The thought stirred her anger. "I mean it. If you try anything, you'll be crying quicker than you can yodel, or yell, or whatever the hell Tarzan does." Brave words for a woman who didn't feel so brave, but then it was all an act anyway. He was playing the wild, unpredictable predator, she the helpless victim; the two lead characters for a juicy *Squealer* story.

She watched him as he watched her, and all the while she couldn't shake the strange sense that he knew what she was thinking. That somehow he

79

felt the emotions swirling through her. The fear and frustration and, most of all, the uncertainty, for as sure as she was that this was a scam, something kept whispering otherwise.

Before she could analyze the strange connection, however, he turned back to his task.

"Don't . . ." She tried to pull away, but one hand locked around her calf while his deft fingers went to work on her throbbing ankle. She struggled to see over his shoulder.

"What are you doing?"

No answer.

"Come on. You don't have to keep pretending. I won't tell anybody that you talked. Just tell me you know exactly what you're doing. Please."

He spared her an unreadable glance.

"You wouldn't happen to be a doctor doing a little acting on the side?" No response. "Maybe a cardiologist by day, and a Tarzan impersonator by night?" She was babbling, she knew. But she needed a distraction from the heat pulsing up her leg, the fire blazing in her ankle. "I could really use a good cardiologist about now." She pressed a hand to her thundering heart, hoping to slow its beat. But the muscle kept pounding away, keeping time with the throbbing in her extremity.

He continued to rub the salve over the injured area, his fingertips smoothing, circling, setting her teeth on edge.

"How about an orthopedic surgeon?" Another frantic gulp of air. "I really think I need a specialist. Or at least a pharmacist." She clamped her teeth shut as he touched a particularly sensitive spot. "Drugs would be good. Some Tylenol with codeine. A double dose."

Unfortunately, he didn't turn to a little black bag and whip out a bottle. His hands went to the small bowl, where he heaped the mashed plants into something that looked like a compress.

"I guess the doctor idea's out, otherwise you'd be using real bandages. As it is, you're inviting a major lawsuit."

He pressed the warm compress over her ankle. Pain wrenched up her leg and through her body to swell in her temples. Tears burned her eyes.

"Enough!" she screeched.

He paused and shot her a frustrated look that said, *Shut up, would ya?* Then he partially turned, his back blocking her view of his ministrations.

She tried to see past him, but he was too large, too close, and the pain too excruciating.

She fell back onto the fur rug and stared at the ceiling of the cave. His fingers worked in more salve, and the fire in her ankle blazed hotter, sending a blast of heat pulsing along her nerve endings. Her body trembled. Her vision blurred and she clamped her eyes shut. Before she could stop it, a tear squeezed past her lashes.

That was when the pressure at her ankle stopped. She forced her eyes open to find him leaning over her, his gaze fixed on the tear winding its way down her cheek. As if he'd never seen a woman cry before . . .

He caught the drop. The rough pad of his finger slid across her cheek, the motion soothing and gentle at the same time. Something glittered in his eyes, a look dangerously close to fascination. Fascination? At a woman's tears?

Before she could dwell on the notion, he turned away and reached for a large club. A scene straight out of Stephen King's *Misery* flashed in her mind.

Whack! He brought the weapon down on a thin strip of wood, not her tender ankle, and her sudden panic eased.

"So you're a carpenter by day."

He gave no comment. He simply pounded away at the wood, then placed the strip over the small fire until it glowed a fiery orange. After that, he bent and shaped the piece, then delivered the same treatment to another strip of wood.

"Whatever your profession, you've obviously earned your first-aid badge in scouting." She watched him fit the cooled strips of wood on either side of her ankle. He bound the homemade splints with twine, then leaned back on his haunches.

"All finished, huh?" No answer, just that piercing gaze burning a hole through her for two full heartbeats. "I guess so." She surveyed his handiwork. "Not bad, Tarzan. You're pretty good with your hands." Uh-oh. Her gaze shot to his, but he merely stared back at her, no glint in his eyes at her unintentional innuendo. "I probably shouldn't be saying that to a half-naked man while I'm flat on my back, but then you're not supposed to understand a word I'm saying anyway."

No flicker of recognition, nothing except deep, intense blue pools that made her think of a midnight swim. "So I really could say just about anything, and you wouldn't have any reaction, right?

Right," she said to herself. "You're the wild, primitive beast raised by gorillas—or in this case it would probably be bears or coyotes since apes aren't indigenous to this region. So which is it, Tarzan? Bears or coyotes?" No response. "What's it going to take to make you talk? I'm warning you, I can gab enough for both of us." Still no response.

"You're really good at playing big, dumb and good-looking." Not a single emotion flickered in his gaze. Nothing. She grinned. "But then maybe it's not so much an act, huh? Maybe you're naturally a little slow-witted." She was baiting him, but he seemed determined to resist. "Oh, well, don't feel bad. You're not much different from a lot of men I know."

Then he stood up, giving her a really good look at all of him, and the breath caught in her throat.

"Okay, so I'm wrong," she managed with a nervous laugh.

He stood well over six feet. Muscles corded his legs, his arms, rippled across his abdomen to disappear beneath the dangerously small loincloth. His chest was sprinkled with silky dark hair, his shoulders broad, powerful . . . *masculine*. Everything about him screamed of his maleness.

Particularly when his gaze dropped and roved her body, stripped her bare, reminding her that for all his gentleness a moment before, he was still a man.

Supposedly a savage man who lived in the heart of the mountains, in a cave with no modern conveniences, no razor to shave the beard that covered most of his face, or scissors to cut his long mane of hair. And other than the fierce growl he'd let loose when he'd first found her, he'd spoken not a word.

Damn, he was convincing. Oscar quality. If he hadn't yet had a break in Hollywood, he'd get one pretty soon if all his performances were as true to life as the Beast of Bear Mountain. A primitive male, raw and untouched by civilization, would draw tons of tourists to the small town of Bear Creek.

"A Tarzan instead of a Bigfoot," she mused. "For psychotic motel owners, Mary and Cecil have all the bases covered. A big hairy ape-man wouldn't sell half as many papers as a buff Chippendales-quality hunk with a little extra facial hair and a great tan. But you really should have rented a chimpanzee to play Cheetah instead of that dog." She motioned to the animal who stared at her with soulful brown eyes. "I always liked Cheetah in the reruns." Adrenaline rushed through her body, and she struggled onto her elbows before she could think better of it. Dizziness swamped her, her stomach revolted and everything faded into a throbbing blur.

He was beside her in the next instant, his strong hands easing her back down.

"I guess I shouldn't make any sudden moves." Her lips were thick around the words, her blurry vision fixed on the shadow hovering over her, surrounding her, it seemed. Long strands of silky hair brushed her face, her neck. His scent, a mingling of fresh mountain air and raw masculinity, spiraled through her nostrils. Heat pulsed from his body and fingertips to warm her flesh.

Something cool touched her lips and she opened her mouth, eager for a sip of water. Her throat felt like sandpaper, and it was entirely too hot in there—

"Ugh," she sputtered as the bitterness washed over her tongue. "That's horrible." She tried to focus on him, but pain still beat at her temples, blinding her. "No—" The word choked into another mouthful of the hideous mixture.

He set the foul-smelling liquid aside, and her head lolled back. She took a deep breath of clean air, of him, eager for something to dispel the awful bitterness lingering on her tongue. Drugs. She knew it, and a moment of fear seized her. He was drugging her, knocking her out. Who knew what he would do then—

A scam, she reminded herself. A harmless scam. The mixture was probably some sort of pain medication to ease her discomfort and make her think Tarzan was a whiz when it came to herbal medicine.

"So how long are you supposed to keep me here and play wild man?" She popped open one eye just as he turned away and started to get to his feet. "How long?" Her hand shot out, her fingers closing around the carved muscles of his upper arm. "Because I'm not really up to a crash course in Wilderness 101. I want to go back to the motel. You saved me, grunted a few times, and doctored my ankle. I've got plenty of material for a story."

A *tabloid* story, she reminded herself, disgusted

at the race of her heart and her urgency to get back to her computer. This was far from Pulitzer material, yet the prospect of writing it rushed through her like fresh wind through a stale room.

That was what she'd been for the past two years. Stale, doing one boring story after another, searching for *the* story to make her career. She needed a break from the constant grind of serious news, and this was it. Unbelievable fluff, but intriguing fluff.

"You can radio Mary and Cecil, or go fetch them or however you guys planned on communicating, and tell them I'm ready to go back now."

She touched him gently. He gave no indication that he understood. Instead, his gaze riveted on her hand, her fingers milky white against his tanned skin. He stiffened, muscles rippling, bunching, and she could practically feel the change in him. The wildness stirring, pushing aside the quiet gentleness he'd shown her. His passive features twisted into a frown. Before she knew what was happening, he jerked away from her as if he'd been burned.

"I'm sorry," she blurted, knowing without so much as a word between them that she'd committed some sort of faux pas. "I know you're not supposed to touch male dancers when they're performing, but I didn't know the same rule applied to actors." Her words followed him out the mouth of the cave, into the surrounding forest as he disappeared, leaving her confused and frustrated and very much alone.

"I want out of here tonight," she shouted after

him. "Tonight! Or Mary and Cecil can kiss their story good-bye."

It wasn't so much the being alone that bothered Tara as it was the quiet that lived and breathed and surrounded her, proof of how alone she really was. Isolated.

Independent, she told herself, battling the fear as she always did. She wasn't alone. She was on her own. Exercising her individuality. Living for herself.

Besides, she wouldn't be here for long. At that moment, he was on some ham radio, contacting Mary and Cecil and relaying her threat. She'd be out of there before daybreak.

The thought eased some of her panic, and she fixed her thoughts on the story. She would do the piece in first person. A true account of a wounded journalist not mauled by the Beast, but rescued by him—with lots of juicy description thrown in about how ferocious the bear looked and how hunky the Beast was. Along with a few shocking tidbits to really tantalize the reader, like the feel of bear saliva on her hand and death pounding on her door.

Hokey, she knew. But stuff like that sold thousands of tabloids every day, and while she might be a serious reporter in another life, she was filling in for Lisa at the moment, and hokey was definitely appropriate.

Her eyelids started to droop, which surprised her considering she was in a strange place, way beyond her comfort zone. But then she was also flying high on some herbal mixture probably meant to knock her out for a little while so Tarzan could take a well-deserved coffee break. He had put on one hell of a performance.

She yawned and fought to keep her eyes open. She really shouldn't fall asleep now, not with Mary and Cecil on their way. But weary exhaustion pressed down on her, and her eyes soon drifted shut. They could wake her up when they arrived. *If* they arrived.

She wanted to think about that last thought, needed to think about it for some insane reason she couldn't name, but it was too late. She drifted into a pain-free oblivion courtesy of Tarzan's foul-smelling mixture. Doctor or not, he certainly knew his stuff.

Chapter Five

Regardless of his crude first-aid methods, Tarzan mixed one heck of a powerful drink. Potent. Awe-inspiring. Tara dreamed one fantastic dream after another, her mind and body blissfully pain-free.

She definitely needed to take Lisa's advice, she decided when she managed to pry her eyes open. She should just find herself a man and have a night of wild, unbridled lust. Then again, it was one thing to fantasize about Brad Pitt or Mel Gibson and project herself into their latest flick. To dream about someone she'd actually met, someone *real*—not a product of the big screen—was another matter altogether. It was dangerous to her objectivity.

Stay calm. Keep cool. Be professional.

She touched a hand to her forehead and frowned. How could she stay cool if she had

dreams that shot her body temperature to dangerous levels? Her hand went to her chest, where her
heart still threatened to explode. Forget calm. And
professional? Ripping off her subject's loincloth
with her bare teeth would be far from business-
like, not to mention its effect on her journalistic
impartiality.

Not that she really had to worry about main-
taining any sense of professionalism. This was a
tabloid story, after all. A hoax.

Her ankle throbbed and kept her from snug-
gling deeper into the rug and giving in to sleep, to
more wicked dreams. The pain urged her to a sitting position and drew her inspection. Her jeans
had been cut away from the knee down, leaving a
good six inches of her bare calf exposed between
the ragged edges and the ankle bandages. Black
and blue bruises mottled the visible area. She
could only imagine what her ankle looked like beneath the makeshift bandages. Grossly swollen,
she was certain from the size of the bandaged
area. And severely bruised, if her calf was any indication, but not broken. Tara had experienced a
broken bone before, and while this pain was severe, it wasn't nearly as bad as if she'd actually
fractured anything. She contemplated undoing
Tarzan's handiwork and checking the bruises herself, then decided against it. She didn't have time.
Mary and Cecil would most likely be here any moment—

The thought stalled as she stared at the mouth
of the cave. It was nearly daylight. She must have
slept for five or six hours.

Ohmigod. Her gaze lit on her watch and her heart thudded. It wasn't daybreak, but evening. She'd slept the entire day away, and without even one of her Sleepy Time pills!

It looked as if Mary and Cecil were determined to let Tarzan give her a good show. Oh, well, they were probably paying him a pretty tidy sum and wanted to get their money's worth.

She wouldn't have minded so much if they hadn't been so determined to do this thing up right, with no modern conveniences as far as the eye could see. Particularly a bathroom.

She gritted her teeth, fought back a wave of dizziness and sat up. She was sore, but not nearly as much as before. She let her body adjust to her new upright state and stared around her. Outside, a few rays of orange brilliance staged their last stand, then surrendered to an army of shadows.

Inside, a small fire crackled, pushing back the shadows to light her surroundings. Various furs covered the earthen floor. Skins decorated the walls. She saw an assortment of clubs, spears, a knife, and a bow and arrow set. A row of pouches, similar to the one Tarzan had used when he'd mended her ankle, hung from the opposite wall. Furniture was nonexistent, no leather sofa or recliner or even a futon. Nothing. Her host certainly didn't have to worry about making the *Better Homes and Gardens* best-decorated list. Maybe the *Field and Stream* Testosterone Top Ten.

Despite the I-am-wild-man-hear-me-roar atmosphere, the dwelling did have a certain warmth, a coziness that wrapped around her and made her feel welcome. Safe. But then that was the point. A real-life Tarzan living in the Smokies, and she'd just landed the role of Jane.

A desperate, I-need-a-bathroom-now Jane.

Getting to her feet wasn't nearly as easy as sitting up. She needed leverage. She crawled across the floor, dragging her ankle and gnashing her teeth against the pain. Bracing her back against the wall, she used her good leg to push herself up.

Several painful moments later, she fought for a breath and tried to ignore the throbbing in her leg. She eased herself along the wall toward the cave opening. Passing the weapon stash, she spotted one knife in particular, a shiny steel blade, whereas the spears had points made out of finely sharpened rock. Mary and Cecil weren't as thorough as they thought. They'd left at least one sign of civilization when setting up this scam.

A scam, she reminded herself when the strange sensation hit her that there was something more going on here. Something bigger.

That was what the motel owners wanted her to think. The more she believed in the Beast, the better the story.

"So far so good," she said, panting as she hopped and rested, hopped and rested on her way to the cave mouth. The dirt floor seemed to stretch and expand. Exhaustion weighed down on her, urging her to give up. She couldn't take much more. Her heart already pounded from the simple effort of getting to her feet. The drumbeat in her ankle had turned into a heavy-metal solo straight off a Van Halen CD.

She couldn't.

She *had* to. She doubted Mary and Cecil had flood insurance on this humble little dwelling.

With one hand braced on the solid rock, she kept going. One inch here, another inch there . . .

The chill night air hit her the moment she hobbled into the shelter's opening. She shivered and strained her eyes. Fog shrouded the area, obscuring the twilight sky and making the fortress of trees surrounding her seem even more impenetrable.

No escape.

No invasion.

The second thought hit her along with a sudden gust of chill wind that snaked inside her clothes and prickled her skin. Behind her, the cave's warmth, begged her to give up. She could barely move, much less find her way out of here in the dark.

Another glance, her eyes straining, and she spotted a nearby tree. It wasn't too far, only a few yards. The problem was, the ground slanted at a nearly impossible angle for someone with two good feet to manuever without sliding all the way down. With her bad ankle, she didn't stand a chance.

Once again she was struck by how remote, how purposefully distant from everything the cave seemed. The sloping ground, the soldiering trees. A perfect place to hide someone. To hide *from* someone.

The thought faded into a cramp and she steeled herself. "You can do this. Just focus, concentrate."

She let go of the solid rock and eased her good foot out onto the slope. "A little ways and you're home free. Then when you're back in civilization, you can give Mary a piece of your mind for not having the consideration to set up a Porta Potti."

She half hopped, half slid a few inches, her arms outstretched, fighting for balance. Okay, this wasn't so bad. She could do it—

Suddenly, her balance flew south for the winter. She swayed, landed on her injured foot. Pain zapped from her toes straight up to her head. Darkness exploded into a thousand pinpoints of light. This was the beginning of the end. A fall to her death.

A pair of strong arms wrapped around her. Even though she couldn't see past the blinding rush of pain, she knew it was him. His strength surrounded her, his body warmed hers, his scent filled her nostrils. *Him*.

Relief rushed through her, despite his feral growl. The sound rumbled through her head, thrummed across her senses and made it very clear how angry she'd made her captor.

All that mattered was that she'd thwarted death. Angry or not, Tarzan had saved her.

Again.

Despite Zane's vow to keep his distance, he found himself cradling the woman in his arms for the second time that day.

She was an idiot. A stupid, stubborn idiot to try to walk in her condition.

An idiot with the widest, most expressive eyes.

She stared up at him, into him. He wanted to look away, but an overpowering sense of familiarity swept over him. He remembered the time he'd gone to the base of the mountain to retrieve a bear cub. The babe had followed an indulgent camper out of the forest and away from the protection of its mother. Rather than let the cub take its chances in civilization—Zane knew the danger that lurked there all too well—he'd gone after the animal. He'd crept into camp and had been about to scoop the cub into his arms when one of the campers had caught him in a flashlight beam.

He would never forget the moment. He'd been paralyzed by the sudden brightness. Fascinated by the brilliance. Fearful of the power behind it.

The urge to run had hit him immediately, and he'd fled into the surrounding darkness.

The same feelings rushed through him now, more intense than before. The urge for survival roared to life, like a sleeping lion just awakened, and he set her down on the nearest rock, needing to get her out of his arms, out from under his skin. He turned away from her.

"Wait!" Tara scrambled to her feet, trying to grab him and keep her balance at the same time. "You can't just leave me out here. It's cold and I have to go to the bathroom and you have to help me find a spot. It's the least you can do. You're supposed to be Tarzan, and he saw to all of Jane's needs." She added when he paused, "Please, I'm dying."

He turned back around, his unreadable eyes holding her captive a moment before he scooped her into his arms and deposited her behind a nearby tree. Before she could tell him to turn around, he slipped into the shadows and she found herself alone in the dark.

For that, at least, she was thankful.

With one hand on the tree and the other grasping a handful of leaves, she managed to do her business in record time. Of course, the wind chilling her bare flesh definitely encouraged her haste. That and the foggy blackness. Back in San Diego, she'd walked through parking lots at midnight, down shadowy streets after sunset. Both had been dark, or so she'd thought. But this gave new meaning to the word. In the city there'd always been a streetlight, a passing flash of headlights or the muted glow from a window. There was nothing here save the tree-shrouded forest.

"Okay." She hugged her upper arms and glanced around. "I'm finished." Silence met her ears, prickled her skin. It was too quiet. Unnaturally quiet. No hum of an air conditioner, no buzz of crickets, no distant clamor of traffic. Nothing.

Just the sound of breathing.

She whirled and bumped into a rock-hard chest.

"Geez, you scared the daylights out of me."

No comment. He merely stood there, staring, sniffing. . . .

Oh, God, he was actually sniffing her, sort of like the way a dog scented out his mate, the way Tarzan sniffed Jane.

He really was a good actor.

Before she could comment, he picked her up as easily, as effortlessly as if she were Kate Moss. His legs didn't buckle and he didn't stumble or make the usual Merle comment about how she should lose a few pounds or go an extra mile on the tread-mill. He didn't grunt or groan or even breathe heavily.

She was liking him more and more, despite the sniffing. Until he spirited her inside and practically dumped her on the fur rug—as if trying to get rid of her as fast as possible.

"Hey, I doubt manhandling the guest is part of your job description," she said as he tossed a fur at her and turned away. "I don't have cooties, you know. Though I wouldn't be so sure about you. There's bound to be all kinds of things you can catch up here smack-dab in the middle of 'Wild Kingdom.'" She shot a suspicious gaze around her. "Then there's the all-important fact that there's no treated water, no indoor plumbing, no Lysol. How long have you been living up here, getting a feel for your character?"

He didn't even glance her way. Instead, he retreated to the far side of the cave, retrieved one of the pouches hanging on the wall and situated himself cross-legged on the opposite side of the fire from her.

That was when it struck her where she'd seen the pouches before. In Cooney Rainer's Indian museum in town. She'd seen one hanging in a display case along with the authentic Cherokee clothing. This guy was Indian. Had she stumbled on the last of the Mohicans? Was he an Indian lost in time?

Wait a second. She hadn't stumbled onto anything. This was a scam. A well-thought-out con.

He wasn't Indian, she reminded herself as her gaze met his. At least not full-blooded. His skin was more suntanned than naturally dark. His hair wasn't blue-black, but brown with tiny streaks of gold testifying that he spent most of his time outdoors. And he had a full-grown beard hiding his features, not to mention a healthy sprinkling of dark hair on his chest. And his eyes . . .

"How long am I supposed to stay here?" She tried to keep her voice level. His presence seemed to fill up the cave, and the sudden urge to stand and run overwhelmed her. "I know they want you to give me the full treatment, but I really think I've had enough." No reply or even a grunt of recognition. "Okay, okay, if you can keep this up, so can I. I'll play along. Just make sure Mary and Cecil know that I have a plane to catch in ten days, and if I'm not on it, there'll be no story."

Ten days.

What was she saying? She couldn't stay here for ten days. Surely they didn't mean to keep her here that long. . . .

Maybe, maybe not. She had no way of knowing, and she was stuck. Without any modern conveniences, no camping gear, no writing equipment, no electric razor . . .

A wave of dread washed over her and she steeled herself. However long, she could do this. She had no choice, and so she would make the best of it. Maybe it wouldn't be so bad. He could have a TV stashed somewhere, a radio, a coffeemaker.

When he untied one of the pouches, she smiled as she watched him heap some of the contents into a crude wooden bowl. "Food," she said, reaching around the fire to take what he offered. Her smile faded into a distinct frown as she stared at the mixture of dried berries and ground meat jerky.

Her nose wrinkled. "I don't suppose you've got a pizza place nearby? One that delivers?"

He simply stared at her, scooped up some of the contents, sniffed, then loaded the food into his mouth and chewed, his bearded jaw working at the mouthful.

Play along, she told herself. "Here goes nothing." She took a bite and her mouth puckered around the sour mixture. *Yuck!* Her tastebuds rebelled and she swallowed the rest without chewing. Oddly enough, despite the hideous taste, her stomach grumbled for more. "Traitor." The declaration met with another stomach grumble. "Okay, okay. You win." She took another bite that proved much easier to swallow than the first. "So it's not a double pepperoni with extra cheese. You've been meaning to cut the fat before it catches up with you. Lean meat, fruit. Two of the basic food groups." She studied the mixture. "And maybe a few you aren't familiar with. Either way, it has to be healthy." Her gaze shifted to Tarzan and she noted the carved muscles of his arms, his broad, hair-dusted chest, his washboard stomach. "Look at you. You obviously get all your nutrients."

He seemed to stiffen under her inspection. Muscles rippled, flexed, and her heart stalled. She took a deep breath.

"It definitely does a body good, but then you're probably drinking those muscle-building shakes and working out when you're not swinging from trees, huh?"

His gaze caught and held hers. The blue depths sparkled, mesmerized her and rendered her speechless, and for the first time she found herself wondering what he looked like beneath his beard. If he had a strong jaw, a chiseled chin. If his lips were half as full and sensual as they looked peeking from beneath the hair.

The sudden desire to see him without all that wild hair sent a wave of panic through her. What was wrong with her? This was a game, a scam. He probably had a weak chin, a scrawny neck, a narrow jaw. Just an average Joe. She tore her attention away from him to concentrate on the food in her bowl. As ordinary and boring as any other man.

"We're stuck here and I intend to play along, but it really isn't necessary for you to keep up the silent treatment. We could talk, pass the time. You could tell me what survivalist course you took to learn how to doctor my ankle so well without modern methods." No response. "It still hurts like hell, but at least it's not broken. I fractured my arm once while roller-skating and I know the agony of a broken bone. It hurt the entire six weeks I had to wear the cast." Still no response. "What I want to know is how long this sprain will keep my ankle out of commission. I could barely hop to the mouth of the cave, and I'm not used to someone carting me around everywhere. I'll need to make rest-room trips, and take a bath. . . ."

She stared at her wrinkled clothes, her grubby hands. Tangles knotted her hair, and she could practically feel the raccoon eyes from her smudged mascara. A shudder rippled through her. "If I have to spend ten days like this, maybe it's a good thing you're not talking, after all."

He continued to stare at her with the same emotionless expression before moving to put away the leftover food. Then he pulled the rug he'd been sitting on away from the fire, from her, near the cave's mouth, and stretched out on his back.

"I guess it's bedtime."

He closed his eyes as if completely oblivious to her presence.

If only she were equally unaware. As it was, it was a long time before she finally managed to tear her gaze from him—the rise and fall of his powerful chest, the sharp ivory teeth of his necklace nestled in the whorls of dark hair, the soft flare of his nostrils, the play of the firelight over his bronzed skin.

More than once, her fingers had itched to reach out, to touch him. Luckily, he lay several feet away, and even the slightest movement of her body sent a bolt of pain, accompanied by a good dose of common sense, straight to her brain. No way could she cross the distance to him, no matter how much she wanted to.

Not that she *really* wanted to. The story, she told herself. That was why she was so fascinated by him, so drawn . . . why she'd made up her mind to stay in this hellhole even though the prospect of ten days of isolation and deprivation made her want to crawl into a corner and die.

But she'd promised Lisa a story, and she wouldn't let her friend down. Not to mention that she really had no choice. She couldn't walk, and she couldn't go back on a promise.

That meant she was here, she was staying, and she *wasn't* touching. Period.

Run!
The command echoed through the young boy's head, sending him flying down the hallway, back to his room, to the dark safety beneath the bed. Where he should have stayed in the first place.

But it was too late. The screams came, following him, shaking him until his breath came in harsh, ragged gasps as he clutched his stuffed bear, fingers digging into the fur as he waited for what would happen next.

The screams died and he heard voices, the faint creak of a door down the hallway, the terrifying thud of footsteps coming toward his room. He saw a blur of shadows out in the hallway. One, two, three, four bogeymen . . .

He snatched the edge of the bedspread down, then squeezed his eyes shut so tight that white dots swam in his head. He welcomed the fuzzy light, letting it push back the darkness and the fear.

"I'm sorry," he whispered, the tears sliding silently down his cheeks as he waited. For life. Or death.

The slam of a door snapped open his eyes; then

quiet settled in. He waited, counting the heartbeats rioting in his chest. Someone would come for him. They had to.

Please!

But no strong arms reached for him, held him, comforted him. There was only fear. It lured him out from under the bed, coaxed him from the safety of the dark as it had earlier.

Again, he stumbled down the pitch-black hallway, but it was different this time. He didn't wonder what waited at the end. He knew.

His bare feet came up against something hard. Wet. His gaze dropped and he saw the man's still form. No face, just a blur surrounded by red. So much red . . .

The teddy bear slid from his limp fingers, splashing into the blood, splattering it. Tears welled in his eyes, but he tried to hold back. Only babies cried. Not big boys. He started to sink to his knees, to beg the form to open his eyes and wake up, to forgive him. Then he heard it. A gasp that sounded like his name.

He stared through the darkness, deep into the room just beyond the body. Inside, blood covered the tangled sheets that had been snowy white only moments ago. His vision blurred with more tears and he blinked before he saw her.

She lay on the floor at the end of the bed, her back to him.

"Help." The voice, weak, and whisper-soft, drew him.

He knelt beside her, felt for her hand. He needed to touch her, to feel her touch him, hear her tell him *everything was all right as she'd done so many times in the past. That she wasn't mad at him, that she forgave him.*

No sweet voice filled his ears. Only the racket of the off-the-hook phone receiver, the tick-tock of a clock, the whir of the air conditioner, the hum of traffic speeding past the partially open window, the distant cry of sirens.

"Please." He pulled on her shoulder, eager to see her face. Then he would know this was a bad dream. One look into her soft blue eyes, and he would see the truth—the reassurance, comfort, love, forgiveness.

It was just a bad dream. . . .

But when he shoved really hard and finally managed to roll her over, he stared into her wide, lifeless eyes and saw only the reflection of himself.

Young. Scared. Unforgiven. Alone . . .

Zane's eyes snapped open to the flickering fire and the woman's form huddled nearby, the furs draping her from neck to feet. Despite the chill that gripped the air, he was sweating. He wiped at the moisture on his forehead, got to his feet and slipped out into the night.

The moon had come out, and the river winked in the light, promising the only relief he knew, where the dreams were concerned.

At least relief from this particular dream. He didn't have it very often anymore. No, most of his nighttime thoughts were filled with images of the woman now back at his cave, and even the ice-cold river had never helped him when it came to her.

But that was a different kind of discomfort, a warm, tingling longing.

But now . . .

He walked to the river and plunged in headfirst. Cool water closed over his head, embraced his body and robbed his lungs of air. He came up gasping and panting, his teeth chattering. The bloody memories dulled as his brain switched from reliving the bizarre dream to taunting him for being so foolish.

"You dreamed of them, didn't you?" His grandfather's voice filled his ears, and he turned to see the familiar black bird perched on a rock near the riverbank.

He shook his head, as if denying it could erase the horrible images, could ease the turmoil raging through him.

"You did. You dreamed of them. Do not lie to me. I know."

"Why? Who are they? Why do I dream of them?" The questions flew from his mind, toward the bird. *"Why?"*

"It does not matter. It is just a nightmare. A bad dream better forgotten."

He shook his head frantically and projected his answer. *"I want to forget, but I cannot. It is there when I close my eyes, waiting for me."*

"Because of the blond woman. She brings the nightmare, causes it. She must leave here."

"She needs help, Grandfather. I cannot turn her away."

Agitated, the bird hopped back and forth on the rock. *"Send her on her way!"*

Zane was tempted. He could turn her out, leave her to fend for herself and find her own way out of the mountains, a two- to three-day trek with two good feet. Then he wouldn't have to deal with the strange feelings she stirred in him. And as much as he didn't want to think she had anything to do with the dream he'd just had, he knew that wasn't entirely true. Tonight's dream had been more detailed than ever before. While he hadn't actually seen the faces, he'd heard the voices clearly. Instead of a jumble of tears and pain, he'd actually heard words.

"Run!" "I'm sorry!" "Help!"

And there had been something terribly familiar about them. Something terrible, period.

Fear rushed through him, whirling, mingling with the remnants of the dream . . . the familiar voices. . . .

Then an image filled his mind. The blond woman as she'd been when he'd first found her. Helpless and at the mercy of the bear. Something tightened in his chest because he knew the sight all too well. The feeling. It stirred deep inside him, dredged from some small dark place he didn't want to think about. He knew what it was like to be helpless, alone, scared, and as much as he wanted to turn his back on her, to bury the nightmare someplace deep as he'd done before, he couldn't.

He stared into the glittering black eyes of the bird and projected his thoughts. *"As soon as her ankle heals, she will leave."*

"Too late. Too late." A loud *cawww* raked across

his nerve endings. Midnight wings riffled, fluttered as the animal took flight.

Zane was left to the only relief he'd found since the dreams had started to haunt him so long ago. His only comfort. His distraction. The river.

Unfortunately, his thoughts soon turned to the woman, the *outsider*, he reminded himself, as if that all-important fact could make a difference. It didn't ease the restlessness inside him, the frustration, the sudden ache that burned through him.

She was here. Real. As much as the realization thrilled him, it made him all the more angry and determined. He sliced through the chill water with relentless strokes, dragging himself up onto the riverbank to stare at the moonless sky and listen to the waterfall rushing to his left.

She couldn't stay here. She disrupted his peace, his solitude, and he wouldn't stand for that. As soon as she could stand on two feet without pain, he would send her on her way. He *would,* and the nightmare would fade away just as it had when he'd first come to the mountain. Only a nightmare. Better forgotten.

He pushed his thoughts aside, cut his mind off and let his senses take over. His feet beat the ground and he fled deeper into the mountains, becoming one with all who lived there.

The beasts embraced him as they always did, welcoming one of their own. While the night stretched over the land, Zane growled as fiercely as a bear, ran as fast as a deer, sensed his prey as keenly as a cougar.

For Zane was a beast himself. Wild. Untamed. And hungry for a mate.

107

Chapter Six

She was stuck here.

The truth struck Tara the following morning when she woke up to find herself very much alone. The fire had dwindled. Sunshine poured into the mouth of the cave, birds chirped from the surrounding fortress of trees, and sweat tickled her brow.

The dulling effect of Tarzan's bitter pain medicine had worn off, and she felt a heavy throb in her ankle, not to mention a major headache at her temples. She threw off the fur covering her legs and examined her injured extremity. It looked even more swollen than yesterday.

She collapsed onto her back, stared at the ceiling and strained her ears for some familiar sound. No morning talk show blaring from the TV, no whir of the microwave, no *ding* of the toaster, no *drip-drop* of the coffeemaker. Nothing.

Her vision started to blur and she blinked frantically. How did people live like this?

Isolated.

Caffeine-free.

Sitting up, she positioned her leg at a comfortable angle and reached for one of the pouches Tarzan had left near the fire.

"Food is food." She took several bites of the meat and berry mixture. "Mind over matter. Just close your eyes, pretend it's a bagel and cream cheese with a double cappuccino." She chewed several mouthfuls; all the while visions of her ideal breakfast danced in her head. Unfortunately, the taste didn't quite fit with the illusion, but maybe next time. She took a tentative sip from the water pouch.

Not bad, but it wasn't a cappuccino, or coffee or a diet soda. A shiver rippled through her. Withdrawal.

She'd had it. She was getting out of here. Today. Forty-eight hours with Tarzan would make a nice fluff piece. She didn't need days or weeks.

Her gaze swept over the collection of pouches and furs, the wall hangings, the weapons. There had to be a means for him to communicate with Mary and Cecil. A ham radio or something. If she could get her hands on it, she'd send out a distress signal.

The dull pounding in her head became an acute searing pain as she struggled to her feet and ground her teeth against the fire streaking up her leg. She hobbled a few steps. It was awkward, painful, but manageable as long as she didn't lean on her injured ankle. She tackled the business of relieving herself first, grateful to find a small vine attached to a root protruding near the cave opening. Either Tarzan had thought to make things easier for her after last night, or the vine had been there all along and she'd simply missed it in the dark.

Not that it mattered. All that mattered was that she managed to complete the grueling task without breaking her neck or sliding down the steep slope at the mouth of the cave.

Back inside, she spent the next hour looking around the cave, poking through Tarzan's meager possessions, and blinking rapidly to keep her headache-clouded vision focused.

Nothing.

There had to be something. Some link to civilization. But it seemed Mary and Cecil were obviously too smart to have let that particular base go uncovered. Finally, exhaustion forced her back to the fur to rest. Just for a little while, she promised herself as her eyes drifted shut. Then she would rip this place apart.

Hours later, the afternoon downpour startled her from a restless sleep—she still needed her Sleepy Time if she wanted any real rest. She climbed to her feet. Back to work.

By the time the rain slowed to a drizzle, the inside of the cave felt like a sauna and she'd unbuttoned all but two crucial buttons holding her shirt together. The material clung to her skin, her hair stuck to her neck and she struggled to breathe, her hands rifling through a stack of furs. No ham radio. No walkie-talkie. Not even a flare gun. Nothing to send out the word she was ready, more than ready, to go back.

She leaned against the cave wall and took mental stock of what she had found. Several pouches full of dried plants, some fruit, more furs, a crude spear collection.

They certainly had covered all the bases. Not a bit of evidence to hint that Tarzan was anything other than the genuine article. If Tara hadn't seen Mary and Cecil's other con job with her own eyes, she might be inclined to believe this was for real.

But, of course, she knew better. She'd witnessed Cecil in his costume, and then that fake search for her when she'd been right in front of their eyes. Obviously all a ploy so she wouldn't suspect them of being the culprits when the real Tarzan showed up.

Not that he was real. A man in this day and age raised in the wilderness like an animal? Hardly. No matter how real these things looked, she thought, reaching for a spear, her fingers trailing along the carved handle. She studied the crude design a moment more before placing the weapon in its original spot. That was when she spotted the jug hidden behind several of the hanging pouches.

She pulled the cork out and took a whiff. The smell burned her nostrils, spread through her senses like fiery tentacles. So Mary and Cecil weren't as thorough as they'd thought. Their expensive actor was nipping at the bottle.

"This stuff has to be one hundred proof."

She took another sniff. *Mmmm.* It didn't smell quite as bad. Not that she was about to drink it; who knew what was actually in it.

"Don't even think it." She told herself. "So what if you've got a major headache and you feel like the living dead? It's not exactly a margarita or a piña colada." She took another whiff and the unmistakable scent of turpentine twinged with apple filled her nostrils. "It smells like some all-purpose cleaner to give Tarzan here whiter-than-white laundry."

Another sniff. Nix the cleaner idea. It *was* alcohol of some sort, but forget a nice quiet zinfandel or even the more potent Jack Daniel's. This was the no-name stuff. The stuff that came with 911 and a skull and crossbones emblazoned across the label. Or it would have, if it'd had a label, which it didn't.

She wasn't drinking it.

Her head pounded faster, pain pulsed up her leg and her own voice filled her head. "Who are you kidding? You're hurt, you're alone, you need a good shot of something and you're out of options."

It burned all the way down, ending in a fireball that exploded in the pit of her stomach and made her insides do flip-flops.

When she could breathe again, she took another drink. It burned, too, but not as bad as the first, and by the time she reached the fourth or fifth sip—she'd stopped counting—the cave was starting to look like it was straight out of a safari layout she'd once seen in *Vogue*. Her ankle felt two hundred percent better—actually she couldn't feel it at all, which was definitely an improvement—and the migraine was practically nonexistent.

Tara managed the few steps to the rug and collapsed, jug in hand, a smile on her face despite the heat, the growing darkness and the all-important fact that she was very much alone.

Even the lack of noise didn't bother her so much—

Okay, so there wasn't really a lack of noise. Her own voice echoed in her ears and she realized she was singing.

". . . if one of those bottles happens to fall, seventy-one bottles of beer on the wall . . ."

". . . happens to fall, two bottles of beer on the wall." Her voice floated out of the mouth of the cave to stop him in his tracks.

There was nothing soft and soothing about her singing. The words were loud, explosive rather than rolling off her tongue. Yet there was something that reached inside him and brought him to a halt. He stood outside in the increasing darkness of night and listened until there was nothing to listen to anymore, his mind absorbing the tone of her voice, the words, the knowledge that he wasn't alone—

The thought scattered as a bird flapped somewhere in the trees; the sound was magnified as were all the sounds of the forest. The buzz of crickets surrounded him, an owl hooted, a squirrel scurried up a nearby tree, all doing their best to distract him from the woman inside.

He stepped into the dark interior of the cave and saw her huddled in the shadows, the fire nearly out, a jug clasped in her hand.

A lopsided smile creased her full lips. She held up the jug and motioned him forward. "Come on over and join the party. I was starting to think you weren't coming home." She held up a hand. "Don't tell me. You caught the traffic on the loop. Drive it myself nearly every day, and I can tell you it isn't pretty."

It was funny how his gaze seemed to have a will all of its own. He didn't want to look at her, at her face flushed just so, the way her shirt gaped where the buttons had come undone, but he couldn't help himself.

She met his stare, and the connection seemed to bring a flush to her cheeks. Soft, quick breaths parted her lips. Her chest rose and fell, pushing against the two buttons that still held the edges of the material together.

His heart thudded. The sound seemed magnified, echoing in his ears, throughout the cave.

"I . . ." Her gaze finally dropped. She swept a hand across her perspiration-lined brow. "Geez, it's hot. Or maybe it's just me. Or the alcohol. Or both." She stared up at him. "Or you. Yeah," she said, her tongue darting out to sweep across her bottom lip. "I think it's you, Tarzan. You definitely upped the temperature in here." She tugged at her neckline, the motion drawing his eyes to the cleft between her breasts. He watched as a drop of perspiration slid down the smooth column of her throat, into the deep valley. . . .

He licked his own suddenly dry lips, his muscles tightening. Fire surged in his loins; his blood raced. His heart crashed against his ribs.

As if she sensed the change in him, the strange emotions whirling and kicking inside him, her fingers went to the buttons. She tried to do up the shirt, but her grasp on the buttons kept slipping. "I really did have too much to drink," she mumbled. Her hand slipped and the shirt gaped open, giving him a better glimpse of the satiny skin beneath. "I guess I should have worn something with snaps. Had I known I was going to meet Tarzan himself, I would have dressed for the occasion. . . ."

Her voice trailed off as his hands replaced hers. He worked at the buttons quickly, as if he'd done the same task just yesterday rather than twenty-five years ago. When he'd buttoned his grandfather's shirt for the last time.

"Look, I know Mary and Cecil want you to play the macho protector, but I'm about to short-circuit." Her voice drew him from his thoughts, and he glanced down to see his hand stalled. "So if you don't mind moving—" Her breath caught as he slipped the button into place, the side of his hand grazing the tip of her breast. The nipple pebbled, making a telling protrusion against the thin fabric of her shirt. His gaze shot to hers, then back to her breast.

He glanced down at his own, seeing the hard pebble. Nothing odd or new. He'd seen it dozens of times, after a freezing dip in the river, a gust of cold air, after a particularly bloody dream.

But there was something different about seeing the effect on someone else. On this woman . . . His fingers ached to reach out, to touch the hard tip, test it.

"If you don't stop looking at me like that, I'm going to start getting the wrong impression. Like maybe you're interested in more than just putting on a good show." She shook her head. "Like maybe I'm interested in more, which I'm not, though I would like to see what you look like underneath that beard."

A piece of wood shifted on the fire. Sparks flew, crackled, and he managed to tear his gaze away from her mouth. He frowned and fixed his attention on the last few buttons.

"Breathe," she told herself, her chest heaving, the material tugging against his strong grip. "Just breathe and it'll be over soon."

The last button slid into place, and he turned his back to her, eager to force his thoughts onto something else and ignore the strange feelings pushing and pulling at his control. The urge to touch her, all of her, mate with her . . .

Her injury. He forced his thoughts to her ankle and set about unwrapping the twine around the makeshift splint. He needed to moisten the poultice and check the swelling. His movements were quick, hurried. He needed out of here, away from her.

"I know seduction's not in the job description, but you don't have to treat me like a leper either," she rattled on, the strange words spilling from her lips. "Obviously you're not exactly thrilled with this little part, but neither am I. I'd much rather be at home. But no. I'm here, stuck with you. A two-bit actor who thinks he's trying to win an Academy Award."

Her voice filled his ears, and an image of her, her generous mouth forming each word, filled his head.

"You're definitely pushing the big, strong, silent type a bit too far."

He busied himself wetting the poultice and tried to ignore the strange feelings whirling through him. Adding more of the wild ginger and spikenard mixture for the swelling, he worked at re-wrapping the bandage.

"Suit yourself," she went on. "I don't need you for company when I've got my little friend here." She patted the jug, then took another long drink.

He paused in wrapping the bandages, his gaze fixed on the way her lips nursed the jug.

When she finished, she swiped at a few drops that trickled down her chin. "And don't think I'm sharing, because I'm not. If you can't be sociable with me, then forget about me being nice to you— *hic!* Oops, I guess I've had a teensy weensy bit too much."

He touched the damp poultice to her ankle and she winced.

"Okay, so I spoke too soon." She took another long drink, then held the jug out to him. "What can I say? I'm nice. You want a drink, GI Joe?"

He rewrapped the ankle, careful not to touch her any more than necessary.

"No thanks, Tara," she grumbled in a deep voice. "I don't drink while I'm on duty, but thanks for the offer. You're awful generous, considering I won't even speak to you.

"That's me," she went on. "Generous to a fault."

From the corner of his eye, he saw her take another drink. A trickle escaped the corner of her mouth and wound its way down her chin.

"Looks like my aim's a little off."

He forced his attention back to binding the last of her ankle. Once finished, he left her to retrieve a pouch he'd dropped at the mouth of the cave.

"All finished, I suppose?" Her voice followed him. "I guess so. Tell me, doc," she said, once he'd returned and positioned himself on the opposite side of the fire from her. "How soon will I be up and around?

"Soon, Tara," she answered herself in that funny deep voice. "All that goop I've been heaping on your ankle is really an antibiotic ointment to speed healing and reduce swelling."

She took a deep breath, her chest heaving against the buttons, and smiled to herself. "Thanks for the reassurance, doc. I feel much better. This stuff"—she held up the jug—"certainly takes the edge off the pain."

He pulled several peaches from his pouch, tossed her one and took a bite out of another.

"Well, I usually like mine in a cobbler, a la mode, but I don't think Mary and Cecil stocked up on any Ben and Jerry's. They really went all out for this setup. Primitive to a fault, with the exception of that knife you have over there and this." She held up the jug. "What I'm really dying to know is where a guy like you—supposedly primitive—got a stash like this." She smiled and caught a hiccup. "Sounds like a bad pickup line, doesn't it? Not that I'm trying to pick you up. I don't pick men up, and if I did, I hope I could come up with something a little better than that—I'm a writer, after all—not that even the cleverest line would work with you because you're so dead-set on playing this thing out to the very end." The words seemed to strike something in her. Her eyes widened and filled with tears and she slumped back against the fur.

"I don't believe this." She sniffled. "I could be here ten full days. How can those two do this to me? I know they're trying to be convincing, but this is downright cruel."

His chest tightened at the anguish in her voice, the sudden despair, and he wanted to reach out. To comfort.

To do much more, he realized as his gaze went to her mouth, to the way it formed each word, the slight tremble of her bottom lip when she moved her mouth just so. . . .

Heat spiraled straight to his groin and he stiffened in torment. She was driving him mad and there wasn't anything he could do about it.

"I can't stay here." She sniffled, as if fighting for control. "Okay, I can. I will. This is a test. If I can't make do with a fake Tarzan for a few days, how will I ever be able to camp out in a war-torn South

American country and write a real story?" She slapped at the tears, wiping her face and sniffling. "I can do this. It's just a few days; then I'm out of here. Fritz will get his story, Lisa will have her byline and I'll be stronger and wiser and—"

"You talk too much," he said in a growl.

"That's because I like to talk. I've always been a—" She did a double take, her red-rimmed eyes widening as if he'd grown an extra head. "Ohmigod! You can talk? Of course you can." She struggled to her elbows. "I knew this was a scam. Why didn't you say something sooner? Stupid question. Of course you wouldn't say anything. You're not supposed to. Don't worry. I won't tell anyone . . ." Her words trailed off as she sat up, only to sway to the side. "Ugh, I don't feel so good."

He set the pouch aside and studied her. "Lie down."

"Where's your radio? I want out of here. . . ." Her complexion went pale and she swallowed. "I really don't feel so good."

"That's why you must rest."

"That's why you have to get in touch with Mary. Tell her I want out of here. Time's up." She swayed, then slumped back to the rug and rested a hand across her eyes. "Are we having an earthquake? Someone's shaking the cave. I can feel it."

"Just take a deep breath."

She took several. "Better," she murmured. "Now I just feel tired. I want to go home."

"You are home. For now."

"No. This is a cave. My house has carpeting and electricity and running water. . . ."

"Sleep."

"At least tell me your name."

"Zane." He knelt beside her and pulled a rug over her. "My name is Zane Shiloh."

"Mine is Tara. Tara Martin, but then you probably know that. I'm a reporter, usually for the *San Diego Sun,* but I'm here as a representative of the *Squealer,* but then you probably already know that, too."

"Quiet, Tara Martin."

"Tara. Just Tara." She sighed. "Zane. That's nice. You look like a Zane." It was the last thing she said, the last word her full lips formed.

Heat surged through him, along with an intense craving to satisfy a hunger he'd never known existed. Until the dreams.

Until this moment.

It went beyond the need to possess, to conquer, to spend himself. He needed . . . to touch her.

It was that simple, that complicated.

She was there, at his fingertips, her heat teasing him, her scent drawing him, yet he couldn't, shouldn't. He'd been warned.

He stretched out next to her, close but not touching. As if he could satisfy his want just a little and still preserve his distance, his safety.

Closing his eyes, he pushed aside the doubts that niggled at him and concentrated on the steady sound of her breathing. So little compensation for years of isolation, yet for now it was enough.

Zane fell sound asleep.

Chapter Seven

"Geez, my head." Tara forced her eyes open to the blinding sunlight spilling through the mouth of the cave. She tried to focus, to think, but the only thing she could do was clamp her eyes shut and bury her face in the rug. "I'm dying."

A strong, cool hand touched her temple and she stared up at Zane, who knelt beside her, a bowl in his hands. He motioned for her to drink.

"Don't tell me you're back to the silent treatment. I've had about all I can take." She swallowed, trying to ignore the bitter taste in her mouth. "I can't believe I drank so much. I never drink. Except when Merle dumped me, but I have a light tolerance for alcohol; two maragaritas and I was plastered." She reached for the nearly empty jug. "I drank almost the whole thing." Heck, it probably wasn't even liquor at all. I drank bug spray or paint thinner or—"

"Whiskey." His deep voice rang in her ears and her head snapped up.

"What did you say?"

He motioned to the jug. "Whiskey, not poison."

"You're talking again."

"Yes, and you talk too much." He held the bowl up. "Drink."

She pressed her lips to the rim and her stomach flip-flopped. "I—I don't think I can do this. I don't feel so good."

"You will feel better once you drink."

"I think I'm going to throw up."

"Drink."

She took a deep breath and nodded. The liquid poured down her throat and she came embarrassingly close to spewing it back out. Her stomach protested and she rolled onto her side, praying she wouldn't toss her cookies. Seconds ticked by, her heart thudded, but finally the nausea passed and a soothing calm spread through her.

"Better?" he asked when she finally gave up the fetal position, sprawled on her back and opened her eyes.

"Much. You should market that stuff. A cure-all. You'd make a killing."

"This is made from hedge nettle. I killed nothing for it, except some plants."

"I didn't mean kill, as in literally. It was a figure of speech. You sell this stuff and you could get rich."

123

"Rich? What is rich?"

"Are you kidding?" She eyed him. "You can drop the wild-man persona. I told you already, I know it's a scam."

"A scam?"

"Mary and Cecil hired you, or maybe the Bear Creek City Council. So tell me, is the entire town in on it, or just the Otts?"

She had to hand it to him. He looked genuinely puzzled. "What is an Ott?"

"Mary and Cecil. Look, cut the act, will ya? I'm willing to play along for the sake of the story—and by the way, that grunting and sniffing you do so much is really a nice touch—so the least you can do is be straight with me. Just between the two of us, who's behind this?"

"You did drink too much. You make no sense." His formal, slightly stilted speech echoed in her ears and a strange sensation shimmied up her spine. Like maybe, just maybe, there was more going on here than a very convincing act.

"You're trying to tell me this isn't a scam?"

"What is this scam you keep speaking of?"

"Make-believe, pretend, an act . . . What am I saying?" She shook her head and tried to ignore the strange doubts jumping inside her. "You obviously know what it is. You're a part of it, and for the record, you're really good. You play an excellent Tarzan."

"Who is Tarzan?"

She sighed. "Give it up. I won't tell Mary and Cecil you talked to me. That bit of information will be our little secret."

"Who are Mary and Cecil?"

"A psychotic motel owner and her big hairy brother." She shook her head. Something was wrong. She could feel it, yet her hunch couldn't be right. No way could this guy be for real. "They're the ones who hired you."

"Hire?"

"They paid you big bucks to save me from the bear and bring me here."

"A big buck?"

She shook her head, frustration cresting inside her. "Okay, you want to play dumb, fine. Go right ahead. But if Mary and Cecil didn't hire you and you're not in on the scam, then how did you get here?"

"I live here."

"This is your permanent home?"

He nodded.

"And this"—her gaze dropped to his loincloth— "this . . . *costume* is your only clothing? You don't have jeans and a T-shirt stashed somewhere?"

"This is what I wear."

"All the time?" Sarcasm dripped from the words.

"Except when I swim."

"What do you wear then?"

"Nothing."

His words conjured a vision of a dark, tanned body dripping wet, and she swallowed hard.

"Look." She shook the image away. "We're way off track here. I'm not buying this act. You *can't* be real."

125

He pounded his chest with his fist. "I am very real. Flesh and blood."

"I know that. I mean real, as in telling the truth. You expect me to believe that you don't know the Otts? That it's pure coincidence they're trying to draw tourists by sensationalizing some story about a Beast who's half man, half animal, and here you are, up on this mountain, a man who looks as wild as a beast? The story come to life? A real Tarzan? You really expect me to think that's pure chance? Luck? That I wasn't set up to see Cecil wearing his ridiculous suit, that it wasn't a ploy to throw me off the real scam—you—and make me believe this whole setup? Do I look like I just fell off a turnip truck?"

"You talk too much." He got to his feet, retrieved one of the spears from the corner and started to leave.

"Where are you going?"

"If we are to eat, I must fish."

"Right. And I suppose you're going to use that? No rod and reel, just a spear?"

He nodded, his face a mask of seriousness, his gaze sincere. "This or my hands. I have no knowledge of this rod and reel you mentioned."

Hysterical laughter bubbled on her lips. "I think you dipped into a little of that skull-and-crossbones stuff yourself. That, or you're starting to believe your own lies."

"I drank no whiskey, and I speak the truth. I always speak the truth."

"No." The word sounded more like an impassioned plea for her own sanity rather than a flat

statement. "There's no way that you, that this"—
she swept a gaze around her—"can be real. That
you can fish with a spear, much less your hands,
or that you actually live here three hundred and
sixty-five days a year, and wear a loincloth all the
time, and live like . . . like Tarzan. There's no way
any of this is real. Uh-uh. No way."

"It is all real, as are you." His gaze pierced her
for several long moments. "*You* are very real." An
odd note laced the words, as if he couldn't quite
believe it himself.

"Well, you aren't," she said. "You can't be."

He didn't reply, merely turned and started to
walk away.

"Wait, Zane." As the name passed her lips, he
stopped at the mouth of the cave. Muscles rippled
as tension gripped his body, as if she'd actually
reached out and touched him.

Perhaps she had. With her voice. Her words.
The most common form of communication, yet he
seemed so . . . startled by it.

"That is your name, isn't it? Zane? Zane Shiloh?"

Slowly, he nodded. "Yes." He glanced over his
shoulder. "Forgive me. It just has been a long time
since I have heard someone speak it."

Right. Disbelief reared its head, but there was
something else simmering inside her. Curiosity.

"How long?" she pressed, the need to know suddenly as fierce as the disbelief.

"Twenty-five summers. Since my grandfather
died and I was left alone."

He disappeared before she could digest the full

meaning of his answer. *Twenty-five summers.* He looked to be in his late twenties, early thirties, tops. Which meant he'd been on his own since childhood. Alone. On this mountain. Far removed from civilization.

If there'd been one shred of truth in his declaration.

There wasn't. There was no way, in this day and age, a man could exist in solitude and not be discovered by some hunter or camper or hiker, even this deep in the Smokies. It was impossible, and she refused to buy it. It was all part of a scam to make her believe she'd stumbled onto a real-life Tarzan.

She'd stumbled onto a real-life Tarzan.

Instinct told her as much, urged her to follow him despite the fact that she might break her neck. She half hopped, half slid from the mouth of the cave, hobbled through the forest, slowing only to wipe the tears from her eyes and catch her breath. The heat sucked the air from her lungs and the pain blurred her vision, but she kept going. While she might act on her gut instincts, she needed evidence to truly believe.

The truth came to her a few moments later as she stood between two trees and stared at the man standing knee-deep in the crystal-clear mountain river.

The sight struck her speechless, and her heart pounded as she watched the scene unfold in front of her.

He eyed the water intently—oblivious to everything else—his gaze sweeping, searching. Then, like Zeus throwing a lightning bolt, he sent the spear slicing through the surface. When he retrieved it, wet and dripping, the crude weapon emerged with a giant fish skewered on the tip. Zane grasped the fish, which was still wriggling and twisting, wrenched it free and tossed it onto the riverbank with two others he'd already caught.

Correction—*speared*. He'd actually just used a crude spear to catch a fish. Tara grasped a nearby tree to keep from swaying. There was no way a two-bit actor could do that. Merle had been an avid fisherman, but he couldn't come close to doing what she'd just witnessed.

More than the act, however, it was the way Zane had looked holding the spear, his movements silent and practiced as he scouted the river, honed in on his prey and made the kill. At that moment he'd seemed more predator than man. Not an actor, but a savage.

The realization hit her, along with a wave of dizziness. She leaned against the edge of a tree and swallowed against the nausea rising in her throat.

Real.

But how . . . ? Why? When? Where?

The questions went on and on, pounding through her brain and making her more dizzy and sick to her stomach. She should have known. He'd seemed too real, too good at portraying his role to be part of any hillbillies' desperate plan. Short of casting Johnny Weissmuller—and she would have known him immediately, since she'd lusted after him in dozens of Tarzan of the Apes movies—the siblings would never have been able to hire an actor who played the part so true to life.

Why hadn't she seen it?

She had. She'd noticed the small clues, the desperate remoteness of the cave, the hodgepodge of his personal belongings—a blending of Indian and manmade—his crude doctoring methods, but she'd rejected the clues because the truth had been too fantastic. Even now she could hardly comprehend what was right in front of her eyes.

Now all those clues took on new meaning as she drank in the sight of him, the water glistening like diamonds in his beard, his chest hair. The sun played off his body, making him seem even darker, more primitive. A feral look crossed his face as he speared another fish.

"Real." The word was little more than a whisper, barely audible to her own ears, yet he turned around.

His gaze scanned the riverbank, pushing deeper into the forest until it pinned her to the tree.

She leaned back and closed her eyes for the space of a heartbeat, as if she could melt into the scenery. When she opened them, he'd already disappeared. Only a faint ripple on the water gave any indication he'd been there in the first place and hadn't been some figment of her imagination.

Hobbling a few steps, Tara sank down onto a fallen tree and tried to make some sense out of all she'd just discovered.

There really was a Beast of Bear Mountain, and it wasn't some scam sponsored by a couple of wacky motel owners. It was an honest-to-goodness man. A wild man. Zane Shiloh.

The name niggled at her subconscious, as if she'd heard it before. Somewhere.

The memory refused to push past the last forty-eight hours. The trek up Marshall Peak, Cecil in his Bigfoot suit, Mary's annoyed voice.

"I told you to hurry up with that suit."

"That makes twice you've screwed up now."

Twice . . .

Twice? A strange feeling hit her then, a shivering awareness that there was more wrong here than a simple con.

From her pocket, she retrieved the missing-person flyer Cooney had given her. The photographer's likeness stared back at her, complete with two nose rings, a choker with a smiley face charm and a tattoo peeking up from under the collar of his shirt. Had he snapped a picture of Cecil in his Bigfoot suit, too? If so, what had happened to him?

Help. She felt the word whispered through the trees, calling to her as it had her first night outside the cave. A shudder worked its way up her spine as one question fought its way past the dozens of others racing through her mind.

Missing . . . on purpose?

Mary had admitted to being the last person to see the photographer. What if he'd snapped a picture and Mary had wrestled him for the camera, to destroy the proof of her con? What if he'd fought her and something had happened? What if

131

the guy had been injured and Mary and Cecil had abandoned him for bear food? What if . . .

Ridiculous. She was getting carried away. There was nothing to prove any real wrongdoing, and Tara believed in hard evidence only. So far, she had only bits and pieces of a conversation that hinted at something sour. And in Mary and Cecil's favor, they'd actually tried to look for her.

For her camera, a voice reminded her.

"We need them pictures."

"When them pictures of the Beast hit the paper, it'll draw folks like flies."

Okay, maybe their search had been self-motivated, but they *had* tried to save her. Or had they?

She remembered the flashlight forcing her eyes closed, then Mary's statement, "She looks dead." Hadn't the woman seen her eyes open for those few seconds?

Obviously not, despite the suspicion gnawing at Tara's gut, and it didn't matter anyway. The poor woman and her brother were most likely lying in a hospital room at that moment, victims of the bear themselves. Tara couldn't forget the fierce growls, Cecil's shouts, the telltale rustling of an attempted escape and Mary's screeching voice. They had been attacked, she felt sure.

Which meant Tara truly was stuck here until her ankle healed enough to make the trek back. Unless Mary had managed to dispatch a search party. Even so, they were most likely combing the spot where Tara had last been seen, and she had the distinct impression she was far, far away from there. Hidden away. Hiding.

Again, the isolation of her surroundings struck her, and her thoughts turned back to Zane. Why had he chosen this place as his home, so far removed from everyone and everything? What was his story?

Before she could wonder about the answers, the hair on the back of her neck stood on end and she felt him—a physical awareness that had nothing to do with an actual touch and everything to do with the fact that she could sense him behind her. Close, but not touching.

"What are you doing here?" His voice, deep and slightly accusing, slid into her ears.

"I didn't believe you. I thought you were part of the scam, but now . . . You are real." As she said the words, the full meaning of that crystallized in her brain.

Twenty-five summers. Alone.

He was a savage untouched by civilization, an honest-to-goodness hermit living in the Smoky Mountains, fending for himself, rushing to the aid of a wounded reporter and doctoring her back to health using only plants and that which nature put at his fingertips.

"This is it," she said incredulously. "A *real* story, not some tabloid trash. It has human interest stamped all over it. Forget the *Squealer*. My editor at the *Sun* will snap this up and give me a great, big, fat promotion. This is major news, maybe even a Pulitzer." She struggled to her feet on a burst of adrenaline and whirled. "You're the story of a lifetime, Zane. The story of my career!"

He glared at her, and she thought fleetingly that she should be afraid. Everything had changed. He wasn't some actor hired to put on a good show, but little more than a stranger.

A stranger who'd saved her from a bear and nursed her ankle.

Those two facts dissolved the fear as quickly as it took root. She'd been with him two days and he'd done nothing but help her. She was many things—wildly curious, hell-bent on getting a story, disgusted at having to work under such extreme conditions—but she wasn't frightened.

Not of him.

But of what he did to her.

She fought to control the frantic beat of her heart. He didn't do anything to her except excite her journalistic ambition.

"This is it, Zane. The story that could send me to the top!" Shock and excitement swirled together, making her dangerously light-headed.

"Fool," he muttered, scooping her into his arms before she could teeter to the side, and sounding none too pleased that he'd been forced to do so.

"You're my ticket to bigger and better things." She struggled to slow her heartbeat, which revved like a primed car at the Indy 500. The story, she told herself, despite the fact that she was all too aware of the strong arms surrounding her, the rock-hard chest cradling her body. "You're my future."

"And you will be the death of me," he muttered, turning to stride back in the direction she'd come.

"I'm not that heavy."

No reply, just a frustrated grunt that somehow sparked her anger more than any smart-mouthed comment.

"Look, if helping me is an inconvenience, you can just put me down. I'll find my own way back."

He kept walking.

"I mean it. I don't need your help." What was she saying?

She wasn't saying anything. It was her wounded ego talking, and, boy, could it talk. "I can make it without you."

He stopped abruptly and deposited her on the ground. Her ankle hit and she winced.

" 'The lady doth protest too much.' "

Her head snapped up and she blinked away the pain clouding her vision. "What did you say?"

"You do not belong here."

"That's not what you said. You quoted Shakespeare. *Shakespeare*. How did you do that? Where did you learn it—"

"This is my home," he cut in, glaring down at her. "*My* home. Only I am safe here. You will die without me, do you understand? You need me to survive, just as I need the deer, the fish, the plants." He tapped his chest. "You need me and so you must do what I say."

His attitude fanned her anger and made her push aside the strangeness of the Shakespeare quote. For now. She planted her hands on her hips. "I don't *need* anybody. I can take care of myself just fine, and I don't take orders from anyone. In case you haven't noticed, I made it all the way down a very treacherous slope without you, and without your permission."

He studied her for several long moments. "That is true, but now you must go uphill."

"So it'll take me longer." She stiffened and jutted her chin out a notch. "I'll manage."

"But now you must escape the bear standing behind you."

"A bear? Behind me?"

He nodded. "Right over there." He said the words so calmly, his expression slightly amused. Not the face of a man staring down a bear.

"Right, and I suppose I've got Godzilla behind my other shoulder."

"I see nothing other than the bear."

"Right. So what's this bear doing? Sizing me up for dinner?"

"I do not think she is hungry. Yet. Only curious. She wants to smell you."

A soft rush of warm air just behind her killed the laughter in her throat. She became keenly aware of deep, wheezing sniffles. She licked her suddenly dry lips and fought for her voice. "You weren't kidding, were you?"

"I am no kid."

"Kidding means not telling the truth."

"I always tell the truth."

"Okay." She took a deep breath. "There's a bear behind me. What now?"

"You could stand very still until she leaves, or you could ask for my help."

"How long until she leaves?"

"I do not know. You are something new and you smell . . ."—he leaned forward and sniffed her—"unlike anything here. She will have to get to know your scent, and that might take a while."

"Oh, God. I have a scent." Of course she had a scent. Probably a pretty strong one. She hadn't had a bath for two days straight. The sniffing behind her turned into a snort, and she jumped. Her arms locked around Zane's neck, and she hung there for a fraction of a second before he swept her up.

"I did not hear you ask me."

Tara chanced a glance and saw the bear, a seeming carbon copy of the one who'd attacked her. The animal reared back on its hind legs. A growl split the air, and Tara's fingers dug into Zane's shoulders. "I'm asking. Get me out of here. *Now.*"

"That does not sound like asking. It sounds like telling."

"Please get me out of here? Now?"

"That is better."

"I don't feel you moving."

"In time. First you must admit that you need me."

"I don't need anybody—" Her words screeched to a halt when he plopped her back down and started to turn. "Okay, okay. I need you." She held her arms out. "Now get me out of here."

"And because you need me you will do what I say."

"I already told you, I don't take orders—" A loud growl drowned her words. The hair on the back of her neck stood on end and fear seized her. "Whatever you say," she blurted. "Just get me out of here."

He didn't move for several moments. Instead, he stared at the bear, long and hard, and some silent something seemed to pass between them. The animal turned and waddled off.

"How—how did you do that?"

Rather than answer, he scooped her up and carried her toward the cave. The slope up the mountain was little challenge for him, even with his arms full. In no time, he deposited her on the ground.

Her bottom hit, she winced and he glared.

"Do not leave here again. You will stay here, inside this cave where it is safe, until your ankle heals. Then you will leave." The words sounded more like a threat than a statement, and goose bumps danced along her arms.

"That could take weeks. I can't spend day and night cooped up inside this cave—" Her words stumbled to a halt when his eyes fired a deep, angry blue. "Okay. Here. Inside." She winced and tried to adjust her ankle. She was too tired to argue, and in way too much pain.

He shot her a suspicious glance. "So how did you manage the slope down?"

"Where there's a will, there's a way, and where there's a way"—she rubbed her sore tush—"there's skid marks on someone's butt."

He frowned. "Do not try such a foolish thing again. You could have caused more damage to the ankle, or wounded something else that would keep you here even longer."

"Geez, Zane, don't be so hospitable. I might start to think you actually like me."

He frowned. "I do not want you here."

"No kidding? I sort of figured that out already. My question is why?"

"You do not belong here. You are an outsider."

"Because I'm not from Bear Creek?"

"Because you come from beyond these mountains. Your ways are different from mine."

"How do you know? Have you ever been on the outside?"

"I have no desire to see the outside. This is my home and you are not welcome. So stay off your feet," he said with a growl. "And let your ankle heal."

"Why are you so angry? I'm the one who should be angry after that little bear stunt. What would you have done if I hadn't thrown myself at you and begged for help? Left me for bear food?"

"You ask too many questions."

"It's my job, and I've got dozens more to ask you, so get used to it."

"Job?"

"What I do for a living. To pay bills, buy food, survive."

"You survive by asking questions?" At her nod, he shook his head. "That is ridiculous."

"It's true. I ask questions, report the answers and make a living off it."

He scowled. "Asking questions will not fill your belly or keep you warm at night. I will do that, provided you listen to me and do as I say. Stay off your ankle." Then he stalked to the cave's mouth and disappeared.

Tara found herself on her own, with the exception of Zane's slothful dog. But she didn't feel the strange loneliness that usually plagued her, or even resentment at his high-handed attitude. Anticipation set her nerves buzzing. This was it . . . Her story. *The* story.

"Pulitzer, here I come."

Chapter Eight

Twenty-four hours after learning Zane was the genuine article, Tara was still clueless as to the hows and whys surrounding him. After silently cooking the fish he'd caught, he'd stayed away from the cave all day following the bear episode, not returning until late into the night. When he did, Tara had already washed up as best she could with the small amount of fresh water left in the water pouch, and had crawled into the furs and closed her eyes. She'd felt his presence for a long while before he approached her, as if he waited to make sure she'd fallen asleep. Then he'd stretched out next to her, and the closeness had scattered her thoughts. It had been a long time since she'd lain with a man. And forever since she'd lain with someone like Zane. Merle had never kept her so warm or made her feel so light-headed.

141

The story, she told herself. So Zane happened to have a great body, as well. She wouldn't let that upset her priorities. Getting close to a man—any man, even Zane—was at the bottom of a well-thought-out list that put her career and her independence and her coveted cappuccino in the top three slots.

She'd vowed to question him the moment he awakened, not really expecting to get any sleep herself. She wasn't good when it came to sleeping in strange beds, which was why she'd loaded up on Sleepy Time, an over-the-counter sleep aid before she'd left the airport. She'd planned to spend the darkest hours collecting her thoughts and hit him with a full interview the moment he woke up. Then Zane slid a strong arm around her waist and she'd melted into his warmth, and into sleep.

By the time she'd opened her eyes, he was gone. She saw him briefly throughout the day, bombarded him with questions, but he ignored all of them, intent on staying silent, aloof, distant.

Not for long, she vowed that night. She fixed her attention on the man who knelt near the fire, a limp rabbit at his feet.

"I need facts, Zane. How am I supposed to write the story of a lifetime if you refuse to answer any of my questions?"

He made no response as he unrolled a strip of soft leather the size of a placemat and placed the animal on top. Next, he retrieved a large bowl of water and placed it to the side, his movements quick, undisturbed, as if he were completely alone.

But he knew she was there. She saw it in the tensing of his muscles whenever he heard her voice, sensed it in the strange current flowing between them. An undeniable awareness.

"This isn't the norm, Zane. These are the nineties. People don't live like this anymore. You're the last of a dying breed. Society will want to know how you've managed to exist all this time without any modern conveniences. How you've stayed virtually untouched by the outside world for twenty-five years, living off the land, totally self-sufficient, no rent or mortgage or credit-card payments. So how did it all start? What brought you to the mountains?"

"You are here to heal, not ask questions." He pulled a sharp-looking knife from the waistband of his loincloth.

"I can do both. . . ." Her words trailed off as she realized what he intended to do with the knife.

At the sound of her fading voice, he spared her a look and saw how pale she'd suddenly turned. "What is wrong?"

She swallowed and tried for a laugh, but it came out sounding rusty and hollow. "I just thought about Thumper."

"Thumper?"

"The rabbit from *Bambi*, the children's movie. Bambi was a deer and Thumper was his rabbit friend."

"Deer and rabbits are not friends. Not here. They are different, just as you and I are different." His blue gaze pierced hers, filling her with a strange electricity that set her nerves humming.

143

Then his attention moved lower, pausing at her chest before dipping lower, roaming over her hips and legs, then back up again. She shifted at the sudden flood of heat between her legs.

Calm, cool, professional. Think story, she told herself. *A big, major story. Nothing else big or major. Certainly not him or any part of him.*

She cleared her throat. "We're both human beings."

Her voice seemed to snap him back to attention, and he frowned. "You are an outsider and I belong here. That is the difference." He said the words as if trying to convince himself, to forget their physical differences and the strange connection that had just sparked between them. "I see food and warmth when I look at this rabbit. I see life. What do you see?"

She swallowed and eyed the limp animal. "Death."

"One feeds the other. The death of one animal gives life to another. The death of this animal will give life to us. That is the way here."

"Did your grandfather tell you that?"

"He tells me many things."

"You mean *told,* as in past tense—"

"No talking." He poised the tip of the blade at the rabbit's chest and the air stalled in Tara's lungs. He paused at her reaction. "Look away. There is no need for you to watch."

"I want to." If he wouldn't talk, she would have to write her story from observation. That meant following each and every thing he did.

More than that, however, she watched because

Zane was right. She was an outsider, way out of her comfort zone with no clue as to how to survive in his world. That made her virtually helpless, vulnerable and completely at Zane's mercy, and Tara had vowed never to be at any man's mercy ever again.

"Go on. Don't mind me. I'm fine."

He didn't move. "Do you not eat meat where you come from?"

"Sure, but I don't catch it and butcher it myself. I buy it from the supermarket, in nice little packages minus the beady black eyes and the cute little whiskers."

"Someone catches it and butchers it for you. That is no different from this. I caught the rabbit; I will butcher it." With a quick motion of the knife, he set about skinning the rabbit, each cut precise, making it obvious he'd skinned animals all his life. *For survival*.

With grim determination, she followed his movements. He performed the chore quickly and efficiently, and in a matter of minutes he was rinsing the cleaned carcass in the nearby bowl of water.

"After I wash the rabbit, I will cook it. Later, I will stake the fur out on a board to dry and use it to make a warm robe for winter. The winters are long and very cold." There wasn't an ounce of emotion in his voice, yet she saw a flicker of desperation in his blue eyes.

Just a flicker, but it was enough to shake her to the core. The magnitude of his words struck her like a dousing of cold water. Winters alone in the mountains with no heat or running water. Nothing but snow and solitude. Isolation.

Safety.

Once again she thought of how far removed the cave was. The perfect place to hide away from someone. Or something.

"Have you ever been down the mountain? Into town?"

"Now we will cook," he went on. He took a sharpened stick and skewered the rabbit before fitting it on a frame he'd situated over the fire.

"Where do you come from?" No response. "Were you born here in the mountains? What about your parents?" She fired the questions at him, hoping for a reply, watchful of a reaction, something to give her some hint as to the mystery that surrounded Zane. "Where are they? Alive? Dead?"

His hands faltered then, and he closed his eyes, searching for something, or hiding. Finally, he shook his head. "I have only my grandfather. He raised me."

"So you don't remember your parents?"

"No questions." He growled, but Tara was already on a roll.

"If your grandfather raised you and he died when you were very young, then who have you been talking to all this time? Your speech is very well developed. You've obviously been using your voice for more than growling and grunting. Who do you talk to?"

He didn't answer. Instead, he bundled the rabbit

remains in the soiled mat of leather and got to his feet. "I must do away with this."

"Your dog?" she called after him as he headed for the mouth of the cave. "Is that who you talk to? Come on, Zane. Tell me something. Anything." Her desperation reached out to him, in the sound of her voice, the pleading in her gaze.

He hesitated. "I have no need to use words with Gilette. She understands without them." He stared at the dog, who whimpered and walked toward him, tongue lapping at his outstretched hand.

"That's her name? Gilette?"

"Yes."

"That's a very strange name. How did you come up with it?"

"It is from *Romeo and Gilette.*"

The words echoed in her head, sparking dozens of questions and making her blood race faster. "That's Juliet, not Gilette."

"Ju-li-et?" He sounded out the new version. "How do you know this?"

"Mrs. Jenkins's eighth-grade English class. The real question is how do *you* know? You've had no formal schooling and you're a good ten to twenty miles from the nearest bookstore, let alone library." Even so, he knew Shakespeare, and not just *Romeo and Juliet*. He'd quoted *Hamlet* to her earlier. The knowledge whirled in her brain, stirring a whirlwind of possibilities. "Did your grandfather introduce you to Shakespeare?"

"No." He shook his head. "Possibly. I do not know."

"How can you not know—"

"No more." The words thundered through the cave and bounced off the walls like a gun blast.

"I know you're not much of a conversationalist, Zane, and I respect that, but this is very important. I want to write your story and I can't do that unless you tell me about your grandfather, your parents—"

A fierce growl sizzled in her eardrums, and Tara, never at a loss for words, found herself suddenly speechless. Zane shot a glare over his shoulder at her, and for the first time since discovering who, or rather, what he was, Tara felt a ripple of fear.

Far greater, however, was the sudden bolt of compassion that struck her as he stood there, framed in the cave's opening, a lone figure surrounded by fading twilight. Isolated. Lonely.

At that moment, she sensed his loneliness more than his anger. It rolled off of him in waves, sweeping over her, mingling with the similar feelings buried deep inside her. The connection that had sparked between them from physical awareness solidified into a strange sort of kinship.

Tara knew better than anyone what it was like to be on her own. She'd spent a solitary childhood with only an occasional glimpse of her parents, who'd never really been parents at all but journalists first.

The story had always come first. Before Tara's first piano recital, her kindergarten graduation, each and every swim meet, high school graduation, and even her wedding.

Not that she blamed them for missing the last.

If she'd been smart, she would have missed it herself. The only event they wouldn't have missed would have been seeing their daughter win the coveted Pulitzer for the story she was about to write. Unfortunately, they'd died in a car crash in Singapore doing a story on feuding rebel armies and would never know that their daughter had followed in their prestigious footsteps.

Not that she was doing this for them. This was for herself, because as much as she'd resented their passion for a good story while growing up, she understood it at that moment as she watched Zane walk away from her, angry and resentful and so determined to dodge her questions.

She wanted his story in the worst way, and she would never give up.

"You've got the silent treatment down to an art form," she said a little while later when he returned. "Come on, Zane. Talk to me."

He gave no response, merely sat across the fire from her, his gaze fixed on the roasting rabbit.

Quiet settled around them, disrupted only by the whistle of the wind and the sound of dripping juices, sizzling as the rabbit cooked. A delicious aroma filled the cave, replacing the smell of blood and death, and Tara's stomach gave a hearty grumble.

"You do like meat," he observed, his expression easing briefly into one of amusement.

The effect was devastating. Her heart jumped, her blood raced and for a full moment, she forgot she'd just won a major coup. He'd said something to her of his own free will.

"I never said I didn't," she said when she recovered her wits. "I've just never really enjoyed hunting."

He frowned at her. "I kill for food, not enjoyment."

"And what do you do for enjoyment?" The moment the question left her mouth, their gazes locked. His eyes glittered hot and bright, an answer to what he'd like to do. Her cheeks heated.

The story, she reminded herself when she caught her mind wandering from his past, to what the next few moments might hold. Would he keep looking at her? Undressing her with his eyes?

She forced the thought away. "Have a heart," she pleaded—there was no place for pride in professional journalism. "Do you know how many reporters would kill for this story?"

"We need more wood for the fire." He climbed to his feet and made a hasty retreat.

"Fine," she muttered to Juliet, who lagged behind and lazed by the fire. "He doesn't want to talk, then we won't talk. I'll just sit back and observe."

So it wasn't the greatest idea, Tara decided the following morning as she sat in the opening of the cave and conducted a visual search for Zane, who'd long since disappeared into the trees. She'd planned to follow him through a typical day, document what he did, hunting or fishing, gathering wood and fruit, talking to the animals or whatever he did to keep his voice from getting rusty. Unfortunately, her ankle prohibited her from doing much of anything except sitting around on her hind end and fighting off boredom.

She didn't even have Juliet to keep her company. The dog had disappeared down the mountain as she so often did. Probably scavenging, as Zane had explained. The dog always returned with some piece of civilization. A spoon. A tin cup. A small tackle box. Even a tube of hand lotion, which Tara had promptly seized.

"Forget this." She'd had enough of staring at the trees and listening to her own voice. A change of scenery was definitely in order. She'd done it once, she thought, eyeing the slope, and she could do it again—regardless of the steady ache in her ankle and Zane's order to stay put. If he wanted her holed up inside, he could darn well confine himself, as well. She'd had all she could take.

After half sliding, half skidding down the incline, she sat panting at the bottom of the slope. She took a deep breath and hauled herself upright. Then, with the help of the surrounding trees, she hobbled at a snail's pace through the forest in the direction she'd taken yesterday. If Zane was at the river, terrific. She'd watch him fish, observe his daily quest for food, and if he wasn't there . . .

Just the thought of water sent a rush of longing through her. While she had the crude wooden bowl and a small amount of fresh water to clean herself, it was a big stretch from the daily shower she'd become accustomed to. She needed a real bath to wash away the dirt and grime and defeat that had settled over her skin.

Defeat? Not in this lifetime. So she had no pen or paper, nothing to record her thoughts, and a very unwilling subject. She fought the sense of futility that swept her. She wasn't ready to give up. Yet.

She hobbled along for several minutes, deeper into the trees until she lost her sense of direction. Hesitating, she strained her ears for some tell tale sound. Nothing, just the faint whisper of a breeze through the trees, promising a coming afternoon shower.

Help . . .

The word floated on the air, whisper-soft and as light as a feather. Yet she heard it as plain as day. A voice in her head.

Zane. Her thoughts jumped, and panic bolted through her. He was hurt, calling out for help, and she had to get to him—

A ripple of water shattered her thoughts, and she hurriedly limped forward in the direction of the sound. She burst through the edge of the forest that surrounded the riverbank and came to a staggering halt. Zane wasn't wounded or bleeding or calling out to her. He was . . . well, *naked*.

Tara simply stared as he climbed from the water on the opposite side of the riverbank. He wore only the bear-teeth necklace. Water sluiced down the tanned perfection of his body, funneling through the hair that covered his chest to soar into a downward spiral that drew her gaze and sucked the breath from her lungs.

As if he heard the sudden frantic thud of her heart, his head snapped up and his gaze locked with hers. Emotion swept his features—anger, dismay, frustration, regret, fear . . .

Fear?

It disappeared as quickly as it had come, giving way to a heated determination as he held her gaze and stood boldly before her. Naked and beautiful and hard . . .

Hard?

She swallowed as her stare riveted on his straining erection.

Her attention didn't go unnoticed. He touched himself then, long fingers stroking his thick, rigid length, the motion enticing, promising.

Embarrassment flooded through her, quickly replaced by a simmering heat. There was no room for shock or shyness or any of those things here. She was standing smack-dab in the middle of utopia, a mountain haven so far removed from civilization that time stood still. Here a rushing waterfall fed a swirling blue pool surrounded by ancient trees and young wildflowers. The scent of crystal-clear water cleansed her mind, while the sight of Zane, so bold and uninhibited, charged her with a strange sense of wantonness. Freedom.

There were no rules here to govern his behavior, to restrict hers. In these mountains, it was survival of the fittest, and Zane was certainly . . . fit. In every way.

He stepped forward then and she knew he meant to slide into the water, to cross over to her so that he could feel her hands on his growing length rather than his own. The desire sparkled in his gaze, open and unshuttered, communicating a

Kimberly Raye

need so profound it awakened her own. Warning signals fired in her brain. She should turn and walk the other way. *Get out of here now. Fast.* Zane was a story. Nothing more.

Ah, but he was much more, she admitted when he stepped from the water to stand dripping wet, still very naked and very hard, right in front of her. So close all she had to do was reach out . . .

Desire shattered into a half scream, half cry that ripped open the silence surrounding them and stalled Tara's hand inches away from her destination.

Worry brightened Zane's eyes and he darted past her, deep into the forest, leaving her hot and panting and wondering what had just happened.

She gasped for several deep breaths and did the only thing a good reporter could do, even one with a sprained ankle: she pulled her raw emotions together and hobbled after him.

Zane outdistanced her and she quickly lost him, but she kept walking, determination pushing her on. The shrill cry continued, luring her on until she reached a small clearing. Her steps faltered.

The sound of his voice, rich and deep, drowned out the anguished call and struck her motionless.

" ' . . . lulla, lulla, lullaby . . . never harm nor spell nor charm, come our lovely lady nigh . . . ' " He crooned to what looked like a medium-size wildcat as he dislodged the animal's paw from beneath two twisted tree roots. " ' . . . good night, with lullaby . . . ' " Minutes later, he stood cradling the frightened animal.

"That was more Shakespeare. *Hamlet?*"

154

"*A Midsummer Night's Dream.*"

"We didn't cover that one in Mrs. Jenkin's class. What happened here?"

"This cub lodged his paw and could not get free. It frightened him and he called out to his mother for help."

"But you came instead."

"His mother roams farther up the mountain with the rest of her cubs. This one probably wandered off and got lost. She would not have found him for a long while, and who knows what danger he would have faced until then."

"And you're no danger? But you have several cougar furs back at the cave. You hunt his kind."

He shook his head and stroked the animal. "Not this young. This cat is just a babe. When he is older and we are evenly matched, perhaps he will wind up keeping me warm."

"But you killed the rabbit, which was much smaller than you, and weaker."

"Smaller and weaker, but fully grown and as fast as lightning," he pointed out. "We were evenly matched. My greater strength against the rabbit's speed. But this cougar . . ." Zane pried the animal's mouth open. "His teeth are not fully developed. Nor his claws as long and as sharp as they will be. He is only a babe. He must grow. Then we will be matched."

"A savage with standards. You harm no babies and hunt only when the opponent has a chance at survival." God help her, she *had* stumbled onto a real-life Tarzan. Strong and noble and good-looking and intelligent.

"That is my way," he said in a growl, as if misinterpreting her stunned reaction as displeasure.

"It's a good way," she quickly said, reaching out to stroke the cougar's soft fur.

Zane held the baby animal at arm's length from her. "Do not touch him. His mother will smell you on him."

"But you're touching him," she pointed out.

"I am part of this place; my scent is familiar. You are different."

"An outsider."

"Yes."

"Yet you were quoting Shakespeare, a book from my world, not yours. Where did you learn it?"

He didn't answer her. Not that she expected him to. He didn't hesitate to comment on their surroundings, his way of life, but his past seemed taboo.

"I will return." Then he walked into the trees and disappeared with the animal in his arms.

Tara, her ankle throbbing, sank to the ground and simply sat there, thinking about all she'd just witnessed, trying to sort through the few facts she had. But the more she knew of him, the more difficult the puzzle. Gentle yet savage. Bold yet fearful. Intelligent yet naive. Man yet animal . . .

She didn't understand him, and worse, she didn't understand herself. Her reaction. The fact that she'd wanted him so badly back at the river she'd been about to touch him.

The story, she told herself yet again. The allure was the story, compounded by the fact that he was dangerously good-looking and she'd been celibate since before the divorce, *and* he'd been stark-naked.

She noticed thankfully when he returned that he'd donned his loincloth.

Without so much as a word, he scooped her into his arms and started back for the cave. She knew the moment he touched her, his muscles tense, almost angry, that he didn't like what had almost happened any more than she did.

Right. She'd liked it, but she didn't *want* to like it, or to dwell on the prospect. Zane was a reporting assignment and nothing more. She stressed that all-important fact, not only to her brain, but to her deprived hormones, and vowed to keep her emotional and physical distance from him.

Zane seemed to have the same idea. Other than glaring at her and warning her against venturing from the cave again, he didn't utter a word. He simply dumped her on the furs and disappeared, returning only after dark, when he sprawled next to her, close, but not touching.

Tara battled the sudden disappointment and resigned herself to the situation. No touching was better. Preferable. Necessary if she meant to write his story. And she did, more than she'd ever meant to do anything in her life.

He wanted to touch her. The need was fierce, pronounced, his body tense and hard since they'd faced off at the river. His skin still tingled from the feel of her gaze, his anger still raging because they'd been interrupted.

But there would be no interruptions now. He had but to turn over, reach out. . . . Just one sweet touch and he could ease the throbbing. The knowledge was instinctive, something he felt deep in his gut. He knew little of the ways between a man and a woman, but he knew the animals. How they lived and breathed and reproduced. And what was a man but an animal that walked upright? What was man but the highest form of predator that hunted for food, be it in the forest or the supermarket of which Tara had spoken. The goal was the same. Survival. And to survive, man had to eat, to drink, to sleep, to mate.

While Zane had become proficient in every other aspect, he'd yet to mate, and he sensed that it was time. He felt it in the tightness of his body, the restlessness that refused him any real rest, the heightened senses so attuned to the woman next to him.

He wanted to touch her, to turn her over and learn her secrets, seek them out and drive his root deep, to spill his seed and seek blessed relief. To survive—

No! He fought the urge. He had to. To keep his distance, see her heal and send her on her way as he'd promised. He wasn't ready to die.

But as he lay there, listening to the shallow sound of her breathing, the soft rush of breath flaring her delicate nostrils, he wondered if death wouldn't be preferable to the ache gripping him. As it was, he felt himself dying from the slow torture of being on fire for a woman within his reach, a woman he couldn't have. *Wouldn't* have, he reminded himself.

She would be his death.

If only she didn't make him feel so . . . alive.

The next morning dawned tense and silent. As she expected, Zane dodged her questions and left the cave in search of breakfast. When he returned with fish and a few fruits, rather than badger him with more pointless questions, Tara let out a frustrated sigh and reached for one of the fish.

"Give me the knife," she demanded.

"Why?"

"So I can clean this. If you're not going to talk, I need to keep myself busy some other way." She took his knife and started to clean the fish. When she'd finished, he simply sat there, surprise and pleasure gleaming in his eyes.

"Not bad, huh?" She smiled.

"Where did you learn to do that?"

"My ex used to fish. He liked the sport, but he wasn't too keen on getting his hands dirty, so it fell to yours truly."

"Ex?"

"As in my used-to-be husband. We were married up until about four years ago, when he left me for a woman with bigger breasts, a smaller waist, longer legs, and fruitful ovaries." At his puzzled expression, she explained, "Ovaries are the part inside a female that produces eggs that make babies." When she said the last word, understanding dawned in his expression. "Merle wanted children, his own rather than adopted ones, and my ovaries weren't up to the task."

"You cannot have children?"

She shook her head and tried to ignore the strange ache the admission always stirred. She didn't even like children, with their spitting up and juice spills and sticky hands. . . . At least that was what she kept telling herself.

"It's better that we didn't have children. They wouldn't have made the situation any easier, though I certainly thought so at the time." She shut her eyes against the rush of old insecurities that swirled inside her. The past was over and done with, and it didn't hurt to talk about it. *It didn't*, she told herself.

Then she opened her eyes, stared into Zane's deep blue orbs, and the hurt eased.

"A child might have proved I was woman enough for him," she went on, "but my barren state wasn't the problem. It was Merle. He was a first-class jerk, and we're getting way off the subject." She wiped her hands on a soft piece of leather she'd drafted to double as a hand towel. "Tell me about this scar." She pointed to the hard ridge of flesh on his shoulder. "How did you get it?"

"You talk too much."

"You started it. You asked me about the fish."

"So now I will finish it. No more talk." He fixed his gaze on the fire, a stubborn expression on his face.

One she knew so well. It was typical male. The classic shut-up-before-you-really-piss-me-off expression she'd seen on Merle's face too many times in the past. It was a look that had sent her scurrying off to the other room to iron or cook or do anything to keep herself out of his line of vision, and the firing line of his verbal abuse.

Shut up, she told herself the way she always had. *Just shut up and no one will get hurt. Namely you.*

She wasn't sure what prompted her to ignore the warning: whether years of docile obedience had finally reached a head and she refused to cower anymore, or if she was so disappointed at not getting her story that she'd rather die fighting for it than sit quietly by in safety. Maybe it was a little of both. Or maybe the lack of caffeine had sent her completely over the edge.

"So what about the scar? What happened?"

"Enough."

"No, it's not." She tossed the makeshift towel down and glared at him. "Just answer one question. *Any* question. Tell me why you're here, why you stay here, what happened to your parents, what happened after your grandfather died. Didn't somebody know you were here? Didn't they care—"

"Enough!" The roar echoed around her and thundered through her head. Zane bolted to his feet and glared down at her, knife in hand, the blade flashing silver fire in the dim light.

Tara trembled, a dozen words held behind her slightly parted lips. Fear gripped her, but its icy fingers weren't enough to keep her sitting down.

She struggled to her feet, grinding her teeth against the pain that bolted up her leg.

Idiot, a lifetime of insecurities hissed. *What are you doing? The guy's mad, he's got a knife. Worse, he's got hands that could do some serious damage if he landed one upside your head.*

But he wouldn't. She knew it deep in her gut, though it went against all reason and logic and her own past experience. Maybe it was the gentleness in him when he tended her ankle or cradled the cougar cub that convinced her that for all his anger he wouldn't harm her.

While Merle had been many things—charming, deceitful, good-looking—he'd never been gentle. Had she not been staring at him through rose-colored glasses, she would have seen it right in the beginning. The barely checked rage in his eyes when she said the wrong thing, wore a color he didn't like, asserted herself by telling him what movie *she* wanted to see.

There was nothing clouding her vision now. She didn't like Zane, much less love him, and while he looked really great in a loincloth, it wasn't enough to drain away her common sense. Not at the moment anyway.

She saw him for what he was, an angry man. A man full of hurt and rage, his eyes gleaming bloodlust. A man who wouldn't harm her, no matter how hard she pressed because . . . just because. He had no morals, no societal restraints, nothing, yet something inside held him in check.

"I just want you to talk to me," she pressed. "Is

that too much to ask? I want to write a story—
you've got a great story: we're a perfect match."

"*We* are nothing, while *you* are loud."

"Is that so?" She planted her hands on her hips.
"Well, you're bossy, mister."

"And you are stupid."

"Stupid? *Stupid!*" she said, the word triggering
the anger and frustration that had been building
for days. "Just who are you calling stupid?"

"You! You are stupid to keep flapping your
tongue when all I want is silence while you are
here. Silence until you leave, which will be soon,
for I cannot take much more." He hooked his knife
in the waistband of his loincloth and stormed outside, into the dark night, as if eager to get away
from her as fast as he could before his control finally snapped.

"Good riddance," she grumbled later as she applied some of his salve to her throbbing ankle.
"Stupid?" She shot an angry glare at Juliet. "Can
you believe the nerve? Imagine him calling me stupid." She shook her head and gave in to the hot
tears that threatened her. "Dammit, I *am* stupid."

Not because she asked him questions, but because she kept hoping for answers. Because she
wanted to hear the sound of his voice rather than
her own. Because with each day that passed, Tara
found herself more and more attracted to Zane
Shiloh.

Chapter Nine

Tara stared up at the ceiling, watching the play of firelight against the smooth rock. She tried to close her eyes, to sleep, but instead she found herself listening for him.

Waiting.

He'd been gone an awfully long time.

She closed her eyes and concentrated on the buzz of crickets, the occasional hoot of an owl—any noise to hold her attention, keep her distracted from the loneliness inside.

Nothing helped. Until she heard the sound of footfalls, the rustle of furs as Zane settled himself down for the night. Not next to her as he'd done for the past few nights when he thought her unaware, but opposite from her, the fire separating them.

Opposite. That summed up their relationship.

Loaded opposites. Reluctant subject and eager reporter. A nature know-it-all and a cappuccino-craving city dweller. Civilized and uncivilized.

Male and female.

Tara did her best to forget the last comparison, but it was much harder than she cared to admit. She cracked an eye open and peered through downcast lashes at him. Stretched out on his back, he had one arm thrown over his face, oblivious to her.

Not that she cared. So what if he didn't snuggle up against her? The sound of his breathing was just enough to soothe the restlessness inside her, a reminder that she wasn't completely alone, and that was all she needed to settle down and grasp the precious sleep that eluded her so much of the time.

Slumber picked her up and whisked her away, and Zane followed. Not the angry man who'd glared at her earlier, but the hot hunk of muscled male who filled women's most erotic fantasies. Tarzan of the Apes. Or, in this case, the Beast of Bear Mountain. Wild. Untamed. Hot. And desperately in lust with her.

The perfect fantasy.

The craving for a whirlpool bath, the itching need for a good cup of cappuccino, the lust for a fresh change of clothes, the desperate hunger for life's essentials—shampoo, soap, a razor, toilet paper, a hairbrush—all faded. For a few moments, Tara forgot the no-win situation she found herself in and retreated into sweet, blissful dreams.

* * *

"Yes," she murmured. "Do it just like that. And that. And this . . ." Her words of encouragement trailed off as Tarzan let loose a loud, lusty yell that curled her toes as surely as did the large, strong hands moving so purposefully over her body.

His touches, soft yet firm, frantic yet oddly controlled, drove her to a maddening frenzy. He was the perfect lover—

The thought shattered into another shriek . . . No, more like a groan. A sob . . . a sob?

Tara left her dreamworld behind for the dim interior of the cave. The fire, little more than glowing embers, fought a losing battle against the chill that pushed its way inside, and she shivered. Then she heard it. Definitely a sob. Full of anguish and fear.

Her gaze found him several feet away in the shadowy interior. He tossed and turned, his sleeping face a mask of pain.

The sight drew her from the warmth of the furs, and she crawled across the earthen floor to him.

"Zane." She touched his shoulder and his eyes snapped open, as if he hadn't really been asleep but lost on the fringe between sleep and reality, in the dark chaos that cradled fear and nurtured it into nightmare. "It's all right." She stroked soothing fingers over his trembling shoulder. "You're having a bad dream."

"A dream?" Wide, glittering blue eyes darted around, as if searching for whatever demon he'd been fighting. "But I heard voices this time, screams . . . death." He stared down at his trembling hands. "I saw it." His fingers curled into fists. "Felt it . . ."

Death. The word blared through her head. A warning. A promise. There was more to this guy than simply BOY FORGOTTEN IN WILDERNESS AND RAISED BY BEARS. He had a past. A deep, dark secret.

The best kind for front-page stories.

The notion dissolved in a wave of sympathy that swept through her as she touched him, felt the bunching of muscles, the quaking of his body.

"Being in night, all this is but a dream. . . ." The deep whisper echoed through her head. Another quote. Another damnable quote, but as much as she wanted to question him, she couldn't bring herself to do it now. She wanted only to soothe him, to comfort.

"Whatever it was, it's gone now."

His gaze captured hers for several heartbeats, and the air caught in her chest. Reflected in the dark depths was the isolation she'd lived with as a child. The loneliness.

"She's gone." His words, whisper-soft and raw with hurt, slid into her ears a moment before strong hands stole around her, pulled her forward and held her tight.

So very tight, as if he could lose himself in her and forget what it was that haunted him. As if he craved the comfort of another human being, the reassurance that he wasn't alone.

As much as Tara wanted to resist—cool, professional indifference was the only way to see any story through—she couldn't help herself.

She'd been needy so many times, sought comfort too many times, and been denied every time. And she did the only thing she could in that moment, faced with her own fear and his.

She held him.

Tara wasn't sure when the embrace changed. When the cold loneliness inside her warmed to a consuming heat. When her hands went from soothing to seeking, and her heartbeat accelerated.

It happened so fast, so easily, that she didn't have a clue until she felt a shudder roll through his body. Not the trembling aftermath of a nightmare, but the shivering prelude to an erotic fantasy. The vise grip around her waist eased ever so slightly. The soft silk of his hair brushed her jaw as he lifted his head from the crook of her shoulder. His lips grazed her neck. She felt his hot breath against her ear, and electricity danced over her skin.

It was cool outside, but her body felt inflamed. Cold and hot. Blazing fire one minute and quivering the next.

Her head tilted back and her mouth parted, waiting, expecting, anticipating. . . .

Nothing.

She opened her eyes to stare up into glittering blue pinpoints of raw flame. His gaze was riveted on her mouth, yet he didn't lower his head. He just stared, as if mesmerized, unsure, frightened. . . .

Right. This guy faced down bears, battled the elements and lived like Grizzly Adams. He obviously feared nothing. Certainly not a kiss.

That meant . . .

The realization crawled up inside her, from the deep, dark place where she'd locked away six years' worth of bitter memories. She'd made peace with herself for being so tolerant, so giving, so damned needy where Merle was concerned, and she'd moved on, eager to leave the past behind. To forgive *and* forget.

"You feel so soft." His deep voice filled her ears. "So much softer than I expected."

She was suddenly aware of the strong hands pressing into the flesh covering her rib cage, the thumbs dangerously close to the undersides of her abundant breasts. She'd never had a buff body, never been lean and mean like the women who hung out at Merle's health club. She'd always been a few pounds over the norm. Not fat, just . . . *soft*.

"Rubens liked soft," she said, sitting up and pulling away from him, suddenly eager to escape the feel of his hands. The hands feeling her.

"Who?"

"A famous painter. He immortalized voluptuous, soft women."

"This painter ee-mor-tal-ized your softness?" His eyes sparkled with anger.

"Not mine in particular. Just forget it." Her mind scrambled for a safe topic. "So who is she?"

His frown faded into a puzzled look. "She?"

"You said, 'She's gone' before we . . . when you woke up." She hugged herself to ward off the sudden chill and keep from scooting back toward him, into his arms, his warmth. "So who is she?"

"I . . . I do not know." He shook his head and

169

turned away from her, his attention directed toward the dwindling flames.

"Come on, Zane. We all need to talk to somebody. Haven't you ever heard that confession's good for the soul?"

"Confession?"

"Speaking what's on your mind, talking about what's bothering you. It really helps to get your fears out in the open. Then you can see there's nothing to be afraid of."

His gaze clashed with hers. "I am not afraid."

"Right. And I'm Madonna."

A puzzled expression creased his brow. "I thought your name was Tara?"

"It is. That was just an expression. A saying."

"Like confession being good for the soul?"

She smiled. "Exactly. For a wild man, you're really quick."

His chest expanded and muscles rippled as he pointed to himself and said with a typical male ego, "I can run as fast as a deer."

"And I bet you're more powerful than a locomotive, too, but that's beside the point, Tarzan."

"You keep calling me this name. Why?"

She stared pointedly at his loincloth. "In civilization, the only man who runs around in a loincloth is either Tarzan, or a Chippendales dancer. I haven't seen you dance, so . . ."

"So I am this Tarzan."

"Not *the* Tarzan. I mean, there isn't any one. It's an image, a type. Johnny Weissmuller was the first to gain notoriety. But my personal favorite would have to be Miles O'Keefe. He did a version with

Bo Derek that was pretty good. Not Oscar-caliber as far as the acting went, but he definitely should have gotten something for best body."

"You liked his body?" Zane's eyes sparkled with something strangely close to jealousy.

She blinked and the fleeting emotion disappeared. Jealous? Right. She was imagining things. The caffeine withdrawal was turning her upside down and inside out.

"Did you like his body?" he persisted.

"I'm a woman, aren't I?"

His gaze narrowed as he studied her, and she had the hunch he was giving some serious thought to her question.

She barely resisted the urge to reach out and smack him.

"Was he quick?" he finally asked. "As fast as a deer?"

She nodded. "And strong and resourceful and hunky as anything."

"Hun-key?"

"Muscular, like you, with loads of sex appeal—" The last words caught in her throat and she shifted uneasily, keenly aware of the intensity of his eyes. "Um, I don't think this is a subject we need to be on right now."

"What is this six peel?"

"It's sex *appeal*"—she cleared her throat—"and isn't the weather nice tonight? A little chilly."

"Tell me more about sex appeal."

"Foggy as usual, but dry."

"What does it mean?"

"Do you think it'll rain tomorrow?"

"What is sex and why is it appealing?"

"Didn't anyone ever tell you about the birds and the bees?"

"Which kind of bird? I know them all. As for bees . . ."

"That's not what I meant. I'm talking men and women. Love. Do you know what love is, Zane?"

" 'With love's light wings did I o'erperch these walls; For stony limits cannot hold love out, And what love can do, that dares love attempt.' "

"More Shakespeare?"

He nodded. *"Romeo and Ju-li-et."*

"Do you know what you just said?"

"Not completely. I know I spoke of love."

"So you read Shakespeare, but you don't really comprehend all of it," she observed, a smile tugging at her lips. "You are human after all."

"What does sex have to do with love?" he asked.

"Nothing, as far as most men are concerned. But in a perfect world, people have sex because they are in love. It's a physical expression of their emotions." She shook her head. "I think we're getting way off the subject here. We're talking sex appeal, not sex, and most definitely not love."

"Tell me more."

She took a deep breath. She could do this. *Calm. Cool. Professional.* "If you have sex appeal, it means you're attractive to the opposite sex. Appealing. Desirable. Now on to tomorrow's weather forecast. I'm betting on afternoon showers, how about you?"

He seemed determined not to let her move to a safe subject. "So this Tarzan has sex appeal?" His eyes reflected the firelight, hot and mesmerizing like the flames dancing in front of them.

She nodded, wondering why it felt so warm all of a sudden. Sure there was a fire, but it had to be fifty degrees outside. Cold, she told herself, trying to summon a shiver. Very cold.

"So he is attractive to the opposite sex?"

She nodded again and wiped at a sudden trickle of perspiration near her temple.

His gaze snagged on the movement, following the slide of her finger down her face, the fall of her hand to her lap. A grin tugged at his lips. "Attractive equals appealing?"

She nodded again. *The forecast for tonight is definitely muggy.*

"Desirable also, I think you said?"

Another nod. *With a slight chance of a heat wave.*

"And I remind you of this Tarzan?"

Ditto. Forget slight. More like a hundred percent chance. She tugged at her neckline. "Geez, the air's awful hot up here." She struggled for a deep breath. "And thin."

Her attempt to evade the question only encouraged him. "So if I remind you of this man and he has this sex appeal that makes him attractive to you because you are the opposite sex—a woman— then, I am also attractive to you?"

"If you're fishing for a compliment, I'm not biting."

"I fish with my hands." He held up the objects in question and Tara caught her breath.

He had really great hands. Large with long, tapered fingers. Capable hands. Powerful. Erotic.

Inspirational . . .

She shook away a sudden image of his hands entwined with hers and tried to concentrate on what he was saying.

". . . you find me attractive? Appealing? Desirable?"

"How did we get onto this topic?"

"Answer."

"I plead the Fifth."

"The what?"

Breathe, she told herself, *and don't look at him. No rippling muscles, no intense eyes. Just don't look.* "You know, Zane, I think you're missing the point of this entire conversation." She took another deep breath and kept her gaze riveted at a point just beyond his shoulder. "It's not about who I find attractive. It's about you and this dream you're having."

"*Just* a dream," he said, as if to convince himself more than her.

She chanced a glance at his face. No grin played at his lips; no suggestive glint lit his eyes. His expression had turned dark, guarded once again. Before she could marvel at how their exchange could alter so quickly, their conversation charged with so many different emotions, he poked at the fire, sending a whirl of sparks into the air.

"So," she said, grateful to be back in familiar territory, "tell me about the *she*, the screams, the death—"

"Enough," he cut in, bolting upright to stalk to the mouth of the cave. "This talk is useless."

"No, it's not." She tried to struggle to her feet,

but only succeeded in flopping clumsily back down to the fur. "It would help if you talked about the nightmare."

He paused, his back to her. "You know nothing."

"I know what it feels like to be afraid, to keep my fears bottled up inside, to refuse to see them in the bright light of day, admit them, deal with them." Only when she'd been close to starving to death in one last attempt to be the beautiful Stepford Wife Merle had wanted, had she finally admitted to herself that she didn't really love him. Worse, that he didn't love her. That confession had saved her life, restored it. "I know, Zane."

Turning, he faced her for several long seconds, as if he wanted to say something. Needed to . . .

"Please," she said. "Talk to me."

"I cannot."

"Why?"

He shook his head and stormed out. Again.

The chill night air pushed into the cave, and Tara huddled beneath the fur, staring at the empty black hole where Zane had disappeared.

"Talking *would* help," she muttered, "only you're so stubborn, you can't see it. Instead, you'd rather let it eat away at you and deprive me of my story."

Oddly enough, it wasn't her journalistic needs that felt deprived as she sat there, cold and alone. Lonely.

A cry pierced the night and sent an army of goose bumps marching along her neck. Her heart did a double thud and the breath caught in her chest. It was the cry of a wild animal. Wounded. Hurting.

Zane.

Tara knew then that it wasn't that he didn't want to admit his dreams to *her*; he didn't want to admit them to himself. He didn't want to remember. The past. The pain.

And there'd been plenty. She sensed it the way she smelled a hot story, heard it in the heartbreaking sound of his voice. She'd seen it as well, in the anguish twisting his face those few moments when he'd been lost in the throes of his nightmare.

Lost and hurting.

The knowledge stayed with her and kept her tossing and turning the rest of the night. She tried to tell herself it was merely her reporter's curiosity, but she knew it was something much deeper that made her think. Wonder. Care.

What had happened to him?

Zane knelt on the ground and stared at the mountain lion lying motionless in front of him. The animal's huge chest gushed red heat onto the forest floor. A knife protruded from its massive body. The first rays of dawn pushed through the trees, lifting the veil of night, showing him exactly what waited for him in the future.

Death.

The fulfillment of the prophecy.

Leaning down, he listened for a heartbeat, his cheek brushing the animal's soft fur. He closed his eyes as regret coiled inside him. He'd had no choice. The animal had attacked and he'd been forced to defend himself.

Still, it shouldn't have come to that. He should

have heard the big predator. Sensed its presence. Smelled the danger.

He clenched his hands, his heart thundering in his chest, the smell of blood strong in his nostrils. He would have. Five days ago, he would have sensed the cat's presence long before an attack, and avoided it as he always did his enemies. Both those who belonged to the mountain, and those who did not.

The outsiders.

The woman called Tara.

Tonight he'd been too worked up to notice any threat, too absorbed in moving as fast as his feet could carry him. He'd run, heedless of his direction, crashing through the underbrush like a stampeding bull. He who usually moved with the stealth of the dead animal before him, the same predatory grace, the same savage intent.

Instead, he'd raged at the night, desperate to outrun the woman. Running away from her questions, the dream . . .

Just a dream.

His gaze dropped to his bloodstained hands and a shudder ripped through him. His heart hammered and he gasped, eager to draw more air into his aching lungs.

He couldn't get enough, fast enough, to fortify himself against the image that fought its way to the forefront of his mind. A small child on his knees, hands covered in blood, tears slipping down his cheeks.

So afraid and alone.

With a frantic shake of his head, he forced the

bloody image back, pushing, shoving it away the way his grandfather had taught him. Finally, it receded, leaving a troubling void to taunt him as he pulled the knife free of the massive cat, wiped it on a patch of grass and hooked it at his waist.

He rubbed his hands on the grass as well, but the blood didn't go away. More followed, running in tiny red rivers from his shoulder where the cat had clawed him.

No matter how he tried to stop the flow, or to push the truth away, the past, he couldn't. Both wounds were too deep. The warm red trickled down his skin, dripping from his fingertips, soiling the grass now the way it had stained his soul then.

That night so long ago.

He closed his eyes, so tired and worn. The image was there, ready to reemerge into his consciousness, and this time, he knew he couldn't fight—

"No!"

His eyes snapped open to see the black bird, feathers stretching, reaching for the surrounding twilight, embracing it the way his grandfather's arms had embraced the boy he'd once been. Sheltered him, from the outsiders and from himself.

"It was just a dream, Zane. Leave it alone."

"It felt like more." It was. He knew it. Deep down, he knew it. "I could feel the warmth on my hands."

"A dream. That is all. All it is now, all it has ever been."

Despite the words, fear clawed at Zane's gut, as fiercely as the lion that had tried to rip his heart out.

"A nightmare, Zane. Nothing more. Let it go."

He wanted to. Needed to. Another shudder ripped through him. So cold. He was so cold now, while his hands were so hot and . . . red.

"It is the woman's presence. She is unsettling you, disturbing your peace. I warned you not to let her stay. Remember the prophecy."

He wanted to deny his grandfather's claim, but he couldn't. It was true. While he'd vowed not to let the woman into his life, she'd burrowed in, dug under his skin with her constant talk, her stubborn glare, her sweet-smelling skin. . . . She made him feel so many things, too many things he didn't understand. One minute he was happy, the next angry. Content then frustrated. Cold then hot. Full then empty . . .

Worse, she breathed life into his fear. The strange nightmares of blood and death had faded long ago. Only when she'd arrived had he started having them again. Stronger than before, the images came to him, accompanied by voices, feelings. The fear rose inside him, a bear just awakened after a long winter's sleep. Hungry, ravenous.

Ready to devour him if he didn't fight back.

"Make her go."

The shout echoed through his head, and his survival instincts took hold, urging him toward the cave, a beast eager to seek out and eliminate any threat.

Man or animal.

Male or female.

Zane closed his mind off to the consequences of

what he was about to do, the guilt. He'd spent his life surviving, living against the odds, defeating his enemies, and she was just that. An enemy. An outsider.

And she had to go.

Dawn was just creeping into the cave when Tara opened her eyes. She knew even before she glanced around that Zane wasn't there. She felt it in the chill of the air, the strange isolation that held her.

She tried to shake away the feeling and busied herself sitting up. Flinging aside the fur, she did a quick inspection of her ankle and blinked back a sudden welling of tears. Still swollen.

"It's not as if you'd walk out of here today even if you could," she reminded herself, sniffling. "Not without Zane's history. Not even for a double cappuccino or a bath or the pleasure of sitting on a real toilet seat."

She forced herself to her feet and half hobbled, half hopped to the entrance of the cave, her movements slow and painful. Staring out into the gloomy morning, she searched for some sign of Zane and wondered if he was still mad at her for pressing him about the dream.

Not that it mattered.

Okay, so it mattered, but only on a purely professional level. She needed him cooperative and willing. Or at least *there*.

Frustration welled inside her, bubbling up like an active volcano ready to spew. Exhaustion weighed heavily on her, along with a night of solitude that had pushed her to the edge. The past few days were catching up to her, the deprivation, the futile attempt to get information from a man who wasn't the least bit cooperative. It wasn't working. She was failing. Miserably.

She paced the cave, desperate to do something. At home, she would have been making coffee, listening to the radio, warming up her computer, ironing or vacuuming or making waffles—

Her thoughts ground to a halt when she spotted him in the mouth of the cave, filling up the entrance and blocking the morning sunlight. His face was a mask of shadows, his gaze the only thing that penetrated the grayness. Twin blue beams caught her with blinding intensity.

She sniffled, wiped at her eyes and patted her wild hair. The effort only made her realize how totally awful she looked.

She snapped then, the words pouring past her lips. "Go ahead and say it. You look like hell. That's what you're thinking." She sniffled and slapped at the tears pouring down her face. "Go ahead. Say it."

Say something.

He merely glared, stoking the fire of failure that already raged inside her.

"Okay, I'll say it for you. Tara, you look like hell. Thank you, Zane. I feel like hell, too." The tears blinded her and she stumbled. Her bottom hit the cold floor, her legs sprawled out in front of her. "And you're clumsy, too," she wailed, the tears spilling over, blotting out everything, including the dark silhouette who moved toward her.

"You have to leave." His deep voice thrummed in her ear, so close, and she felt the familiar heat from his body. But there was something else, as well. A tension that surrounded him, held his body tight, distant.

"You think I like it here?" she said in a blaze of anger. "Well, I don't. I'm going stir-crazy. I can count the cracks in the ceiling only so many times. I can't write a thing, not without my backpack. It had everything in it, pens, paper, my tape recorder. I haven't had a chocolate cupcake in what seems like forever. I look like hell. My clothes smell and I haven't had a shower in days. I hate it here, and I hate you because you won't say anything to me." Determination raged with her sense of failure, and she shook her head furiously. "This is the last place I want to be, but I have no choice. I can't leave, even if I wanted to, which I don't because a good journalist doesn't just walk away from the story of a lifetime. I'm not a quitter and I'm not leaving." The tears came fast and furious as she indulged in the one luxury still available to her: a good cry.

"You will," came his strangled command. "You have to. *Now.*" The last word was little more than a growl, and a wave of alarm bells rang in her head.

Something was wrong.

The thought hit her a moment before she felt his hands close around her neck.

Chapter Ten

Zane ceased to think as his fingers gripped her neck. There were no thoughts, no feelings, no guilt. Just cold, calculated intent.

Survive. Survive. Survive.

A cry burst from her lips. Her head swiveled toward him. Shock twisted her features. Her cheek brushed his hand.

He felt the wetness a moment before his gaze dropped and he saw her tears. They slid over his bloodstained fingers and washed away the telltale crimson. The past. The truth.

Abruptly, his hold broke. He stumbled backward, his gaze fixed on the clear streaks her tears had made on his skin. Clear. Clean.

"I have to get out of here." She sobbed, crawling on the floor, away from him, from danger, like a wounded rabbit eager for escape. And he didn't blame her. How could he?

She was right to fear him. He'd almost killed her.

Almost.

His gaze shot to his hands again, still wet with her tears, and his fingers closed, as if he could hold the moisture. The salvation.

"You're an animal!" She hefted one of the leather pouches and threw it at him. It hit his scratched shoulder and pain splintered through his body. Another pouch followed before he managed to duck, this one full of water. It caught him in the side of the head and splattered to the ground. Liquid seeped across the floor of the cave in a creeping brown puddle. "You're worse." She threw another pouch, but he managed to duck this time. "You're a . . . a *man*! I can't believe I thought you were different. I fantasized about you. I actually wanted to *touch* you—"

The harsh cry of a raven drowned any more accusations. The pouch went limp in her hand. Zane turned at the sound of wings beating the air, but saw nothing. Only the sun peeking over the treetops, dispelling the shadows, promising light to fill the dark places inside him.

But they were already filled.

He stared at his hands again, saw the trails of wetness, and for a few heartbeats, the restlessness inside him eased.

And the fear.

* * *

"That's what you get for trusting a man." She scrambled around the cave after Zane left and gathered what supplies she could. Several furs, a knife . . . Outside the sun topped the trees, showering the cave in light and dispelling the early morning shadows. Daylight was coming and she had to get out of there. To safety.

She grabbed the empty water pouch and her hopes plunged. What little fresh water there was now lay in a muddy brown puddle at her feet. And even if she did have a full pouch, it wouldn't last her the several days it would take to find her way off the mountain. Nor would the small amount of dried berries and odd roots stashed in the cave. Reality weighed down on her. She would dehydrate, starve, die of exposure, or fall and break her neck before all was said and done if she tried to leave.

And she didn't want to die.

She closed her eyes and remembered the feel of his hands at her neck, his fingers squeezing, strangling. Her heart thundered, tears choked her and she buried her face in her hands. She still couldn't believe it.

He'd gone from remote and gentle as he'd been on that first night, tending her ankle, giving her food and water to drink, to being hostile and aggressive, and it was all because of her.

Because she'd badgered him with her questions. She'd kept at him, pushed him too far—

"No. It wasn't your fault." She recited the mantra she'd learned during therapy, during those dark weeks following Merle's abandonment. She'd learned that his behavior was *his* problem. She'd never asked for the emotional abuse, never instigated it by not wearing the right color dress or cooking his dinner just so. He'd been responsible. His own shortcomings had made him lash out, and hers had allowed her to put up with it.

No more. Zane was responsible for what he'd done.

Just as she was responsible for saving herself.

Her fingers tightened on the knife. Yes, it was up to her to protect herself, to stay alive. Any way she had to.

And she would. Tara was a survivor, and she would make it through this, and live to write the story. One way or another.

She spent the rest of the day waiting for Zane to return, knowing she had to face him. Leaving was out of the question, and so the time had come for a showdown. Either he tried to kill her again and she defended herself and whatever happened, happened, or they lived out the rest of her recuperation in tense, tolerable silence.

Her nerves were a jangle of fear and desperation and anger. Fear led the pack in the beginning, spurring her to find a strategic place in the cave, so that she wouldn't be caught unawares when he finally showed up. Then came desperation. She wanted the entire confrontation over with.

Finally, anger settled in, making her heart pound faster as the day wore on and he didn't return. Hunger gnawed at her belly, thirst clawed at her throat, and her temper flared. So that was his game. Leave her here to starve to death and dehydrate. That way he didn't have to get his hands dirty. Nature would do it for him.

The thought conjured a mental image of him, blood staining his fingers as he'd skinned and cleaned the rabbit. All right, she admitted, so he wasn't afraid to do his own dirty work, but he still couldn't face her for some reason.

Shame? Remorse?

That same picture flashed over and over in her mind, and she discarded the silly notion. Zane felt no remorse. No shame. He killed when necessary, for food and warmth—survival—without batting an eye.

Until tonight.

The day gave way to night and she built up the fire, eager to see clearly when the showdown came. Exhaustion hit her hard and fast as she settled down to wait, the warmth of the furs lulling her, surprising since she'd always had such trouble getting comfortable at night, secure and content only when tucked into her own bed at home. Her eyelids drifted shut, the knife gripped in her hand.

She didn't really sleep. She found herself caught in that restless place just this side of sleep, her eyes closed but her other senses still functioning, her ears alert, her muscles tense, ready.

The soft shifting of fabric brought her wide-awake. Her eyes snapped open, but she didn't see a savage standing over her, waiting to rip her heart out. Just the ceiling reflecting flickering firelight. Her gaze shifted to the cave's mouth and she spied a familiar red bundle.

It couldn't be. Hooking the knife in her waistband, she struggled across the floor, her fingers reaching for the canvas. It was! Joy coupled with relief as she yanked open the fastenings and pulled out the contents of her lost backpack, feeling like a child on Christmas morning.

She was so absorbed in unpacking, she didn't see him slip inside. She soon felt him, however. His presence. His gaze. Her skin flushed hot, then cold, the hair on the back of her neck stood on end and she glanced up.

He leaned against the far wall, arms crossed, watching her. No apology burst from his lips, no remorse twinkled in his eyes. His face was the usual expressionless mask, and her blood boiled.

"If you think bringing me my backpack will make up for what you did, you've got another think coming." Anger made her voice short and clipped. "What you did was unforgivable." She unpacked several more items, conscious of the weight of the knife at her waist, the distance of her hand from the weapon.

"What did I do?"

The sound of his voice surprised her. She'd become accustomed to having to coerce even the most minimal answer from him. Her head snapped up, her gaze colliding with his.

"You tried to kill me."

"If I had meant to kill you, you would be dead, Tara."

Her name rolled off his lips, so deep and mesmerizing, and for the space of two heartbeats, she forgot about the knife and found herself caught in the magic of his eyes, the intensity that scrambled her thoughts.

Quickly, however, she broke the trance and glanced down at her pack. "You grabbed my throat," she said accusingly, marveling at the hurt that bubbled inside her. She should have expected no less from him. He'd made his dislike of her no secret. *An outsider.* "You wrapped your fingers around my throat."

"Yes." No apology, just the simple acknowledgment.

She cast a skeptical glance at him. "But you weren't trying to kill me?"

"If I had tried, you would be dead."

"Then what were you doing? My birthday's still two months away, so don't tell me you were taking measurements for one of those bear-teeth necklaces you wear."

"I was not." The words rang with truth and conviction, and she felt her anger dissolve a little. "But I would not need to measure for such a thing. I could judge the size by looking at you."

"I was being sarcastic, Zane." She shook her head and touched fingers to her still-tender neck.

His gaze followed the action and she could have sworn she saw regret in his gaze. It disappeared as quickly as it had come, but not before the sight had cooled her anger another degree.

"Then what were you trying to do? If you didn't want to kill me—"

"I did not say I did not *want* to kill you. I said I did not try. I did want to kill you . . . to be rid of you. I told you to leave, but you refused."

For some reason, the admission brought tears to her eyes, and she didn't see him walk toward her. Not until it was too late and he was kneeling in front of her.

Her hand went to her waist and her fingers closed around the handle of the knife, just in case. "Well, thanks for the honesty, at least." The words trembled from her suddenly shaky lips. "But just because you don't like me, doesn't mean we have to be at each other's throats—"

"I do like you," he cut in. "I do not want to, and there are many things I do not understand, but I do like you. Your hair . . ." He reached out to test the weight of a wayward curl.

His skin brushed hers, and a tingling warmth spread through her. She closed her eyes, her hand going limp around the knife. She was crazy to allow his touch, to desire it after what had happened, crazy to let go of the knife. . . .

But it was still there, still close if he made any threatening move or did more than just touch her hair.

Her blurry gaze snagged on the bar of travel-size soap she'd pulled from the pack, and she froze. Suddenly, she tuned in to how awful she must look, her clothes, her hair.

She dodged his curious fingers. "Please don't."

Immediately, his hand fell away, but his gaze remained steady, intense. "Your hair is so—."

"Dirty and filthy," she filled in for him. "And if you like me so much, why do you want to get rid of me?"

"I do not."

"But you just said—"

"Come." He didn't wait for her response. He scooped her up into his arms and headed for the mouth of the cave. Her hand went to the knife, but then he started to descend the mountain and she was forced to slide her arms around his neck to hold on.

Not that he would have dropped her. She knew it on an instinctive level, in a part of herself she wouldn't have trusted under normal circumstances. But this wasn't normal. This was much more. Darkness. Heat. Him. Her. A treacherous, sloping mountain.

She held on, reassuring herself that the knife was simply an arm's length away should she need it.

But he was closer. Much, much closer.

The chill night air stole around them, but Tara didn't feel the cold. He was too warm, too big, his arms too tight around her as he carried her from the cave, down the mountain with the careful, sure footing of a man who'd maneuvered the path many times.

A strange sense of comfort crept through her, and she stiffened. This was the last guy she should feel comfortable with. Safe? No way.

"For the record, I'll have you know I don't want to go anywhere with you. I don't trust you at all, buddy, even if you did find my backpack. . . ." Her words faded into silent awe as they cleared the trees and she found herself staring at a shimmering pool of water. She'd seen the river before, but never at night. It glittered like a giant, depthless mirror.

Fleetingly, she considered that he might have changed his mind about strangling her and decided to drown her. The thought passed quickly, however, when he eased her down the length of his body and set her on a nearby tree stump at the water's edge.

The descent took her breath away. She felt every bulge of muscle, including the one that said that for all his intent to kill her, he did, indeed, like her very, very much. Well, one part of him did, at least.

Zane knelt at her feet and carefully removed the wrapping from her ankle while the moonlight played off the dark curtain of his hair. The sight was almost as inviting as the water twinkling beside them.

Almost, but she'd been days without a real bath, and so she tore her gaze away from him to stare at the mirror of silver. The waterfall rushed in the distance, but where she sat, everything was calm, quiet. Peaceful.

Her gaze went back to Zane, the gentle movements of his hands, the unreadable expression on his face. While he looked the same as always, stoic and serious and hard, something had changed in him. The angry tension that had coiled his body tight since her first prying questions had somehow eased, his rage spent. Or at least put aside.

She wouldn't quite let herself believe in him, despite everything in her that told her she was now safe, and that it had something to do with his attempt to kill her.

Thrill to the most sensual, adventure-filled Historical Romances on the market today...

FROM LEISURE BOOKS

As a home subscriber to Leisure Romance Book Club, you'll enjoy the best in today's BRAND-NEW Historical Romance fiction. For over twenty-five years, Leisure Books has brought you the award-winning, high-quality authors you know and love to read. Each Leisure Historical Romance will sweep you away to a world of high adventure...and intimate romance. Discover for yourself all the passion and excitement millions of readers thrill to each and every month.

Save $5.⁰⁰ Each Time You Buy!

Each month, the Leisure Romance Book Club brings you four brand-new titles from Leisure Books, America's foremost publisher of Historical Romances. EACH PACKAGE WILL SAVE YOU $5.00 FROM THE BOOKSTORE PRICE! And you'll never miss a new title with our convenient home delivery service.

Here's how we do it. Each package will carry a FREE 10-DAY EXAMINATION privilege. At the end of that time, if you decide to keep your books, simply pay the low invoice price of $16.96, no shipping or handling charges added. HOME DELIVERY IS ALWAYS FREE. With today's top Historical Romance novels selling for $5.99 and higher, our price SAVES YOU $5.00 with each shipment.

AND YOUR FIRST FOUR-BOOK SHIPMENT IS TOTALLY FREE!

IT'S A BARGAIN YOU CAN'T BEAT! A Super $21.96 Value!

 LEISURE BOOKS *A Division of Dorchester Publishing Co., Inc.*

GET YOUR 4 FREE BOOKS NOW—A $21.96 Value!

Mail the Free Book Certificate Today!

Get Four Books Totally FREE – A $21.96 Value!

▼ Tear Here and Mail Your FREE Book Card Today! ▼

PLEASE RUSH
MY FOUR FREE
BOOKS TO ME
RIGHT AWAY!

Leisure Romance Book Club
P.O. Box 6613
Edison, NJ 08818-6613

AFFIX
STAMP
HERE

Intent, but not attempt, she reminded herself, remembering his words, the feel of his hands. If he had, indeed, tried, he would have succeeded.

But he hadn't tried. Something had stopped him, and that same something had brought him to some realization.

This was the result, she thought, noting the celestial light that sculpted his shoulders, his arms, the chiseled perfection of his brow and nose, the rest of his face lost in the beard. A strong, calm man with a touch of wildness about him. Wild yet gentle, she noted as he removed the last of the bandages and trailed his fingertips over her swollen ankle.

"It is still huge."

Among other parts, she thought, her gaze sweeping the rest of her body hidden beneath the tattered jeans and rumpled shirt. Clothing that felt a touch looser than it had a few days ago. Then again, it could just be another hallucination courtesy of her caffeine withdrawal.

He turned and busied himself gathering up the twine and splints, while her attention shifted to the water.

Anticipation sizzled through her, and her hands went to the buttons on her shirt. She'd slid three free before she realized Zane was watching her, his hands paused in collecting the bandages, his blue gaze riveted on the expanse of flesh she'd exposed.

"Turn around. This isn't a peep show." Not that he would want to peep at her, she reminded herself.

Then she saw the hunger brightening his blue eyes until they gleamed in the darkness with an intensity that sent a shiver through her. He wanted to.

The realization made her hands tremble and reminded her of the other day here at the river, when he'd faced her, gloriously nude and uninhibited. He'd wanted to touch her then, as much as she'd wanted to touch him.

Of course he wanted to. Unwrapping the package was always fun; it was afterward that the disappointment set in. When you realized the shiny paper, the huge bow had all been a disguise for the not-so-great gift inside.

"Turn around," she said again, her voice louder, more insistent. Desperate.

After several frantic thuds of her heart, he stood, gave a last, lingering glance at her bare skin, then turned away.

She took a deep breath and stifled the sudden disappointment. Disappointment? More like relief.

"I still don't trust you." She said the words more to convince herself as she made quick work of her shirt and pants, her gaze riveted on his stiff back. She stashed the knife beneath her pile of clothes. Then, still clad in her bra and panties, she slid off the tree stump, into the water. Cool liquid closed around her heated skin as she waded out several feet.

"Okay, you can look now," she called out when the water topped her shoulders and lapped at her chin. Her gaze swept the now barren riverbank.

Had he peeked and been scared away?

Probably. Maybe.

And maybe he was just giving her some privacy.

She pushed the possible answers aside and fixed her attention on the water, the way it slid over her fevered skin, embraced her, washed away the dirt and grime and made her feel human again.

And a touch wild. She smiled and floated on her back, her gaze going to the blanket of stars overhead. She was, after all, swimming nearly naked in the moonlight in a secluded mountain wilderness far, far away from civilization, from cappuccino makers and whirlpool baths, remote controls and hot rollers, electricity and indoor plumbing.

And for the first time, the fact didn't bother her.

"I still don't trust you." Tara sat on her side of the fire, her legs stretched out in front of her, and brushed her damp hair with a travel-size hairbrush she'd had the good sense to stash in her backpack.

Zane knelt beside her and applied a warm poultice before rewrapping her ankle with the twine and homemade splints. While she was relatively dry, with the exception of her drenched hair, Zane was gloriously wet. After helping her back onto the riverbank, he'd taken one look at her dripping wet in her scanty bra and panties, and promptly jackknifed into the river while she scurried into her clothes and dried off as best she could.

Drops of moisture glided down his arms and glittered like diamonds with the play of firelight.

The sight turned her mouth dry and she licked her lips.

He caught the action out of the corner of his eye and turned toward her, his gaze intense. Watchful.

Always watchful.

While she hadn't actually seen him at the river while she'd been bathing, she'd felt his presence. Close by, as if watching over her.

But this was different. A sizzle of awareness went through her.

Stop that! She didn't want to be aware of him in that way. He posed a threat. He'd wanted to kill her, for heaven's sake!

"I don't care how you try to color it, or that you brought me my pack or helped me down to the river for a bath; you still wanted to kill me."

"I did," he said in that straightforward manner she was quickly coming to hate. Honest men were overrated.

She shook away the thought. What was wrong with her? Honesty was great, particularly when it came to men. No worrying about what they were thinking. *You simply ask, and bam, you have an answer. Admirable.*

The trouble was, she felt more like punching him than giving him a medal.

"You know, Zane, you might try being a little more subtle."

He fitted the splints back into place around her ankle and applied the last of the twine before sparing her a glance. "Su–tool?"

"It means not being so blunt," she said as he sat back, crossing his legs to watch her brush her hair.

"Making your point without beating someone over the head with it."

"Beating?" He shook his head. "I have no wish to beat you."

"You just wanted to kill me."

"Yes."

"You could definitely learn some subtlety." At his puzzled expression, she added, "Don't be so straightforward. Hint around at the truth rather than plowing head-on with it. You could have said something like, 'I didn't really want to kill you, not exactly.' "

"You wish me to lie?"

"Not lie, but you don't have to be so . . ." She shook her head. "Just forget it."

"Forget what?"

"Nothing."

"All right."

She threw the hairbrush at him. It landed squarely on his chest before he caught it. "All right? No, it's not all right. How do you think I feel knowing you wanted to kill me?"

He studied the hairbrush, a thoughtful look on his face as if the possibility that she might have feelings had just struck him.

"Awful, that's how," she went on. "Afraid that you might try it again. Angry that you could probably succeed and there isn't a damned thing I can do about it. And disappointed." The last two words were out before she could stop them. She stared into the fire, deliberately avoiding his gaze.

"Why are you disappointed?"

The million-dollar question, she thought. One

she couldn't begin to explain because she herself wasn't even sure. "Just forget it."

"No." He inched around the fire, closer to her. His hand forced her chin to meet his gaze. "Tell me."

She shrugged free and turned back to the fire. "I—I didn't think you were a killer. I mean, I know you can kill and you do when necessary, but I never would have thought there would be so much rage. . . . When you touched me, I felt it." She closed her eyes as the memory swamped her. His fingers biting into her flesh. Tight, tighter . . . "I misjudged you."

That was it in a nutshell, what bothered her the most. She'd read him wrong. She who'd been hurt once because she'd refused to see a man as he really was, who'd vowed never to look at anyone with blinders on again, had done just that. She'd drawn all the wrong conclusions, focused on the gentleness she'd seen rather than the raw savagery that kept him alive in a wilderness where only the strong survived.

"I will not kill you." The words were quiet, sincere.

"Oh, yeah? How do I know that?"

"Because I am telling you so."

A hysterical laugh bubbled on her lips. He was a savage. She'd seen his ruthlessness, felt it. His statement was utterly ridiculous.

And true.

She didn't admit it to herself right away, until later that night after he'd disappeared yet again.

When he returned, he dropped several worn books into her lap. The leather volumes were ragged at the edges, the pages yellowed and faded.

"These are yours?" She read the titles, from *Romeo and Juliet*, *Hamlet*, to *A Midsummer Night's Dream*, and suddenly a few of the puzzle pieces fit together. His strange quotes. His formal speech. "Where did you get them?"

"I have had them since I was a child."

"Were they your grandfather's?"

"I found them in his cabin, but he never read them to me. I do not think he liked them. He tried to take them from me once, but I hid them away, far away. When I read"—he held one of the books, his fingers trailing over an open page—"I feel something inside. As if I know the words already, not the meaning, but the words."

"Maybe you've heard them somewhere before. In your past, maybe a part you don't remember."

"Maybe. I do not know for sure. I know only that when the quiet gets to be too much and I crave the sound of a voice, I read the words out loud and it helps me. I feel . . ."

"Less alone," she finished for him, and he nodded.

She met his gaze then, those intense blue eyes that shone with truth and honesty and a strange glimmer that made her pulse quicken. The knife pressed against her side where she'd tucked it away after her swim, but its presence gave her little reassurance.

As Tara stared into Zane's deep blue eyes, his

solemn words ringing in her ears, a precious clue
to his past sitting in her lap, suddenly she didn't
fear for her life so much as she feared for her
heart.

Chapter Eleven

Over the next few days the atmosphere between them became one of camraderie. They read Shakespeare together, with Tara explaining the passages she understood to an eager Zane, who proved a quick student. In return, he gave her survival lessons that included how to skin a rabbit, stake out a fur and differentiate between the types of herbs and roots that grew in the mountains.

Tara also talked more of her past with Merle, her desire to be a journalist and her newfound freedom. In return, Zane opened up a small amount and spoke of the four years spent with his grandfather.

As it turned out, Zane's grandfather had been none other than the Cherokee medicine man Cooney Rainer had mentioned when she'd been in his museum. From his grandfather, Zane had learned the use of various herbs and plants—which explained his ability to treat her ankle, not to mention the pain reliever he'd concocted the first night she'd spent in the cave.

But while the old man had taught Zane some of the Indian ways, he'd also introduced him to the white man's ways. Zane knew what a radio was, as well as a cookstove and various cooking utensils. He knew of flashlights and what matches were used for. He could even shuffle the deck of cards his dog Juliet had scavenged from some campground beyond the mountains.

The Cherokees had adopted many white ways back in the early 1800s, and so Zane's upbringing between the tender age of four and the time of his grandfather's death had been filled with a blending of the cultures. The old and the new.

The years following? He didn't speak of them, nor did he mention the first four years of his life.

Tara didn't push. She contented herself with learning as much as she could from what he freely told her, and gloried in the fact that she could now put her thoughts on paper. He'd found her backpack!

"What is this called?" Zane finally asked on the third evening after her nighttime swim as he fingered one of her treasures from her coveted backpack.

"A hairbrush. You use it to brush your hair, which is what I am doing. Didn't your grandfather have a hairbrush?"

Zane shook his head. "He used a comb." He took

the brush from her and tested the weight in his large hand.

"This doesn't pull as hard as a comb on the tangles."

He glided the brush through his dark hair, his hands firm around the handle. "This is better than a comb."

"It's a necessity when you have a rat's nest like mine to untangle."

The brush stopped midstroke. "You have a nest of rats?"

She smiled and held up several damp curls. "My hair. It's curly under the best circumstances, frizzy in this climate and full of tangles . . . a nest. It's a figure of speech."

He handed her back the brush. "Like confession being good for the soul?" His gaze dropped to the fire and he stared, as if searching for the answers to the universe.

"No, that was a saying." She turned her attention to her backpack. Pulling out various items, she showed him each one, from a travel-size toothpaste and toothbrush, a small sewing kit with a tiny pair of scissors, a pack of moist towelettes, a disposable razor, a small bar of soap, a bottle of Sleepy Time—the over-the-counter sleep aid she'd picked up in San Diego—her battery-operated curling iron and single-cup coffeemaker, several packs of coffee, leftover cupcakes, her pens and paper and microcassette recorder.

If only she'd thought to bring a change of clothes, but the hike was supposed to be only overnight, and she'd had no desire to change clothes in front of Cecil or his squirrels.

The isolation of her situation gripped her for all of five seconds as she sat there and surveyed everything she now possessed in the entire world. Then Zane leaned forward, as if he saw the turmoil on her face, and touched her, and it faded in a rush of sensation that tingled from her head to her toes.

"Thank you," she said, blinking frantically. "For my backpack, the nightly baths, and for talking to me the past few days."

"You are welcome." He released her, his eyes intense, studying everything about her until she felt like a bug under a microscope. Probing. Sizing her up.

She stiffened. "Please don't look at me like that."

"Like what?"

"The way you're looking at me." She rubbed her arms, partially shielding her breasts. "It makes me uncomfortable." *Hot, hungry and desperate, too.*

"Why?"

"Because I'm not used to it." *I'm not ready for it.*

He seemed genuinely puzzled. "No one looks at you in your world?"

"Not like you're looking at me." She averted her gaze and stared into the fire. "Like you want to see everything, beneath my clothes, inside my head."

"I do." The deep voice slid into her ears and compelled her to look at him.

She met his gaze and the words escaped before she could stop them. "So do I."

Fire leaped into his eyes and heat flooded her cheeks as she realized what she'd just said. "I meant the part about looking inside your head, into your past. *Only* that part.

"How about the scar on your shoulder?" she rushed on, eager to move on to a new subject. A safe subject. "You never did tell me how you got it."

"Shortly after my grandfather died."

"How did he die?"

"He was standing on the riverbank, fishing; then he fell."

"Did he hit his head?"

"No," he finally said. "He was hurt before he fell. Inside. A hurt I could not see."

And? She managed to catch the word before it left her lips. She'd vowed not to push, to let him open up on his own.

He lifted his gaze to hers as if he'd heard anyway. "I was frightened. I pulled him from the water and ran down the mountain. There was a man my grandfather called friend. A ranger. He was a good man, though I had never met him. Still, I knew he would help. He was my grandfather's friend and so I tried to find him." He stared into the fire. "I should not have, but I had to do something. All the medicine Grandfather had taught me was useless. I could treat many illnesses, but I could not help him." His gaze dropped to the fire once again, as if he could see the past in the flicker of orange flames. "I was useless. I ran down the mountain so fast, I lost track of how far. I only knew I had to find the ranger."

"Did you?"

"No." His gaze went to the empty moonshine jug

205

Kimberly Raye

Tara had drained on her second night in the cave. The container sat in the far corner, collecting dust. "I found several men surrounded by those jugs."

"You stumbled onto a group of moonshiners?"

He shook his head. "No. The sun was high. The moon was not shining."

"Moonshiners are people who make liquor illegally. Like wine or whiskey, or whatever was in that jug. That's what those men were doing. Ohmigod . . ." She made several mental notes. "So what happened? Did they see you? Help you?"

He pointed to the scar on his chest, the one she'd traced so often in her fantasies, with her hands, her lips. . . .

"I approached and one of them pulled out a weapon."

"They *shot* at you? Moonshiners? They must have been doing something more."

He shrugged. "I remember the man was very nervous. He fired wildly into the underbrush where I was hiding. I do not remember much after that. Just voices. Footsteps. Then I found myself here." He gestured to the cave. "My grandfather saw that I was brought here, far away from the men and danger."

"But I thought your grandfather was dead at that point."

"His body, yes, but his spirit was much too strong for death."

"So his *spirit* brought you here? Picked up your wounded body and *carried* you?" Disbelief laced her words, but Zane seemed unaffected.

"The animals did it for him," he said solemnly.

206

"You have a strong connection to the animals, don't you?"

"They saved my life. They do so every day, whether easing my solitude like Juliet here, or providing food or warmth." He patted the rugs. "I am grateful to them, respectful. They accept me, even those that are my enemies."

"You talk to them."

"Yes. With my mouth, my mind."

"You're telepathic," she said, remembering Cooney Rainer's claim about the medicine man who talked to the animals.

"What is te-le-path-ic?"

"You can communicate with your mind. With your thoughts." Realization dawned. "That's what you did with the bear that time. The one standing behind me. You looked at him and he went away."

"It was a she, and I told her you meant no harm."

"With just a look."

"With my mind."

"Did your grandfather teach you to communicate telepathically with the animals?"

"Yes and no. He taught me how to direct my thoughts, but the connection was already there. My heritage, he told me. A gift I was born with."

"He was your mother's father."

He cut her a sharp glance. "How do you know?"

"In Bear Creek there's a man who runs an Indian museum. He's Cherokee, too. He told me about an old medicine man who lived in the woods and talked to the animals. Said he had a daughter who could do the same. I bet she was your mother, Zane. Do you remember—" She caught herself as he shook his head and she saw the all-too-familiar shuttering of his gaze.

"Never mind," she blurted, eager to keep the line of communication open. "So this became your home after the animals brought you here?"

His expression eased and he nodded. "It is better. The cabin was too close to civilization, to the men who hurt me. They pushed up into the mountains, looking for me, to see if they'd killed me, but the animals hid me well. They found only my grandfather's cabin and his body."

"What did they do?"

"They raided the cabin, taking what they thought useful and destroying the rest. They did bury him in a shallow grave that I found later, a long time later, after I healed. I was very sick."

She shook her head as the reality of what he was saying hit her. "My God, you were only eight years old. A boy, Zane. Those moonshiners shot at an eight-year-old boy, and they nearly killed you."

"Yes." He rubbed the dog's head. "They tried to kill Juliet's grandmother, as well. They were starving her, keeping her hungry and agitated so she could defend their land while they were away. I saw her when I stumbled on them. She came at me before they tried to shoot. She went for my throat, but for some reason, she could not sink her teeth in. She would not." He stroked the dog affectionately. "After I healed, I went back for her, and one of those bottles, but I did not enjoy my taste nearly as much as you did." He grinned.

"Thanks a lot. I don't usually drink so much, you know."

"So you said." His smile faded as he turned his attention to Juliet. "The dog had all but wasted away when I reached her. I brought her here, gave her food and water."

And love, Tara added silently.

"She grew strong and she eventually gave birth to a litter of puppies, all male and one female. That female was Juliet's mother. She was strong, as well. She nursed her litter through a terrible winter, and Juliet was the only one to survive. You would not die, would you?" The dog responded by licking his hand affectionately before returning to the plastic doll's head she'd stolen from a camp far down the mountain. His gaze hardened. "Though you had better stop scavenging. You are liable to get into trouble venturing so far away."

"So your grandfather died and you came to live in this cave. With Juliet. What about Children's Protective Services?"

"What?"

"An organization that looks after children. When your grandfather died, they should have stepped in, taken you to a foster home until your family could be located. Didn't the ranger notify them about you?"

He shook his head. "He did not know about me. No one did. I lived in the shadows whenever my grandfather met with other people."

"Why?"

The minute the question was out, she wanted to snatch it back. A cloud came over his expression, a thunderstorm of anger and frustration that twisted his features and warred with the part of him that had finally decided to open up to her. He finally shook his head. "No people. That was better."

"What about family? Your mother and father—"

"I remember no family. Only my grandfather," he cut in. "He raised me, taught me to read and write. To hunt. To use the herbs and make powerful medicine. To survive."

No people. The statement echoed in her head, feeding her curiosity, clutching at her heart. He tried to make himself sound so simple, but there was so much more. So much anger and rage, despite the recent change in him, and she wanted to know why. To know him. "But why didn't your grandfather enroll you in school in Bear Creek?"

"I told you, he taught me himself."

"But the authorities would have insisted—"

"No one knew about me. Grandfather saw to it. He told no one. He raised me, protected me."

"By hiding you from the world—"

"What is this?" he cut in, his attention shifting to her camera, and Tara knew he'd said all he wanted to for the moment.

She resigned herself to being patient and picked up the camera. "It takes pictures. Unfortunately I don't have any film left. I shot an entire roll of Cecil wearing that stupid Bigfoot suit."

"Cecil?"

Tara spent the next few minutes relaying the story about Mary and Cecil and their scam to drum up business.

"This is the scam you thought I was a part of?"

"Of course. I mean you, your very existence and the fact that you've lived here so long with no contact with civilization is unbelievable."

"I have seen other outsiders besides you. A few campers, hikers who wandered too far up into the mountains."

Tara quickly realized that some of the reported sightings, those that talked of a shadowy figure, part man and part beast, had been true, an image fed by fear, but nonetheless factual. While others, the one Mary had mentioned of a monster eight feet tall, ripping up tree roots, had been a hoax.

"What is this button for?" Zane's question drew her back to the camera.

"This is the flash. The film's out, but I think this still works." She pressed the button. The bulb flashed and Zane froze, like a deer caught in headlights.

The fear lasted a heartbeat; then he bolted to his feet and fled the cave.

"Zane! Wait! I know some people are camera shy, but since I wasn't actually taking a picture, I didn't think . . . Aw, shoot." He was gone and she was alone.

"Story of my life," she grumbled. "Story of my life."

The urge to sit and feel sorry for herself was incredible, the feeling of sudden isolation overwhelming, but more intense was the desire to record everything she'd just learned. She started to reach for her microcassette recorder, then quickly changed her mind. While she'd had the presence of mind to pack an extra set of batteries—just in case—enough to see her through until her ankle healed and she finished her story, she had only one blank cassette with her. That she intended to save for something really juicy.

Not that this bit of information wasn't ripe. It was her first big breakthrough where he was concerned, and her pen flew over the pages, recording every last detail, along with several observations she'd made over the past few days.

When she was finished, she reread her words, and an overwhelming sadness filled her. Eight years old, wounded and alone.

Lonely.

Much to her dismay, the truth fortified the already strong connection between them. She couldn't afford to feel anything for him, least of all sympathy. He wasn't a kindred spirit, but her subject. Her future. Her dreams.

Yes, he was definitely the stuff her Pulitzer Prize–winning dreams were made of. That and a few baser thoughts. Lusty thoughts, for as much as she tried to deny the chemistry between them, she couldn't. The awareness was always there, in her breasts, her belly, her thighs—whenever and wherever he looked at her. Hell, even when he didn't look at her. She had only to think of him . . .

And she did that plenty. Too much.

Then again, the way she was feeling really wasn't her fault. She was living a major female fantasy. The civilized city girl stranded in the jungle with Tarzan as her protector. Her hormones were bound to react, against her better judgment, of course.

But she wasn't about to let him start calling her Jane. Fantasy and reality were two very different things, and Tara wasn't so pent-up sexually that she couldn't tell the difference.

Not yet anyway.

"Turn her out, Zane. Take her halfway down the mountain and leave her." The raven sat in the tree-top, his beady black eyes fixed on the man who stood beneath. *"Before it is too late."*

Zane shook his head, fear and something else, something stronger, fighting a battle deep inside him.

An old medicine man . . . who talked to the animals. He had a daughter . . .

"My mother—" he started, his words drowned by the piercing shriek of the raven.

"You have no mother. No father. Just me. I will always be here for you, to protect you, but I cannot if you do not listen to me. This woman is dangerous. She must leave. You must make her."

"She knows nothing of survival. I would be killing her as surely as if I ripped her heart out with my own hands, and I cannot do such a thing. I could not." He stared down at his hands and felt the warmth of blood, death, his past.

He clamped his eyes shut and felt her tears, washing him, cleansing him—

The loud *cawww* of the bird shattered his thoughts. *"You have given her life; now she will be your death."*

"She eases the loneliness inside me." The sound of her voice, the way each syllable trembled from her lips, soothed the ache in his chest. It didn't matter whether she spoke softly, or sang in her loud, slightly off-key voice. He liked it. Needed it. He'd been alone so long.

It was his way, he reminded himself. Yet the knowledge did little to soothe the battle that raged inside him. Fear fighting loneliness. Anger warring with need. The past fighting with the present.

"She talks to weaken you," his grandfather's voice whispered through his head. *"Not help you. You must harden yourself to her. Drive her away, give her to the mountains. They will take care of her."*

"They will see her dead."

"If her will is weak, she will die. If it is strong, she will live. It is not your responsibility, but nature's. Turn her away."

But it wasn't an option he would consider. He didn't know what was happening inside him, the strange feelings, the stirring, but he knew that it would be far worse if she left.

Worse than death?

Yes, he realized. The truth sent him back to the cave rather than deeper into the mountains to run with the animals as usual, to lose himself in his senses and forget his maddening thoughts. Instead he sought out the sweet woman with sunshine hair and rounded curves and eyes that drew him the way the cool river did on a hot summer day.

*   *   *

A strange tingling in the pit of Tara's stomach drew her from peaceful oblivion, toward a more lively plane where dreams reigned and Tarzan himself waited for her with open arms.

Her blood thrummed, her heart kick-started and soft, panting breaths parted her lips as the heat increased and she became aware of the soft butterfly touches at her breasts. . . . Touches?

She cracked one eye open to see a tanned thigh kneeling beside her. Goose bumps danced along her flesh as cool fingers stroked the skin just above one breast. Her nipple sprang to life.

Her peeking eye traveled upward to see Zane leaning over her, his dark figure silhouetted by the bright morning sunlight spilling through the cave's mouth, making him more shadow than man.

A figment of her wishful dreams . . .

But this was much more. She was fully awake, her body fully alive, and he was really touching her, the sensation a hundred times stronger than anything she'd felt in her fantasies.

Her one-eyed gaze snagged on his face, which was so intent, staring at the area he caressed, marveling at the response he drew from her with the flick of his thumb at the very tip of her fabric-covered breast.

She sucked in a breath as the crest peaked, throbbed, and Zane's touch lingered. Warming her. Caressing her.

"It's not nice to touch someone when they're sleeping. It's called taking advantage."

He didn't react. No panicked apology at being caught red-handed. No remorse.

"You are not asleep," he said simply.

"But you thought I was."

"Yes."

"It's the same thing."

"How can it be when you are fully awake?"

"You didn't know that."

"I know now."

"And you're still touching me."

"Yes."

"So . . ." She struggled for a breath as his thumb circled the sensitive area. "Stop." *Please.*

"Why?" His forehead wrinkled. "Does it hurt?"

"Yes," she ground out, and swallowed a bubble of laughter when he snatched his hand back as if he'd been burned.

"I am sorry."

She struggled up onto her elbows. "It's okay. I mean, it's not okay that you touched me without my consent, but it wasn't a bad hurt." Heat rushed to her cheeks, and she wanted to swallow her words, but he looked so worried, she couldn't help herself. "It was more like a good hurt, and for the record, I'm sorry about last night with the camera flash. I should have warned you."

"I do not know what happened. The light . . ." He shut his eyes, blocking out whatever it was that pushed into his mind before he stared at her. "Forget the camera. Tell me about this good hurt you spoke of."

"Well, it's like this." She reached out and fingered one of his male nipples which was surrounded by silky dark hair. It pebbled beneath her touch, and he jerked at the first moment of contact. "It hurt, right? That's why you jerked away?" At his nod, she added, "But it wasn't a bad sort of hurt. It stirs a pain, but it's different from real pain. It's more shocking than anything else. And you can't touch someone like that unless they give you permission. Which I didn't."

"I can touch you without permission."

"No, you can't."

"Yes, I can." To prove his point, he reached out and she slapped him away.

He leaned over her then, his knee gently pinning one arm, his grip strong on her other. With his free hand, he brought her nipple to throbbing life. It strained through the thin material of her blouse, demanding release and another sweet touch.

Fear, her sanity screamed as hunger spiraled through her when he touched her again, and again. *Fear would be a really good emotion about now*. He was physically stronger, obviously capable of subduing her and doing what he pleased.

Or what she pleased.

She battled the thought and tried to summon her courage, and her voice. *Scream. Cry. Do something to make him stop.*

Maybe she would have, if she'd truly been afraid, and if she'd truly wanted him to stop. Zane held her down with unrelenting strength, but there was no rage in his grip, no malicious intent in his gaze. Just curiosity, wonder and something else.

Something that deepened his eyes to a sparkling

midnight blue and made the air stall in her lungs. No man had ever stared at her in such a way. As if he wanted not only to devour her whole, but to take slow, sweet bites and savor each one, savor *her*.

A shiver went through her, and her nipples grew harder, more insistent.

His mouth parted, and her mouth parted.

His tongue darted out to wet his bottom lip, and hers followed suit.

He leaned forward, and she strained upward.

The soft rush of his breath whispered over her skin, and she shivered. A moan trembled from her vocal cords, and a bloodcurdling shriek filled her ears.

Abruptly, Zane's hold loosened. His head snapped around just as a black bird streaked over them, slapping at the walls of the cave before finding its way back in the direction it had come.

Then it was gone.

There was no calm after the storm, however. Juliet barked up a frenzy. Tara's heart kept up its breakneck speed, and Zane's chest heaved with each ragged breath.

"I guess if I were the superstitious type, I'd definitely say Fate was trying to tell us something."

"Superstitious?"

"Believing in things you can't see, like spirits or chance or destiny. If I believed in such things, I'd say somebody's trying to tell us that this"—she pointed to him, then herself—"you and me, isn't such a great idea."

"But you do not believe in such things?"

She shook her head, and the small motion seemed to ease the sudden tension gripping him. "Definitely not," she said. *Probably not*, a small voice added when a shiver rippled through her, a strange sensation that had nothing to do with Zane's nearness and everything to do with the strange bird. A familiar bird. Hadn't he been back at the motel on her first night?

Ridiculous. A black bird was a black bird. There had to be hundreds of them in the mountains. It wasn't the same one. And then there was the strange voice she kept hearing when she ventured outside the cave. The desperate *Help!*

She forced the notions aside suddenly keenly aware of the bright light, Zane's presence and what he'd been about to do.

What she'd wanted him to do.

What *he'd* wanted to do. The realization stunned her. He'd actually been touching her with heartfelt desire, not in the dead of night when he could pretend she was someone prettier or thinner. A brunette rather than a blonde. A supermodel rather than a frumpy housewife.

Zane had wanted to see her, test her body's reaction, feel it against his tongue.

The truth stunned her for a long, breathless moment, until reality sideswiped her. Of course he'd been fascinated, eager. He'd never seen a woman before, not like this, not if he'd been living up here, isolated since the tender age of eight.

It didn't matter that she was flawed.

He was a child spying his first piece of peppermint candy, his attention focused on eating rather than the not-so-perfect shape of the sweet or the fact that it might be crushed.

She fumbled with her buttons and fought back the disappointment that welled inside her.

"What is wrong?" Those all-seeing eyes noticed the sudden change in her.

"Nothing."

"You did not like my touch."

"That's not it. It's just . . . I'm a fifty-seven Chevy in sore need of a paint job, and you're a kid fresh out of auto shop."

"What are you talking about?"

"Me. Sure I've been bathing in the river, but it's far from my usual skin-care routine. No raspberry-scented shampoo or body wash, nothing."

"Raspberries? What do raspberries have to do with this?"

"You see, if we were going on a date in the real world I would at least be able to prepare, treat myself to a facial and a leisurely bubble bath, do up my hair and makeup, make sure that I smelled good."

"Like raspberries?"

"Exactly, but I can't do any of those things, not that a few minutes ago could be likened to a date or anything."

"What is a date?"

"Where a man and woman get dressed up and go out. To spend time together, get to know each other."

A grin tugged at his lips. "To touch?"

"That, too, though things usually go a little slower. We'd probably have dinner a few times first. Then you would work up your nerve to kiss me."

"A kiss?"

"Where a man and woman touch lips, like this." She held up her palm. "This is your mouth and this is how I would kiss you." She demonstrated and he chuckled. "Laugh all you want, but a good kiss can curl your toes. Anyhow, kissing is first base. Then later, after a lot of kisses, you might hit second base." Her gaze dropped to her chest. "Second base is touching above the waist. Then there's third, and finally comes the home run." She remembered the passionate glaze to his eyes and her body's fierce response. "But that comes much, much, *much* later, and it's irrelevant here because you and I haven't even had a date, and you shouldn't go around touching someone without first asking."

"Unless they smell like raspberries."

"Even then it's not nice to . . . to touch someone that way while they're sleeping."

"You were not asleep," he pointed out.

"But you didn't know that."

"I did. I felt it here." He reached out, his fingertips skimming the top portion of her left breast. "In your heartbeat."

The air snagged in her lungs before she found the strength to breathe and push his hand away. "You're doing it again."

"You are not asleep."

"But I didn't give you permission." She scooted away from him and started straightening the furs, throwing all her focus into the quick, swift movements of her hands. "You know, Zane, our relationship is already on shaky ground by that little murder attempt of yours the other night."

"I have already told you, I will not hurt you."

"Says you. I'll admit that you've been trying to restore my faith in you, with the backpack and answering my questions and helping me down to the river. But waking up to find you groping me is a step backward. A violation of trust. Not that I trust you. Not completely."

"I will not hurt you." A glimmer lit his deep blue eyes, and he grinned. "Not a bad hurt."

That was the trouble. It wasn't the bad hurt she was afraid of. It was the good hurt, the delicious ache he stirred with his seeking touches, his searing glances.

She let loose a frustrated sigh and scooted toward the water pouch, pushing away his hand when he tried to help her. She needed space and air and a healthy dose of caffeine, none of which she was likely to get if he didn't leave her in peace. "Don't you have a rabbit to catch or some bears to wrestle or a deer to track?"

He said nothing, simply stared at her long and hard, as if trying to figure something out. Finally, he stood.

"I know this is your place." Her voice was softer, laced with desperation. "But I really need some time to myself. Just until dark."

"Dark," he agreed; then he turned and walked away, not hurrying as he had each time in the past. He went because she asked. Because she needed it so desperately, and somehow, some way, he sensed that, respected it.

The quiet closed around her, and Tara, a woman who hated being alone, welcomed the solitude.

Chapter Twelve

A day of solitude was great, but tiring, Tara decided later as she collapsed in the mouth of the cave to watch the sun set.

After Zane had left, she'd drunk all four packets of the "emergency" instant coffee she'd stashed in her backpack, ate the remaining cupcakes and made dozens of notes for her story. While she still had questions about his years since his grandfather had died, she had many more questions about the years prior to his coming to Bear Mountain. An old Indian medicine man had taught him to live off the land and survive, but someone else had taught him the love of Shakespeare, as well as the fear she'd glimpsed when he'd had the nightmare.

Yes, he'd learned the fear early on.

The sun dipped lower. A burnt orange color edged the treetops. The wind rippled, swaying the branches and sending a play of shadows across the ground at her feet. She stared at her wrapped ankle. A shiver worked its way through her body as her thoughts turned from Zane's past to what had happened between them that morning, what had been happening since she'd first met him.

A connection that had nothing to do with facts, and everything to do with chemistry.

She closed her eyes, feeling his touch, hearing his voice, and another shiver followed, then another, until she was forced to admit that no matter how bad she felt at being Zane's first and only woman by default of the sprained ankle that had landed her here, she also sort of liked the idea. At least when he touched her, he wasn't comparing her to anyone else. No one firmer or younger or more passionate. He didn't know any better, and while, professionally, she believed that knowledge was power, personally, a little ignorant bliss could be quite satisfying.

She'd been thinking about him all day, and had long passed being simply aroused. She'd passed aroused that morning. She was on fire. Aching. Quivering.

She reached up and touched her breast, stroked the nipple just as Zane had, her fingertip tracing tiny circles around the ripe bud. It pebbled, pressing against the lace of her bra, eager for escape. For more. For him.

Her eyes snapped open and scanned the surrounding fortress of trees. She saw only a forest of green. Heard only the occasional chirp of a bird or a distant, unrecognizable growl that made her forget her lustful thoughts and reach for Juliet, who'd stayed throughout the day to keep her company until Zane returned.

Until dark.

"He promised he'd be back when it got dark, so where is he?" she asked Juliet. "So he's not out at some nightclub with another woman, or sucking back brewskies with his buddies, but he's still not here." The dog turned soulful eyes on her. "Don't go taking up for him. He's late."

Agitation turned to full-blown anger as dusk settled in.

"Don't even try to cover for him," she told Juliet. "He's in hot water."

The night chill set in, sending goose bumps racing along her flesh and cooling her anger.

"He's coming back," she told herself. "And when he does, I'll give him a good piece of my mind, unless . . . unless he's hurt." She turned a worried gaze to Juliet. "Oh, my God, what if he's not back because he can't make it back? What if he's hurt? Dead?"

Help! The word whispered on the wind, carrying through the trees to send fear shivering up and down her spine.

Her imagination, she decided. It had to be. It wasn't Zane's voice she heard. Just a voice. A man's voice. A lost voice . . .

Before she could stop herself, she pulled the missing-person flyer from her pocket and studied the picture. The smiley-face choker, the tattoo peeking up at the neck of the T-shirt. The earring in his ear, his nose.

Help! The word came again, and in a rush of fear, Tara folded the paper and stuffed it back into her pocket.

"I overdosed on the caffeine today," she told Juliet. "I've been withdrawing so long, my system doesn't know how to react to the sudden boost. I'm imagining things."

The dog licked her hand reassuringly, but the thought that Zane could be hurt followed her back inside the cave as the wind grew colder, gustier, and she could no longer wait outside.

"I'm overreacting, aren't I?" Juliet barked and Tara tried to shake away her worry. She crawled into the furs and closed her eyes. Juliet stayed near the mouth of the cave, settling down in her usual spot, but she didn't close her eyes.

"Can't sleep either, huh?"

The dog yawned.

"Men," Tara mumbled. "Can't live with them, can't live without them. But we can sure try. Zane's probably out stargazing while I'm here worried sick." Instead of making her angry, the prospect sent a wave of relief through her. She focused on the emotion and closed her eyes. "I'm definitely overreacting." She clamped her eyes shut and refused to think about Zane broken and bleeding in some gully. Zane ripped to shreds by the claws of a vicious bear. Zane floating in the river after hitting his head when he accidentally dove into a shallow part—

She tossed onto her side, pushing the image away, searching her mind for a better one.

As if on cue, a hot, heated memory popped into

her mind, his hand at her breast, his lips parted, ready to suckle her. A hollowness yawned deep inside her, and she tossed onto her other side, catching her ankle in the process. A yelp burst from her lips.

And then he was there, looming over her, worry bright in his eyes as his gaze swept her from head to toe.

"I . . . uh, my ankle," she said, a riot of emotions whirling through her. Relief that he'd come back, anger that he'd taken his sweet time, and delight because he was really here. Safe. "You're back."

He ignored her last comment, his eyes roving her once more. "What is wrong with it?"

"With what?" She tried to focus on what he was saying, but rather than hearing his words, she found herself absorbed in the way his full lips formed them. He had a really great mouth, a tad too full for the ordinary guy, but a model . . . He'd make a great model. Dark, brooding, his mouth sensuous and promising and so very kissable . . .

It suddenly struck her that for all her erotic thoughts, she hadn't once imagined kissing him and how wonderful it would be. How . . . new. He'd probably never kissed anyone before, probably didn't even know how, but she could teach him. Boy, could she ever.

". . . is wrong with your ankle that caused you to cry out?"

She blinked away the picture of Zane and his very kissable lips and said, "I, uh, twisted it when I turned over. Where have you been all day?"

"Around."

"Why did you stay gone so long?"

"You said dark." He gestured toward the mouth of the cave. "It is dark, and I am back."

"Yeah, but it's been dark for hours," she said accusingly. "You should have been back when it first got dark. That's what you said. Dark."

"It *is* dark."

"Yes, but there are various degrees of dark. This is dark dark, while sunset is plain old dark. That's when I thought you would be back. At sunset."

"You should have said sunset then."

"I did. I said dark, *implying* sunset."

"That is ridiculous."

"No, it's not. It's perfectly reasonable, and you're inconsiderate. Did you ever stop to think I might be worried when you didn't come back at the agreed-upon time?"

"It is dark and I am home," he ground out again. "Just as we agreed."

"But this is dark dark; we said dark."

"I am going to sleep."

"Now I really don't trust you. First you try to kill me, then cop a feel while I'm sleeping, then you lie—"

"You talk too much."

"Yeah, well, we've established that." She blinked at the sudden rush of tears to her eyes. Of all the times to cry, now was not one of them, not when there were other things she would much rather be doing, like touching him, making sure he was real and this wasn't some figment of her worried imagination. "I thought something bad had happened to you."

He reached out, his voice deep and soft when he spoke. "This is why you are upset? Because you thought I might be hurt?"

She nodded and dashed a traitorous tear from her cheek before she chanced a glance at his face. A satisfied male grin tugged at his lips and she stiffened. "Of course it bothered me. A bear could have eaten you, and where would that leave me? Stuck here, that's where, with no clue as to where I am and nobody to bring me food. I would have starved."

The grin didn't falter, and she realized he wasn't buying her explanation.

"It wasn't you," she pressed. "I really could care less about you. You wanted to kill me. I'd probably be better off if you hadn't come back, except that I really don't know where I am and I doubt Juliet's half the hunter you are and—"

"You still do not trust me," he finished for her.

"Exactly," she replied as he urged her back down to the fur. "What are you doing?"

"Putting you to bed."

"I'm already there, and I can cover myself just fine on my own, thank you very much." But he wasn't put off. He tucked the furs around her while she glared at him, then smeared a wayward tear from her cheek. "Maybe I'm not sleepy," she said.

He raised an eyebrow. "After all this talking? I am tired just listening." He lay down next to her, but he didn't touch her. Rather, he sprawled on his back, so close, so warm, so frustrating.

The fear that had been knotting in her stomach

slowly unraveled as she watched him. His chest rose and fell with deep, even breaths; his muscles gleamed in the firelight. He was alive, and though she shouldn't care one way or another, she did.

He sighed.

"You sound tired."

"I am." He cracked an eye open at her. "You are exhausting."

"From something besides my talking, I mean." She leaned up on one elbow and studied him. "What kept you so long?"

"I was looking for something."

"What?"

"Raspberries, Tara," he murmured, before putting his back to her and settling down to sleep. "Raspberries."

"This isn't exactly what I had in mind." Tara stood knee-deep in the river the following afternoon and stared at the pouch of raspberries Zane thrust at her.

"You wanted to smell like a raspberry."

"I wanted raspberry-scented soap and shampoo. This is not the same thing." Something flickered in his eyes, and she had the strange thought that she'd hurt his feelings somehow, and, oddly enough, that was the last thing she wanted to do.

She had every right to throw the blasted raspberries back in his face after he'd tried to kill her, but she couldn't summon the anger. He really was making an effort to earn her trust. To please her.

"Why?" Her gaze met his. "Why did you find these for me?"

"You wanted them. Did you not?"

She nodded, a smile tugging at her features. She pushed aside the deeper meaning of the question and tried to focus on the moment at hand.

"If you do not want them—"

"Of course I want them. I'll just have to improvise." She lifted the pouch to her nose and took a whiff before casting a glance at the river. The rocks broke the surface of the water in a circular shape on the far side, forming a small, isolated pool. "How about helping me over there and I'll see what I can do with these?"

Minutes later, she sat on a rock at the edge of the small pool, her backpack next to her, and dumped the pouch of raspberries into the secluded portion of water. The scent of ripe fruit and fresh air and crystal-clear water filled her nostrils, titillating all of her senses.

"Turn around," she said, but she needn't have bothered. Zane had already blended into the forest, as if he didn't want to see her naked any more than she wanted him to.

Especially in broad daylight. Over the past week, she'd become accustomed to the midnight swims, to the cover of darkness that preserved her modesty, or rather, her ego. This was too bright. Too revealing.

She slid out of her clothes and slipped into the raspberry-scented water as fast as possible. Sinking down, she let the water rise to shoulder level, the soft ripples lapping gently against her skin. *Ahhh . . .*

She grabbed the small bar of soap, rubbed her

hands and worked up a small lather, then attacked her hair. Her legs came next as Tara smoothed the soap over her skin and shaved her legs.

By the time she pulled her clothes back on, her hair was squeaky clean, her skin smelled of mountain water and raspberries, and her legs were as smooth as a baby's bottom. She felt better than she'd felt in days.

Almost.

She eyed Zane, who'd materialized the moment she'd finished dressing, and her fingers tightened on the disposable razor she'd scooped off the rock.

"You want me to trust you."

"What?"

"That's why you're being so nice. To make me trust you, right?"

"I simply want you to know that I no longer wish to kill you."

"If that's true, then prove it."

"How?" Suspicion brightened his gaze.

She held up the razor and studied it. "I've been wondering what you look like underneath all that hair." Hopefully not so good. Then maybe the sight of his not-so-perfect face would kill this strange fascination she had for him.

It's just the image, she told herself. *Like being attracted to someone at a Halloween party. The costume is the lure, but strip it away and you find a plain old, ordinary person. End of fantasy.*

"Let me shave off the beard with this." She showed him the razor and indicated the tiny metal edge visible just beyond the plastic rim. "It has a sharp blade right here, and when you sweep it along your skin, it cuts the hair off. Come on, Zane." Days of wondering, of fantasizing, boiled over. She had to know. To see him. Now. "Trust is a two-way street." She played her trump card. "You want me to trust you; you trust me." Leaning forward, she touched the softness of his beard.

He caught her wrist, his fingers tightening. Fire flashed in his eyes the way it always did when she touched him. *Get away, get away, get away.* The warning echoed in her head as it always did, but she didn't obey this time. She couldn't.

She wrenched away from him and reached out again.

He stiffened, but he didn't try to dissuade her this time.

"Please." Her voice was suddenly small, desperate, and, oddly enough, she didn't care. She needed . . . so many things. To see his face. To gain his trust. To fortify her own.

She needed this.

And he understood.

She saw it in his eyes, in the slight nod of his head, and the next thing she knew, she was sitting at the river's edge while he sat in the small raspberry-scented pool in front of her, his broad shoulders level with her waist. She spent the next several moments pruning his beard with her small sewing scissors. Then with surprisingly shaky hands, she lathered what was left of his beard, smoothed the soap down the strong column of his throat. Her fingers glided over muscle, feeling the banked tension beneath. He sat so stiff, so watchful, but she wasn't about to let his wariness keep her away. The moment of truth was upon them.

She dunked her hands into the pool to rinse off the suds. Water sloshed, wetting the already damp fabric of her blouse, but she was oblivious to anything save the man at her fingertips. She reached for the razor.

The blade caught the fading afternoon sunlight, twinkled, and his hand shot out to grip her wrist.

"Trust me," she whispered, and he let go of her hand. She touched the razor to his throat. He went rigid, but he didn't resist.

The situation was oddly empowering and very erotic. The scent of raspberries surrounded them, but there was something more. Something wild. Him.

His scent—raw male and a touch of savage—filled her nostrils and created the most damning thoughts of two bodies tangled together, touching and twisting and kissing. Sex at its most primitive level. Passionate. Desperate. Breath-stealing.

She inhaled and immediately regretted it. The scent grew stronger, the impressions more vivid, and her hands trembled so badly she wondered if she could actually do this.

She could. She had to.

She slid the edge up his throat, carefully around his Adam's apple, touching him with the razor, but not her hands. She repeated the sweeping movements, dunking her razor after every slow glide over his skin. With each motion, a tingle sizzled up her spine, pulsing to all the strategic points of her body.

She became keenly aware of her damp shirt, of her nipples tight and aching.

Zane seemed just as aware. He stopped watching her. His attention fell to her chest and she stopped breathing altogether. She fixed her gaze on a portion of his jaw, seeing only the small patch of hair that still remained. Just a few more seconds, she told herself, touching the razor to the area. Another smooth stroke, a desperate *bam, bam, bam* of her heart and . . .

Just as she swept the last of the hair away, he touched her. A tentative fingertip at the hard peak of her nipple. A gasp parted her lips. Her stare swiveled to him, and for a full moment, she forgot all about the hand touching her so intimately.

Her gaze riveted on his clean-shaven face.

A sob caught in her throat, a sound of pleasure and pain. He was even more handsome than she could have imagined. He had a strong jaw, a firm chin and lips that were much too sensual for a normal man.

But Zane was far from normal.

He was the stuff fantasies were made of. Not just because of his looks. While he was handsome, all right, his features were a tad too harsh, almost cruel. Yet there was a wonder in his eyes, a curiosity that gleamed from the inside out. That made him at once appealing and threatening. He was primitive and raw and so . . . male.

And he was touching her.

Chapter Thirteen

Tara knew she should push him away and stop this madness right now before it went any further and he touched more than just the sensitive tip of her breast.

Stop it now.

She was here to get his story, not to initiate him into the joy of sex.

Sex and joy in the same sentence? Something was terribly wrong with her. Sex had never been a joyful experience. One of obligation. A lesson in humility and obedience. An affirmation that Merle was right and she was far less a woman than she should be. Frigid. Barren.

Ah, but Zane thawed her icy inhibitions. And when he looked at her the way he did right now, she actually felt . . . whole. Fruitful, as if she could birth an entire generation.

The realization hit her like a sizzle of electricity that skimmed from her head to her toes and made her entire body ache for more.

More of what he was doing.

More than what he was doing.

Tara stared deep into Zane's eyes and saw her own desire reflected in the glittering blue orbs. He wanted her. Wanted to stroke and coax and see her respond. Wanted something he'd never experienced before, yet his body craved it as if he already knew. Craved her.

And she craved him.

"I want to kiss you." His deep voice slid into her ears, skimmed her nerve endings, and her skin prickled. His voice was like the rest of him. Dark, mysterious, intense. "Can I?"

"Yes," she said softly, and knew she was agreeing to much more than a simple kiss.

A shiver worked its way up and down her spine, and she closed her eyes in delicious anticipation. Like a radio picking up a certain frequency, Tara tuned in to Zane. His deep breaths filled her ears, the scent of him inflamed her senses, and the wanting in his eyes. . . . Ah, the wanting did the most amazing things to her. Just one look from him and her nipples ached. A wet heat pooled between her legs. Her skin came alive, utlrasensitive to the warmth of the sun filtering down through the trees, the soft breeze whispering through the branches, and the heat of his fingertips as they worked at the buttons on her blouse.

Her eyes snapped open just as he slid the openings free and a soft breeze rushed over her lace-covered breasts. Before he could finger the front clasp of her bra, she grasped the edges of her shirt together.

"I . . . This is going a little too fast."

"There are no skipping bases allowed in this dating custom of yours?"

"What?"

"Second base." He touched her nipple, and desire speared her. "This is second base and I have not completed the first one. That is why you are so hesitant?"

"First?" She tried to gather her control and think past the heat swamping her senses. Something about baseball and dating and . . .

"The kiss." And before she could grasp what he meant to do, he pulled her down into the water, across his lap, and touched his lips to hers.

Her lips parted instinctively, and he followed her lead. Soon their tongues were tangling, stroking, and their relationship altered from that of teacher and student to equal, hungry partners. Every reason why she didn't want him to see her naked disappeared in a rush of sensation. Her hands abandoned her shirt to slide around his neck, her fingers burying in the dark silk of his hair.

Zane unhooked her bra as if he'd had eons of practice. His hands slid the cups aside. The rough pad of his fingertips plucked and pulled and rolled the sensitive tips of her nipples until she cried out.

He stiffened then and pulled away from her, worry shining through the unfulfilled hunger mirrored in his gaze.

"Did I hurt you?"

"Yes . . . no . . . A good hurt."

His expression eased and a grin curved his lips. The sight pumped her blood faster and threatened to send her heart into overdrive. She was so devastated by his expression, so mesmerized, that she didn't even notice when his gaze dropped. Not until she felt the tightening response in her nipples.

He was staring at her and she was naked, very naked, from the waist up.

Instinctively, she moved to cover herself, but he stopped her.

"Trust me, Tara." He echoed her earlier plea, and her hands went limp. He moved them aside, slid her arms free of the material and tossed her shirt to the rock beside her pack and the forgotten razor.

It was only her breasts, she told herself. It wasn't as if she'd stripped completely bare. The water lapped at her waist, hiding a not-so-flat tummy, and if she leaned back just so, her breasts looked perkier.

Still, her stomach coiled, dread winding tighter, tighter, as she waited for his reaction.

He gazed down at her and surprisingly, no condemnation lit his eyes. No demoralizing glint that made her feel like a field horse at a thoroughbred auction. No disgust or, worse, pity. Nothing but blue heat that warmed her on the inside as well as the outside.

"Second base is good," he murmured. "Very good." He touched her lovingly, reverently, as if she were a beautiful flower, as fragile as the white, cottonlike wildflowers that grew around the river, their leaves so delicate a deep breath would scatter them.

She wasn't, she reminded herself as a shudder rippled through her body. Her breasts could have been any woman's and he would have been equally fascinated. She was simply . . . female. A representative for womankind.

But it didn't matter, not with his lips parted and his gaze fixed so intently on her, as if she were a seven-course meal and he was about to break a week-long fast.

He leaned over her, his breath warm on her throbbing skin, and she closed her eyes, waiting to feel his mouth, his tongue. . . . *Nothing.*

Nothing?

Her gaze snapped to attention to see him over her, staring at his reflection in the mirrorlike water. He touched a hand to his smooth-shaven face and simply stared for a long, drawn-out moment, as if he were staring at a ghost.

"Zane?" She struggled upright and touched his shoulder. "Zane, are you all right?"

He swiveled in her direction and she saw the fear in his eyes. The terror.

Zane Shiloh had seen a ghost, all right. He'd seen himself for the very first time, and the sight had struck some chord.

"What is it, Zane?"

He shook his head frantically and slipped from the water, leaving Tara staring after him as he raced for the trees as if the devil himself chased him.

241

The devil or something much more dangerous. His reflection and what it meant to him.

Zane raced deeper into the trees, pushing himself, summoning his speed and trying to force everything from his mind. To cut himself off and become at one with the forest. But he couldn't.

The images followed him, swirling in his mind. He'd seen the face before. In his nightmares . . .

He came up hard against something in the doorway. Something big and wet. His gaze swiveled to the fallen form and he saw the face. His own face . . .

He ran until he couldn't run anymore. Until the sun dipped below the treetops and he collapsed against a tree trunk. The images didn't dull and he clamped his eyes shut. The face remained in the black backdrop of his mind, taunting, shoving and tugging at his memory.

There was no escaping through his senses, no cutting himself off from everything except what he could see, hear, smell and touch. There was no salvation this time.

Only her. She offered the one way for him to lose himself. For those few moments with her in his arms, her rounded bottom cradling his hardness, he'd thought of nothing save the feelings coursing through him, boiling his blood and making his body achingly hard. She offered release. . . .

"Death."

The word pushed into his head, the familiar voice drawing his attention. Even before he heard the rustle of leaves, the wings slapping at the air, he knew his grandfather was near. Watching over him.

Watching . . .

"Make her leave, Zane. Now, before it is too late. You must. She is the reason you are hurting. The reason the nightmares will not rest."

"No! It is me." Zane pounded a fist against his chest. "It is my face that stirred the image. My own face that haunts me."

"Because of her. She stripped your face of its whiskers, pulled you from the darkness into the bright light of day. She will do the same to your soul with her never-ending questions, and then it will be too late. Who you are will cease to exist. She will not leave, and so you must run deeper into the mountains to safety. Go now before she destroys· you!"

Zane heard the anguish in the raven's thoughts, felt it deep inside him in the tightening of his chest, the painful thud of his heart, and he pushed to his feet. What his grandfather said was true. Tara wouldn't leave, not until she knew all there was to know about him. She'd said as much herself.

"Abandon the cave. You will find another. A new home far away from here, from everyone, where you will be safe. Go, Zane. Now. Leave here. Leave this woman."

Zane started through the forest, but he didn't head deeper into the mountains. He ran the path he'd just traveled, his feet carrying him back toward the river. To her.

"No!"

The raven beat the air behind him, screeching and clawing, as if trying to grasp him, to draw him back, to save him from the fulfillment of the prophecy. He resisted, shrugging away from the talons that ripped at his shoulder.

"Do not go! Death will steal you, Zane. Death!"

But as Zane rushed back the way he'd come, he knew it wasn't death that awaited him, but salvation. He felt it in the hunger stirring deep in his belly. While Tara was indeed an outsider, she was also a woman, and he needed her.

Isolation wouldn't make the nightmares go away, for he carried those inside him. On the outside as well, he thought, touching a hand to his smooth cheek. Running away from Tara wouldn't defeat what hunted him. But running to her . . .

She would ease what gripped him. Physically. Emotionally.

He didn't know how he knew. He simply did. The way he knew an animal was friend or foe even before it materialized, or the coming of a storm long before the sky turned gray and the heavens opened. The knowledge was instinctive. In his blood. Part of who he was.

She was his release, his escape, his refuge, if only for a little while, and he didn't think beyond that.

He ran faster.

Tara sat on the riverbank and hugged Juliet, eager to stay warm against the coming chill. Dusk had already fallen, and night would soon follow.

Where was he?

Had the sight of her naked breasts scared him away for good?

She pushed away the thought and concentrated on the sound of her own voice as she told Juliet one of her favorite stories.

". . . and they lived happily ever after. Wasn't that a good one?"

Juliet responded with a yawn before sinking down onto all fours and resting her snout on her paws.

"Thanks a lot, Juliet." She ignored the pang of hurt. Juliet was only a dog. No way could she really appreciate the merits of *Beauty and the Beast.* "You could at least look a little excited." Juliet closed her eyes and Tara sighed. At least she wasn't talking to herself all the time. Juliet might not be an avid listener, but she was there. Faithful company while Zane had left her.

And at such a crucial moment. She'd been about to . . . They'd been about to . . .

She shook away the thought, slid her clothes off and slipped into the cool water for a bath, desperate for something to distract her from him. She swam out to the middle of the river, ducked her head beneath the liquid and let the coolness soothe her feverish skin. And men thought they had the market cornered when it came to cold showers. They worked just as well for women. Tara just wished she didn't need one.

But the things he'd done to her. Or rather, the things he'd been about to do to her . . .

Her skin heated all over again, despite the chill

water, and she closed her eyes, slipping into one of her favorite fantasies. This one took place at the river and had been heating up her free moments since he'd first brought her to bathe. She was swimming by herself, moonlight reflecting off the water, and then she felt a touch on her shoulder. . . .

Her eyes snapped open and she whirled.

And there he was, just the way she'd pictured him in her fantasy, but even more sexy because he was real, solid. He was right in front of her, drawing closer, closer, and he wanted her.

His arms slid around her as he pulled her against his chest and claimed her mouth in a kiss that was savage, desperate, as if he wanted to lose himself in the act.

He did. She sensed it, and it touched something deep inside her. Her arms stole around his neck, pulling him closer, holding him as if she never meant to let go.

She didn't, not for the next few moments anyhow, not until she had this man in a way she'd been dreaming about for days.

His hands moved roughly over her back, scorching and searching, and as much as it delighted her, she grappled for control.

She tore her mouth from his. "I . . . we have to slow down. Calm down."

His movements stopped, and she felt the tension gripping his body, as if he fought so desperately to hold back that which was inside him. She felt the heat and size and hardness of him against her belly, and an ache deepened inside her.

"Tell me what to do." His voice, raw with passion and pain, thrummed through her body, and she shivered. "Show me."

She wanted to. God, how she wanted to. But could she?

She had such limited experience where sex was concerned. She'd been a virgin with Merle, a naive, inexperienced, faithful little virgin so eager to please, to gain the sort of love she'd only dreamed of. Love that didn't really exist except in fairy tales.

She would never know that lay-down-your-life sort of love she'd always wanted. Dreamed of. No meeting of souls or hearts. No springing forth of life from something precious and beautiful. She'd given up on that a long time ago.

But she could have this . . . this meeting of bodies, sharing of pleasure. While she was far from an expert, she knew what made her feel good. Knew what her body craved.

Sex had always been more of an obligation than anything else. She'd always been on the receiving end, always on the bottom for those few moments of panting and sweating.

No more. This would be different. Fulfilling. Heaven.

The water lapped at her waist, soft and caressing against her belly button. She dipped her head and drew his nipple into her mouth. His hand came up, his fingers threading through her hair as he held her to him while she laved the tip, suckled and relished the deep groan that rumbled from his chest. Searching fingertips wandered down his chest, sifting through the silky hair that funneled down his abdomen. She moved her hands lower, below the water, where she skimmed the silky flesh of his manhood, and a cry tore from his lips.

He grasped her wrist and stilled her exploration for a long moment, as if trying to gather his control and understand the fierce emotion raging through him, marching across his features as she watched. Excitement, fear, desperation, desire . . .

She pulled free and wrapped her fingers around him. His hips bucked sharply, driving his swollen flesh deeper into her caress. She gripped him, stroked him, pleasured him and marveled at how he seemed to grow larger in her hands.

Awareness sizzled through her, and her gaze locked with his. Fire burned in his eyes, hot, intense, eager.

He caught her hands in his own, pulled them to his lips and kissed them, his tongue tracing her knuckles before he placed a kiss on each palm, a gesture of gratitude for the magic she was showing him, and it touched her more than anything else she'd ever felt.

She slid her arms around his neck and pulled him to her. The kiss was long, slow and deep, with Tara setting the pace, drawing out the delicious dance of lips and tongues until her entire body trembled. He followed her so perfectly, mimicking the deep thrusts of her tongue with an added urgency that was highly erotic.

"Your turn," she said breathlessly, pulling away from him to allow a few inches of distance between them. Moonlight danced across the water, caressed her bare torso.

He fixed his attention on her breasts, and self-consciously she folded her arms, blocking his view. He caught her hands, urging them to her sides. Then he reached out and touched her so softly, sweetly, that tears stung her eyes. She blinked as a honeyed warmth unfurled inside her. Then he grew more bold and leaned her back over one steely arm. A raw, hungry sound rumbled from his throat as he urged her breast toward the wet heat of his mouth. He fastened his lips around her nipple, sucking hard, and she forgot everything save the thrumming of electricity that swept through her body and brought every nerve to charged awareness.

He suckled her, his mouth hot and greedy, and she trembled. The sensation went on forever; then he lifted his head and stared at her, seeing the response in her glazed eyes and parted lips. Leaning down, he delivered the same delicious torture to her other breast for several sweet, breathless moments until both her nipples were dark red and wet and painfully erect.

Then his hands trailed down her sides, spanning her waist, slipping between her legs. At the first probing touch of his fingers, a cry burst from her lips.

His hand stilled and his gaze riveted to hers. "Did I hurt you?" he asked, his voice thick and husky and filled with barely contained need.

"I . . . no. I've just never felt a man's hand . . . there. Like that."

"Like this?" He slid one finger into her and watched her keenly.

"Yes." The word was a breathless whisper that seemed to please him.

"Do you like it?"

"Oh, yes."

"Then I am doing this right?"

"Definitely yes."

There were no more words thereafter as he touched her slow and deep, and heat sparkled through her. Her body trembling, she cried out, clutching his shoulders, holding on lest she float away from him, as small and lightweight as the hundreds of lightning bugs that surrounded the river, twinkling in the darkness like stars.

She grasped his neck and wrapped her legs around him. The buoyancy of the water lifted her, making her seem weightless, all the while supporting her injured ankle. No way could she have moved in such a way on land, not with her injury, but the river was different. She lifted herself just until she felt the thick, pulsing tip of him at the moist heat between her legs.

He went rigid then, waiting—anticipating, she realized from the tremors gripping him—as if his body knew exactly what came next.

What happened between a man and a woman was instinctive, primitive, the most basic form of communication, as old as time itself. The body knew in a way the mind never could.

Tara lowered herself onto him inch by slow inch. A gasp lodged in her throat, mingling with his deep, delicious moan. When he was fully embedded inside of her, she buried her face in the crook of his neck and tried to calm her hammering heart.

While she'd felt a man in this way before, never had the emotions felt anything like this . . . strange and blissfully new and frightening all at once. Heat sped along nerve endings, stirring new sensations, and a wave of discovery washed over her. She became acutely aware of the water lapping at her bare bottom, the wet silk of his chest hair chafing her nipples, the cold hardness of the bear-teeth necklace pressing into the soft mounds of her breasts, the frantic beat of his pulse against her lips.

His hands cupped her buttocks, holding her to him as if relishing the feeling of being buried hilt-deep in a woman just the way she herself was savoring the throbbing fulfillment.

"You feel . . . like home," he murmured, his voice deep and raspy and heartbreakingly sincere.

She smiled and kissed his eyelids, the tip of his nose, then his lips in silent gratitude. And then she started to ride him.

Chapter Fourteen

Zane was dying. His grandfather had been right. Tara meant his death, and this was it. With each shimmy, each slide of her body, sensation burst through him, and he knew that one more movement, one more breath from her, and he would burst into a thousand pieces.

From far away, he heard the shriek of the raven, the wings beating at the air, felt the talons rip into his back in one final attempt to save him from destruction.

He closed his eyes, focused on the feelings rushing through him, and tuned out his surroundings, the way he did when he closed the door on his humanity and ran with the animals.

This was his last run, his final race through the forest, and he intended to enjoy every moment. To savor the rush of adrenaline, the fresh scent fillings his nostrils, the woman embracing him, grasping him so tightly it was as if she'd been crafted just for him.

His heart pounded, his lungs gasped for air and the pressure inside him built. Blood rushed hotter, faster, and he gripped her smooth buttocks, mimicking the pattern she'd set, his own pace more frenzied, desperate as he urged her up and down his engorged length.

Her cry pushed past the ringing in his ears, and he bucked hard and fast and deep one final time; then he exploded.

It wasn't death that followed, however, that swooped down to suck him up, but life. Sensation. Tremors racked his body. He held tight to Tara and relished the delicious spasms that gripped him as her body milked his. He'd never felt more alive, more vibrant, more invincible than he did at that moment. With her. Inside her.

He opened his eyes to find her collapsed against his chest. Smoothing his hand down her slick back, he soothed the shivers from her body and carried her up the riverbank.

Leaving the water behind, he knelt on a patch of soft, dew-covered grass and eased her down.

"No," she said when he started to pull away. Her arms snaked around his neck and she held him tight, as if she didn't want to let him go, and something shifted inside him. "Not yet. Please."

Her plea mirrored his own, and he rolled onto his back, settling her on top of him, his manhood still deep inside her, their hearts beating against one another, legs tangled. It was nothing he'd prepared himself for. He knew the ways of nature, how beast mated with beast, but there were no soft touches afterward, no lingering feelings that kept male and female together. Nothing like what he felt at the moment.

For all his wildness, his kindred spirit with the animals, his savage soul, Zane knew he was different. He'd felt it before, and the truth had always saddened him. Until now. For the first time, he savored who he was, what he was—a man. Simply a man. And she was his woman.

He held her tighter, closed his eyes and welcomed sleep.

Chill wind swept over her skin and drew her from the pleasurable warmth of sleep. Tara opened her eyes, leaving the darkness of oblivion behind for a softer blackness. She gazed down at Zane's sleeping face and watched him for several long moments.

She saw him sleep so rarely. He was always sprawled on his back, his arm across his face, hiding. Or lost in a nightmare. Rarely did he look so peaceful, so spent.

A delicious ache pulsed between her legs, and she shifted ever so slightly, feeling his body's response deep inside her own. Even asleep, he was fully attuned to her.

That should have frightened her. It would have under normal circumstances. In civilization, no way would she have ever let a man get this close to her. Before she knew it, he'd be moving in, turning her life into his, and if he were anything like

Zane, she would gladly let him. She would lose herself in loving him, pleasing him, pleasuring him, and there would be nothing left when he finally did leave.

Not this time.

She ignored the strange ache that gripped her at the thought. This was perfect. Every woman's fantasy. Her fantasy, right?

The most they could ever have—the most she wanted, she reminded herself—was a week of lust while she finished her story and her ankle healed.

This . . . thing with Zane was nothing more than sex in its most basic, primitive form. One man, one woman, no emotional ties, no repercussions. No threat of disease or pregnancy. No thinking, just feeling.

And what feeling . . .

She shifted again and a sizzle of electricity rushed from the point where they still joined, to set her ablaze. She sat up, positioning her leg at a comfortable angle as she threw her head back and closed her eyes, not wondering what he was thinking, or what would happen next.

Just feeling . . .

She moved, a delicious lift and slide that made her heart pound faster and stole the breath from her body. She knew she should wake him up, but she couldn't pause long enough to lean forward. There was something oddly exciting about being in such control, setting the speed, seeking out her own pleasure.

"You are so beautiful." His deep voice echoed in her ears and her eyes snapped open. Like a child caught with her hand in the cookie jar, she felt herself blush.

"I didn't mean to wake you."

"Did you not? How could I sleep through such exquisite torture?"

She smiled. "I'm torturing you?"

The laughter in his eyes faded to something deeper. Hungrier. He touched one erect nipple. "Exquisitely."

"Oh." She couldn't help herself. She smiled. While she was more concerned with her own pleasure than his—this was her moment in the sun, her reward for so many years of unselfishness— the fact that she excited him made her happy.

"Please continue," he murmured.

His palms rasped across the tips of her breasts and she closed her eyes, her head thrown back as she relished the rush of sensation.

"Is that a yes?"

"Ah . . . yes," she said softly, resuming the lift and slide. "Yes, yes, *yes* . . ." And Tara gave herself up to the second-best climax she'd ever had, the first being only hours before with this very man. A man who made her feel very much like the woman she was. For that alone, she could have fallen in love with him—if she'd been inclined, but she wasn't. Love was the farthest thing from her mind.

No way. Nohow. Never, *ever* again.

"What happened to your back?" Tara asked him several hours later when they returned to the cave. Zane knelt beside her, applying a poultice to her ankle, now sore from their lovemaking on the riverbank. The first time, in the river, had been different, the injured limb buoyed by the water. But with it tucked under her, pressing into the soft moss while they'd . . . while she'd . . . Needless to say, it now hurt.

Zane, always so attuned to every change in her expression, every flash of discomfort, had mixed a fresh poultice and proceeded to doctor her immediately after he'd carried her inside and placed her on the comfortable furs.

Tara trailed her fingertips over the raised red welts on his muscled shoulder, the marks still raw and tender. Guilt ebbed through her.

"Did I . . . do this?"

He flashed a grin at her. "Sort of."

"Sort of? What kind of an answer is 'sort of'? Either I did or I didn't." She stared at the stubby nubs of her own nails she normally kept well manicured and polished. But then, she hadn't been living in Timbuktu, miles from her nail file and electric nail dryer.

"You were responsible," he said, "but it was not your claws that sank into my flesh."

"Then whose?"

"My grandfather's. He does not like you."

"Zane, your grandfather's dead. You told me so yourself."

"I also told you his spirit lives on."

"You really believe in ghosts?"

"No. I believe in spirits. The soul. My grandfather's lives on in the raven."

"Your grandfather's a bird?" At his nod, she

added, "I know a lot of people believe in reincarnation, but I can't quite buy it."

"Reincarnation?"

"Where the spirit is reborn in the form of something else."

"My grandfather was not reborn. The raven is his spirit animal. His connection between this world and the other. When he died, his body faded to dust while his spirit rose, strengthened and filled the body of this raven, who will carry his soul to the next world, to Oblivion when the time comes."

"You really believe that?"

He gave a solemn nod. "It is true. Maybe not in your world, but here . . ." His gaze swept their surroundings. "The mountains are a very spiritual place, Tara. They hold the souls of many who lived and died here before, both man and animal. While their bodies faded into the earth, their spirits rose. Some crossed over, content to go in peace, while others stayed. They live and dwell here."

"Why?"

"Perhaps their work on earth was not finished, or they are frightened of what waits for them, or there is some truth they seek to tell the world, or they are just stubborn."

At his words, Tara remembered the desperate *Help!* she'd heard so many times, the plea carried on the wind, echoing through the mountains, reaching out to her, calling her. A spirit lingering in this world?

A burning in her pocket drew her gaze. She could see the flyer, the image burned into her mind. The missing photographer. The *dead* photographer . . . No. She had no proof, nothing but the strange words of a wacky motel owner.

"That makes twice you've screwed up now."

And the hunch that something was terribly wrong.

But that wasn't enough. Tara sought facts and nothing more. She forced the notion aside.

"So the mountains are strong and they feed your grandfather's spirit, which lives on in a raven. How do you know it's really him and not just a plain old raven communicating telepathically with you?"

"I hear his voice. It is him."

"Maybe you just think you hear him, because you miss him," she pointed out.

"I do miss him. I miss the way he used to sit with me by the river and show me how to fish and tell me stories about when he was a boy, and how he used to pick plants and explain the value of each. I miss all of that because things have changed. He is no longer with me as he was before. He is different now, but so am I. I am a man, and he is a raven."

"You're half-right, anyway."

He frowned. "Why are you so quick to disbelieve? Have you no faith at all, Tara?"

His words stirred years of bitterness, of futile hopes and desperate prayers. "I have faith, all right. In myself, my work." Partly truthful, she thought, her arm slipping about her waist to cradle the part of her that would never nurture a child.

"And what about Kanati, the Great Spirit? The earth? The moon? Have you no belief in those things?"

"The earth, yes, because I walk on it, the moon because I see it most every night, but a Great Spirit?" She shook her head. "No . . . maybe. I don't know. I used to pray when I was a little girl. I prayed for my parents to come home, for them to stay with me or take me with them, or at least call, but they never did. I kept praying. I prayed that Merle would love me. That finally my life would be complete. It never was. I prayed that I wouldn't die in that hospital after Merle left and I nearly starved and exercised myself to death. I prayed that I would live. That was the first time my prayers were answered. Maybe that was the first proof I had that any Great Spirit exists." *And now*, a voice whispered. *You have now. This man, this passion.* "Let's just say I'm not completely convinced. When I walk away with my Pulitzer, then I'll believe in a higher power."

"Tell me more about this Merle. What kind of man was he?"

"A jerk."

"Jerk?"

"A selfish jerk. He thought only of himself, of what he wanted. If he was dissatisfied with himself, he projected that onto me. I wasn't pretty enough or nice enough. I didn't keep the house as perfectly as he expected, or cook quite as well as he wanted. That's the sort of man he was, if you can call someone like that a man. He was spiteful and mean, and at times simply cruel."

Anger flashed in Zane's eyes and warmth shot through her. "Not physically, other than a little pushing and shoving, but, boy, did he do a mental job on me. I lost myself when I was with him. I became wrapped up in his way of thinking, warped. I actually thought there was something wrong with me."

He touched her cheek, his fingertips brushing away a stray tear. "There is nothing wrong with you. You are perfect."

"I talk too much."

"True, but still perfect."

"I can't skin a rabbit."

"You will learn."

"I don't want to learn."

"So you are not so perfect." Humor danced in his eyes, and his words coaxed a smile. Then a seriousness came over his expression. "This Merle was a fool."

"That's what I keep telling myself." If only she believed it. Logically, she did. She'd gone through all the counseling, done her best to build up her self-esteem, and she'd succeeded. She had a good job, her own place, and she liked herself. But there was still that last, lingering doubt, that tiny voice that kept whispering, "Maybe it *was* you."

A voice that faded away the minute Zane's strong fingers stroked the curve of her cheek.

"I never want to find myself in that kind of situation again," she went on. "That's why this—you are so perfect. What we have is just temporary. I don't have to give up my life. You don't have to give up yours. We have a good time, then go our separate ways." She knew that, wanted it, but somehow saying the words made her chest hurt. That and the fact that he didn't protest. "So you talk to this raven?"

"He warned me about you, about what you would do to me."

Her face flamed at the memory of exactly what she had done to him. What she wanted to do again. "Forgive me if I have a hard time picturing you having a birds-and-the-bees talk with a raven."

Zane looked puzzled. "We did not talk of birds and bees, but of you."

"The birds and the bees are a nice way of referring to what happens between a man and a woman."

"Mating," he said, his gaze burning into her, the memories obviously still fresh on his mind.

"Yes, that's another way to put it." She took a deep breath to cool her suddenly pounding heart. One look from him, and her body did the damndest things. "What did he say about me?"

"He does not like you."

"A raven doesn't like me. I'm terribly hurt." Silence ticked by and something prickled at her conscience. "Okay, why doesn't he like me?"

"He is afraid you will hurt me."

The words hung between them for several long moments as she gathered her courage to ask the question that suddenly held more importance than any she'd ever asked before.

"And you?" She stared at his profile, watching for some change in him. A telltale tensing of his muscles, a frown. "Are you afraid? Are you sorry that we . . . that I showed you how two people . . ." She couldn't bring herself to say *mate*. "How it is between a man and a woman?" she finally finished. For someone who'd promised herself to be bold, self-confident and a risk-taker, to live the fantasy, she sure stumbled around a lot when it came to talking about it. "Are you sorry?"

"No." The word held such conviction that her chest ached and she barely resisted the urge to throw herself into his arms. "I would never be sorry for such a thing." He flashed her a smile, then finished wrapping her ankle. "Tomorrow you will soak it in the stream. That will help to ease the swelling."

"Sure thing, doc."

"And we will be very careful in the future." He flashed her another heated look that told her he was envisioning a very busy future between them, and handed her a handful of muscadine grapes before settling himself beside her.

She studied his profile. "You didn't answer my first question. Are you afraid of me?"

"I should be." He stared into the fire as if deep in thought. "My grandfather is always right."

"Not in this case. I won't hurt you, Zane. I would never hurt anyone, especially you." Her hands trembled as she trailed them over the vicious marks on his shoulder. "You helped me when I first came here, took care of me, you still do. And you make me feel . . . special. I thank you for that."

"You are special." He bit into a grape. Juice trailed down his chin, and he cast her a hungry look. "I have met no other like you. No one with sunshine in her hair, or skin as soft as a flower petal, or breath as sweet as the peaches that grow farther down the mountain."

The words washed over her in a deep, soothing rumble, food for her deprived soul. She peeled the skin off one grape and bit into the sweet flesh. "Keep going."

"No one who sings as sweetly of things I have no knowledge of, or who smiles as brightly at the prospect of a mountain bath."

"You should see me at home with my whirl-pool."

His hand touched her chin and he urged her gaze to meet his. "For now, this is your home. Here. With me."

"With you," she agreed. *For now.*

They spent the next hour eating and talking, and then they made love again, with Tara showing Zane all the places she liked to be touched. After that, she gave him as much pleasure as he gave her, caressing him in all the right places and keeping him busy for the entire night so he didn't have time to sleep and dream of the face he'd seen down by the river.

The face that haunted him, hunted him, and begged him to remember.

But he wouldn't. Zane had made that vow to himself a long time ago, when he'd traded his fear for peaceful dreams and a lifetime of isolation.

No past. No pain.

* * *

Get up, get up, get up. . . . *The words replayed in his head like the Christmas record he'd scratched when he'd been playing with his sword.*

He hadn't meant to scratch the record. One minute he'd been listening to "Jingle Bells" and waving his new toy, and the next, scratchhh . . . *Ruined.*

"I told you not to play with that sword in the house, Zane. We'll play outside, after Christmas dinner. Then we'll come in, get Barry the Bear and read your favorite story."

No more dinners or stories or anything.

The blood drenched his socks, creeping through to warm his cold feet. Not a good warmth like hot chocolate, stealing through his bones. But bad. Wet. Sticky.

Get up!

He tried to force the words to his lips, but they stalled in his throat. His teeth clenched, his tongue heavy and limp and useless as he stared down at the man sprawled at his feet, bleeding all over the carpet, staining his blue and yellow Mighty Mouse pajamas.

He fixed a tear-filled gaze on the man's face, but he couldn't see. Not clearly.

He couldn't.

He didn't want to.

Too much blood. Too much death.

Get up, get up . . .

"Get up!" Zane surged upright, his voice bouncing off the walls to disappear into the pitch-black night that hovered at the cave's mouth. He buried his sweat-covered face in trembling hands and clamped his eyes shut. As if he could shut out the nightmare, push it away until all that remained was blessed nothingness. Peace.

His gaze went to the woman sleeping beside him, the naked curve of her shoulder exposed above the fur robe. He reached for her, needing to chase away the dreams and lose himself deep inside her.

And for the rest of the night he did.

"You had the dream again last night, didn't you?" Tara asked the next morning as she sat at the stream's edge, her ankle resting in the cool water. Zane sprawled a few feet away from her, his back against a tree trunk. He popped raspberries into his mouth, his gaze fixed on her bare legs. "You did."

"Your legs are smooth."

"Thanks to my razor. Speaking of which, I'd be glad to shave you again."

He shook his head, his expression closed. "No. No more shaving."

"Tell me about the dream."

"No." He popped another raspberry into his mouth and let his gaze slide down the length of her thigh, down her calf. "Now is not the time for talking. Let us do something else."

"You have a one-track mind."

"If that means I think of you, then I have the mind of which you speak."

"You were crying last night."

"You were killing me with your sweet body." He gave her a lazy grin. "It is a wonderful death."

"You were crying before we . . . *Before*."

"You must have been the one dreaming." And with that, he popped the last raspberry into his mouth, stood and walked into the forest.

She turned to Juliet, who still lounged nearby. "Mmm, he didn't threaten my life. I'd say that's definitely an encouraging sign. He's softening." The dog whimpered. "Okay, so maybe he's not throwing himself at my feet and begging me to listen to his story, but he's coming along. He'll be pouring out his past in no time at all. I give him a few days, tops."

A few days passed, and Tara knew little more about Zane's nightmares than she had in the beginning. She learned only that he was little more than a boy in the dreams. The cries in his sleep resembled those of a child, filled with a child's fear, a child's pain. It was the man who turned to her, however, and sought comfort in her embrace. Funny, but she couldn't seem to bring herself to question him during those dark hours. All she could think about were his tears, his desperation.

She chalked her strange reaction up to over-active hormones. The guy was ultrasexy, and obviously it was affecting her rational thinking. She'd tapped into thirty years of repressed sexual energy, so of course she was overwhelmed by him. For a man with no previous experience, he'd turned into an expert lover, so in tune to every sound she made, every breath she took. He watched her eagerly, drinking in the knowledge of what pleased her as if he cared for nothing else but her pleasure.

He was a man unlike any other.

A man a girl could easily fall in love with.

If she were looking to fall in love, which she wasn't. She wanted a few days of great sex, and a prizewinning story.

The sex was no problem, but the story . . .

"I'm stuck," she mumbled to herself as she knelt by the stream one morning. She wore only her shirt as she scrubbed her underclothes and jeans and wished frantically that she had the luxury of a washing machine. There were some things she certainly wasn't going to miss when—if—she ever managed to write Zane's blasted story.

And other things she'd miss terribly . . .

She forced a sudden image of Zane aside and concentrated on sifting through what she knew of his past. "Let's see . . . He's been on his own since he was eight years old, here, living in isolation. Prior to that, he was with his grandfather for a few years, and before that . . ." A blank, as if a wall had been ressurrected to block out his earliest years. He had no impressions, no memory of his mother or father, or how he got there. She shot a frustrated look at Juliet, who lounged a few feet away, tongue hanging out from the hot morning sun.

"If I'm going to write this story, I have to know at least the basics—where he came from, how he got here, who brought him." Juliet whimpered sympathetically and Tara smiled. "You've been here with him for a long time, a companion, a confidante. Does he talk to you about the dreams? I can't shake the feeling that there's something there. If he would just break this stupid vow of silence he's got going and tell me about them."

"Better to forget."

His deep voice echoed in her ears, and her head snapped up to see him standing on the riverbank a few feet from where she knelt. The sunlight played off his powerful torso. Muscles rippled, flexed as he hunkered down and cupped his hands and took a long, cool drink. Water trickled down the smooth column of his throat, now covered with over a week's growth of stubble, since he'd refused her offer to shave him.

His deep blue gaze zeroed in on her, pinning her to the spot, and awareness shot through her. Her unclad legs curved under her, her body bare beneath the thin covering of the shirt.

She clutched the wet clothes in her lap and searched for her voice, eager for a distraction from the suddenly palpable tension between them. "Sometimes it's better to remember. Whatever you see in your dreams obviously bothers you. If you faced it, got it out in the open, maybe you wouldn't wake up in a cold sweat every night. It's not healthy."

"Is that what concerns you? My health? Or are you simply eager for more information for your story?"

"Both," she said honestly. "I'd like to see you get a good night's rest, and I'd like to see me write the best damned piece I can—which isn't going to happen unless I know more. I need background to make the readers understand who you are. I know all about you from about the age of four on, but what about before? How did you get here? Were you born here? Are your parents alive or dead? Did they purposely bring you here? Why, how, what, when, where—I need to know them all. I want to know what you see at night. Is it your past? Your future? What haunts you, Zane?"

She expected him to get angry or simply walk away, but he did neither. Rather, he stepped toward her, and she knew the moment of truth had come.

Chapter Fifteen

Zane stopped inches away, his body blocking out the sunlight as he towered over her. "What haunts *you*, Tara?" Blue fire burned in his gaze, searing her face, searching as he stared at her, into her.

"I don't know what you're talking about."

"Do you not?" His eyes gleamed, hungry and dangerous. She swallowed and clutched the newly washed clothes in her lap.

Her naked lap.

She became instantly aware of the coarse rock beneath her bare bottom, the water from the wet laundry trickling down the insides of her bare thighs, the heat between her legs.

"I want to see you." He leaned down, the sun blazed at her, and his large hands reached for the dripping bundle she clutched. "Now."

"Now? But it's broad daylight, and we just

made . . ." The word *love* poised on the tip of her tongue and she snatched it back. "Uh, mated, and I'm really busy. I've got laundry to finish, and my writing and—"

"Now." He pulled the wet clothes from her grasping hands and tossed them to the riverbank with a resounding smack, leaving her completely open and vulnerable to him.

Panic zipped through her and she took a deep breath. *Calm down. It's not as if you're entirely naked. You've got a shirt covering all the major parts. The not-so-perfect breasts, the slightly too-large thighs, the I-wish-it-were-flatter stomach.*

"Now," he repeated, his fingers going to the buttons on her damp shirt.

She caught his hand. "You—you can't." Her reaction was silly. She'd been intimate with him more times than she could count over the past few days, but suddenly she felt as frightened and apprehensive as a virgin on prom night. For all their lovemaking, they'd never done anything in broad daylight, out in the open with so much . . . light.

"Why not?" He shrugged free of her grip and worked at the first button of her shirt. It slid free in a heartbeat and he moved to button number two, then three.

"Don't do that. *Please.*" The last word came out as little more than a sob. His hands stilled, fingertips burning through the thin covering to scorch her bare flesh. "I—I know what you want, but I can't."

"Why?" Such a simple question.

Such a complicated answer, she thought, fear

coiling fast and deep in the pit of her stomach. *I'm far from perfect. I haven't got a Cindy Crawford stomach or Tina Turner legs or a Pamela Anderson chest. I'm adequate. Average.*

The only words that stumbled to her lips were, "I just can't. Not now. Not here."

"You can."

"I don't want to."

"Liar." He stroked her flesh through the damp fabric of her shirt. "Your body wants to. It is your mind that is holding you back. Close your eyes, Tara. Close your eyes to the daylight, shut your mind off and simply feel. *Feel.* Then if you do not wish for me to touch you, to taste you, then I will stop."

The deep, soothing rumble of his voice lulled her eyes closed, and though she trembled violently, fear and panic and the warm feel of his fingertips making her pant, she did as he instructed.

Don't think. Just feel.

"Just feel," he murmured again, echoing her thoughts. He urged her backward until the rock met her back, her legs draped over the side and dangling in the water.

Water lapped and swirled at her calfs as Zane stood waist-deep in the water and positioned himself between her legs.

The warm heat of the sun slid across her skin as he parted her shirt, stripped it away. Her eyes snapped open and she started to protest. "Please. I don't want you to see me."

"Is that your fear? That I will see you?"

"No."

273

"Then what is it?"

"That you won't like what you see. That you won't want to make love to me anymore. That you won't—"

"Ssshhh," he murmured, touching his fingertip to her lips. "Do not worry, sweet Tara. I will always want to make love to you. 'Love looks not with the eyes, but with the mind.'" Then he leaned over her, blotting out the sun, easing her sudden panic, and she lay back down, eyes closed, body blazing for more of what he'd promised.

He parted her legs, fingertips sliding over the soft skin of her thighs, rasping her nerve endings to life. He moved his hands over her thighs, up and around until his large fingers slid beneath her buttocks. He drew her to him, sliding her body along until her bottom lay at the edge of the rock. He spread her legs wider, and then he touched the wet heat between them. She arched toward him, wanting more even when she'd said the opposite only moments ago.

An eternity, it seemed. But he'd been right. She wanted this, and suddenly the need took precedence over a lifetime of insecurity. She opened wider, her legs falling open, begging him, and he answered.

He stroked her, slid his rough fingertip over the softness of her skin before plunging it deep inside. The pleasure almost shattered her, and she fought to drag air into her lungs. He stroked and explored until she writhed, and then he put his mouth on her.

The shock of feeling his kiss at her most private

part sent a bolt of panic through her. No man, not even Merle—especially not Merle—had ever kissed her there. She reached for Zane's head, suddenly desperate to pull him away and beg him to stop, but somehow her hands had a different idea. Her fingers threaded through the dark silk of his hair, holding him closer, urging him to continue.

And he did.

He tasted and savored, his tongue stroking, plunging, driving her mindless until she came apart beneath him. She shattered into thousands of weightless specks that caught the faint breeze and floated toward the morning sun like the whisper-soft petals of the featherlike mountain flowers that surrounded the riverbank. One breath, and like a flurry of white, she scattered.

She opened her eyes to find him staring down at her as intently as if he could see clear to the bone. Her legs were spread, her shirt bunched beneath her, her breasts like twin sacrifices to the sun blazing overhead. She was completely exposed to him, vulnerable, afraid. His gaze swept the length of her, leaving nothing untouched by his visual caress, before brilliant blue eyes met green and he murmured one word that changed her life forever.

"Beautiful."

And it was at that moment that Tara finally admitted to herself that she was falling in love with him.

Love? Was she crazy? Hadn't she learned anything after six years of pure hell with Merle? Ob-

Kimberly Raye

viously not, she thought as she stared at Zane, who still slept next to her. The first rays of dawn caressed the chiseled planes of his face, making him seem darker, more intense, and a shiver rippled through her.

Not from fear, but from anticipation. Of his touch, his kiss, the intensity in his eyes when he looked at her, the answering ache that flowered in her chest.

Yes, she was falling in love.

Falling in love, but not actually *in* love, not yet. Which meant there was still hope.

She grabbed one of Zane's spears to use as a cane and limped to the entrance of the cave. She had to get out of here. To think, and she couldn't do that with him so close. He short-circuited her rational thought, and she had to figure out her next move. Drinking in the fresh morning air, she tried to still the frantic beating of her heart.

Maybe it wasn't love at all. She could just be overreacting, misinterpreting strong lust for something more. Zane was so sexually overwhelming, and she had been so deprived, such a mistake would be easy to make.

Even as the hope whispered through her head, she knew in her heart it was futile. It was love, all right. She was falling hard and fast, something she'd vowed never to do. Even worse, she was falling in love with the first man she'd gone to bed with since the divorce.

Okay, so they hadn't actually been in a bed yet. They'd been everywhere else, including the top of the waterfall after Zane had helped her over her self-consciousness yesterday.

Love. She closed her eyes, wishing at that moment that the sun would send down a ray strong enough to shrivel her on the spot. When that didn't happen, she knew it was up to her. She had to stop herself from feeling anything for him. Lust, love, compassion, anger—anything. If she didn't, she would be heading for major heartache. Her feelings would grow, blossom until the logical part of her lost complete control to the emotional part. She would fall so hard, so fast for him, she'd lose her perspective, her *self.*

She had to do something.

She shot a glance at her notebook, which was brimming with information, yet still lacking the most crucial piece of the puzzle. The first piece. The beginning that had led to all of this. To Zane the wild man. The man she craved as much as her next breath.

Blinking back a wave of frustrated tears, she stared out at the surrounding landscape.

If only her story were finished.

If only she could walk without the blasted cane.

If only she weren't falling in love.

"What is wrong with you?" Zane asked later that afternoon as he sat across from her, knife in hand as he whittled a tall piece of wood he was fashioning into a new spear handle.

She ignored his question and asked, "How long does it take to make one of those?"

"In the winter, when I am forced inside and can

277

do little but this, several days at most. In the summer, perhaps a few weeks."

"Don't you ever wish you could spend fifteen minutes, drive to the hardware store and buy one?" She stifled a hysterical giggle. "But then if you could drive to a hardware store, what would you need a spear for? You could hit the nearest McDonald's for dinner, go to Neiman's for clothes. You wouldn't have to make everything yourself."

"That is my way." He said, ignoring the incomprehensible references.

"But it isn't mine," she reminded him, or maybe she said the words more for herself. "It isn't."

"While you are here it is." He indicated the furs in her lap and she glanced down, seeing the half-finished coat she'd carefully stitched over the past several days. The reality of what she was doing hit her like a slap to the face. She stared down at her hands, and suddenly she saw only the cracked tips of her once well-manicured nails, her callused palms.

She'd slipped into the role of Tarzan's Jane so easily she'd forgotten her lust for nail files and hand lotion and polish. She'd forgotten everything except sewing the coat together, enjoying the monotonous act while daydreaming about Zane.

Geez, she had it bad. Beyond bad.

"You never answered my question. What is wrong?"

"Nothing." *Everything.* She laid the coat aside. "I'm just going a little stir-crazy. I need some air." She struggled to her feet, and Zane was beside her in an instant, helping her up.

She shrugged away from him and surprised them both.

"Something is bothering you."

"I just need to go outside for a little while. Sit by the river."

He nodded. "It is hot. I could use a swim."

"Alone," she snapped when he moved to put away his knife. "I want to be alone." His gaze caught hers and hurt flashed in his blue eyes. "It's a woman thing, Zane," she said, her voice softer. "Sometimes a woman needs some space to be by herself." To *be* herself, she added silently. No man clouding her thinking, making her act in ways she would never dream of if she weren't so enslaved emotionally.

"Then I will give you space." No argument about what he wanted or needed. Just . . . space.

Irritation gnawed at her. Why couldn't he argue a little? Act overbearing, selfish, manipulative? Be a little more like Merle? It would be easy to feel nothing for him then, to shut herself off. So easy.

"I really need some space."

He carried her down to the river and, as promised, slipped into the forest to hunt for dinner and left her to some blessed solitude.

The solitude remained blessed for all of five minutes. The river wasn't the sort of neutral place that lent itself to objective thinking. They'd made love too many times there, shared too many moments, and when she looked at the water and mulled over her dilemma—her story wasn't finished and she couldn't walk without the cane, certainly not well enough to make it back to civilization—she didn't see answers or possibilities; she saw only deeply tanned flesh, rippling muscles, intense blue eyes. *Him.*

"This isn't working," Tara told Juliet, who'd wandered up to the riverbank and flopped down, her head resting on her paws. "I have to get out of here, to find someplace that doesn't remind me of him."

She grabbed the spear doubling as her cane and the notebook she'd brought with her, and pulled herself to her feet, despite the pain that assailed her. The ground sloped slightly as she entered the forest, the slant too subtle to throw her balance off but enough to make walking less work as she hobbled along, gaining distance and a clear head with each movement.

What was it with her and no-win relationships?

Zane isn't Merle, a small voice whispered.

"So he's not a bastard *now.* I didn't think Merle was either. Not until it was too late." But there'd been signs. Signs she'd seen, but ignored, such as when they'd picked out her engagement ring. She'd wanted a diamond, but Merle had talked her into getting a small pearl. Then there'd been the wedding cake. She'd wanted ultradecadent marble cake with chocolate-dipped strawberries and buttercream frosting, while Merle had pushed for angel food cake with lemon sauce when he knew she hated lemons. He'd won, setting a precedent for the next six years. Whatever he wanted, she agreed to.

She walked and walked, clutching the notebook, racking her brain for some clue that Zane was just as manipulative. While he was bossy at times, frustrating, he wasn't beyond stepping back and letting her take the lead. Both in their lovemaking and socially-like today, when he'd agreed to leave her alone. No questions, no pouting, no messing with her head.

Okay, so he was as far removed from Merle as a man could get. He was nice, caring, a gentle yet persistent lover, resourceful, spiritual rather than materialistic, and he thought she was beautiful. She still had a major problem on her hands. He was a primitive man and she was a modern woman in sore need of a manicure, a cappuccino and the comfort of a real bed, not to mention that she had the story of a lifetime hanging over her head, and she was *not* falling in love with anybody.

They were polar opposites. Zane was haunted by death and she had a zest for life. He was the ultimate predator and she his prey. He embraced nature while she thrived in civilization. She had to go back.

She shook her head. Of course she was going back. There was never any question about that. She tightened her grip on her notebook. Leaving sat at the top of her priority list, right under finishing her story.

The loud screech of a bird punctuated her thoughts and she turned just as a sleek black raven settled into a branch overhead.

Just a bird.

She took a deep breath and turned, her gaze slicing through the tree-shrouded forest. "Juliet?

Here, girl. Here." But the dog was nowhere in sight.

Tara took a step forward and the bird screeched again, sending a dance of goose bumps down her spine. She stopped and tried to calm her racing heart. It was just a bird, despite what Zane had said about his grandfather.

"Just a harmless bird," she told herself. She held the notebook to her chest and called to Juliet. Silence answered, a still, unnatural silence, as if the Apocalypse had come and she were the last person left on the face of the earth.

In a terrifying instant, Tara realized the forest had grown darker, more shadowy. Dread churned in her stomach as she glanced upward, forcing her attention past the sleek black bird poised so attentively above her. She expected to see the sun high overhead, but only a faint orange glow edged the treetops, testimony to the sinking truth that morning had turned to afternoon.

How long had she been walking?

Too long. She'd been so absorbed in her thoughts, she'd completely forgotten the time. Frantically, she turned to start back in the direction she'd come, but there was no discernable path. Suddenly the trees seemed closer, a united wall that surrounded her while the raven watched like Big Brother.

Lost.

No. She couldn't be. She chose a direction and took a step forward. The bird let loose another blood curdling *cawww*, as if warning her not to move, not to take another step. Her grip on the cane tightened and her heart lurched.

Calm. Cool. Professional.

It was just a bird. No reason to panic. She resisted the fear clawing at her and took another step forward.

Another loud screech raised the hair on her arms. Wings rustled, branches shook and the bird took flight. She ducked, holding the notebook up to protect herself just as sleek black wings slapped the air near her head in a scene straight out of Alfred Hitchcock's *The Birds*.

She took off at a half hop, half trot, desperate to get away, but the bird kept after her as if trying to pull her back, to halt her progress. Tara was too frightened to stop, to turn, for fear she would get a faceful of vicious scratches.

The bird's pursuit drove her deeper into the trees, wings flapping at the back of her hair, claws grasping at her shirt, ripping through the material enough to draw blood. Just when she was ready to burst into tears, the foliage thinned. Moments later, she burst from the trees and found herself at the back door of an ancient-looking log cabin.

Wrong way, wrong way, wrong way! the bird seemed to screech.

Or maybe the right way, Tara thought as she dodged the frantic raven and rushed for the back door. She pounded for several moments with one hand, while the other clasped her notebook and fended off the bird. Blood streamed down her arm.

With her book, she smacked at the raven as hard

as she could. The animal gave a piercing shriek and took flight in an explosion of black feathers. Tara drew in a deep breath and tried to calm her racing heart. The raven was gone. For now.

She surveyed her bloodied arm. While there were numerous scratches, none were very deep. She ripped a strip off of the bottom of her shirt and wiped away most of the blood. Hobbling around to the front of the cabin, she climbed the three steps onto the porch, all the while straining her ears for some telltale sign of the bird's return.

As she gripped the wooden railing that ran the length of the porch, the view snagged her attention and she turned, sucking in a deep breath, all thoughts of the crazed bird forgotten.

Awestruck, she simply stared. The cabin was lower in altitude than the cave, she thought, but built at such a spot that it seemed poised on the tip of the world, staring out over a blanket of treetops and an endless stretch of mountains. Beautiful. Breathtaking. Inspiring.

A shrieking *cawww* shattered her momentary awe, and she hurried toward the front door, banging against the wood for all she was worth.

"Help! There's a crazed bird chasing me—" The door creaked open beneath the pressure of her fist. "Hello?" She walked inside and found herself standing in the middle of a broken disarray.

Years had spread a layer of dust and cobwebs over pieces of broken furniture, shattered dishes and an overturned bookshelf. Tara knelt near the scattered volumes and picked one up. Dusting off the cover, she stared down at the title. Shakespeare's *Macbeth*. Awareness sprang to life inside her and her heart pounded faster. She picked up another book. *Herbs and Various Uses*.

She knew even before she saw the remains of what had once been a medicine pouch—so similar to the one Zane carried—that this was the cabin he'd mentioned. His grandfather's cabin. Where Zane had spent his early years before the old man's death.

Excitement bubbled through Tara, and she forgot all about the strange raven that now hopped back and forth on the front porch, shrieking into the fading afternoon sunlight. The threat seemed inconsequential, and she slammed the door on the bird. Putting her notebook aside, she set about picking through the mess. Zane's past was here. She knew it, smelled it the way she scented a hot story.

She spent the next half hour searching, only to come up empty-handed. The place had been picked over, vandalized, probably by the moonshiners Zane had mentioned. He'd said they'd followed him to the cabin to make sure he was dead. They'd buried his grandfather. They'd probably trashed the place, too—

The thought stalled as she pushed aside the shell of an old chest and saw a trapdoor cut into the floor beneath. Rummaging around, she found an old butter knife and quickly used it to pry open the square panel. A smile split her face as she stared down into the secret compartment. The last piece of her puzzle.

* * *

Zane fought the strange sense of panic that had gripped him back at the river when he'd found Tara missing. He had to focus, to think only of following her footsteps. Of finding her before the afternoon rain, he thought, glancing at the swirling dark clouds overhead. For then her trail would be washed away, the air cleansed, and tracking her would be nearly impossible.

He picked up his pace. Several times he stopped, studied the branches, the marks on the ground, sniffed the air and let what lingered of her scent fill his nostrils.

She was hurt. The knowledge festered inside him, drove him faster. His arm pulsed with a fiery sensation. Sticky. Wet. He glanced down more than once, convinced he was bleeding. He saw nothing save smooth, tanned flesh sprinkled with dark hair.

It wasn't his own wound he felt, but hers. He was connected to her, not only in body since they'd mated, but in soul, as well, their spirits linked.

"No!"

The word exploded in his head, like a loud clap of thunder. The raven streaked down, flapped to the ground and brought Zane to a staggering halt.

"Turn back."

"No, Grandfather. She is hurt. I can feel it. I must help—"

"You have done enough. Turn back."

"I cannot. We are linked." He clutched his hands together and entwined his fingers. "We are one."

"She is Death. You would defy me and willingly

embrace Death? Welcome it?" The bird squawked and fluttered. *"No! I will not let you do this."*

"It is already done." Zane stepped past the bird and continued his quest.

The animal screeched, beating the air, following. Claws scraped at Zane's back, his shoulders, fighting so hard to hold him back. But where the raven was a powerful creature in spirit, Zane was far more powerful in body. His legs pumped faster, his arms flailing to ward off the sharp claws that came at him. The frantic words fired through his head like a rapid burst of gunfire, each louder than the first. More desperate.

"Leave her. She is nothing to you. She brought death to our refuge. Defiled our safe haven. Let her go while there is still a chance. Forget her and come back, Zane. Do not leave me. Come back. . . ."

The first few drops of rain hit him, sizzled across the raw wounds on his back, and he ran faster, leaving the raven behind. The rain fell in earnest by the time he broke free of the trees. He squinted, his gaze slicing through the downpour, searching. He spotted a bloodied piece of her shirt, and something in his chest shifted. Two strides and he snatched up the soiled material. His breath caught, and fear unlike any he'd ever felt before gripped his heart.

Then he heard the shift of wood followed by the soft sound of Tara's voice above the downpour, and relief washed through him, as cleansing as the rain. He rounded the cabin, climbed beneath the shelter of the porch. Wood creaked and the door opened.

She sat on the floor, an old shoe box in her lap, a mess of newspaper clippings scattered around her.

"I don't believe this." She shot him an incredulous glance before turning back to the newspaper in her hand, oblivious to the steady trickle of rain from a huge hole in the ceiling. "I knew your name sounded familiar. I read about this case in my investigative journalism class. The senseless murders of Margot Wolfe—the famous zoologist who supervised the birth of the first black bear born in captivity at the Chicago Zoo—and her husband, David Shiloh, a literature professor at the University of Chicago. They were both found dead in their home, stabbed to death, the result of a burglary gone bad. A reporter covering the story actually got a photograph of a crucial piece of evidence, a fragment of a baseball jacket one of the robbers had been wearing. Apparently, he'd caught his sleeve, and the logo had ripped off. The police missed the torn material during their initial sweep and had no leads until the reporter came forward with the photo. It provided the key lead in the investigation that led to the conviction of a four-man robbery conspiracy that had been operating throughout Illinois." She held up another clipping that included a faded black-and-white photograph of a small child clutching a tattered bear, surrounded by police as he was being led from his home. Just a boy, any boy.

Her gaze met his and she murmured, "This is you, isn't it? They were your parents."

He started to protest, to tell her that he had no

knowledge of the clippings, the murders, the people of whom she spoke. Then she shifted and he saw the tattered white teddy bear sitting in her lap, the dark rusty stains marring its worn fur. The sight unlocked something deep inside him, opened a door that had been closed for so long he'd forgotten it even existed, and the first images rushed through, slamming into him, rocking his senses.

The pitch-black beneath the bed smothered him, choking him. He had to get out, to the air, the light. He had to.

"I knew the name Shiloh sounded familiar; I just couldn't figure out from where. You're that Shiloh. I don't believe it. I simply don't believe it . . ."

Her words faded and Zane shook his head, fighting the memories the way he always had, struggling to push them back, barricade the door, but this time he couldn't. They rushed out, rolling over him in great waves that made him shiver, despite the oppressive heat and humidity engulfing the room, as blistering as the sweat baths his grandfather had taken. Zane's teeth chattered and he sank to his knees, feeling the cold inside him: death.

The blackness of the hallway was softer, but he still cried, still afraid as he crept silently forward.

"I'm so sorry, Zane." Tara scrambled across the floor toward him, cradling the stuffed bear, Zane's bloodstained past in her hands. "So very sorry."

He stopped just outside the doorway and shrank against the wall, his bear clutched tightly in his hands as he saw the first shadow. Then one turned to two, three, four that moved back and forth, around the bed where his parents slept. The bogeymen—

"No!" He raised his arms to block out the truth. He didn't want to see any more, to feel the knife slashing at his insides, shredding his heart. His grandfather had been right. This was the prophecy coming to pass. Tara had found the cabin, opened his past, unlocked the death he'd thwarted for so long, and now it was devouring him.

The pain smashed over him in dark waves, sending an echo of violent tremors through him. His stomach heaved, his lungs burned and blackness edged his vision.

The cold hand of death reached for him, but he felt only warm, soft, urgent fingertips. Life, not death.

"It's all right," she murmured, her sweet voice pushing past the roaring in his ears. "It's going to be all right. Remember, Zane. Face what frightens you and it'll be all right."

With her hands on him and her soothing words rumbling in his ears, he stopped fighting the visions and let himself see.

Chapter Sixteen

*He leaned back against the wall, his heart thudding,
fear clawing at his gut as he saw one of the bogeymen go rigid and turn toward the doorway as if he'd
heard something.*

*Zane's heart pounded; he felt the frantic in-and-
out of his breathing, the sob burning his throat.*

*He clamped his eyes shut and prayed for his
mother to wake up. To scoop him into her arms,
cradle him, and tell him this was just a bad dream.
There was no such thing as the bogeyman. No shadows slipping in and out, back and forth. No shadow
standing in the doorway, looking for him—*

"Zane!"

*His mother's frantic voice shattered his thoughts,
and the stuffed bear fell from his suddenly limp fingers. His eyes snapped open to see the shadow in the
doorway whirl toward the bed. His mother*

screamed, his father lunged up, and the shadows closed in.

Zane ran as fast as he could back to his bedroom, crawling under the bed, clamping his eyes shut until he saw nothing and heard only a faint buzzing in his ears. No shadows stabbing his parents then scrambling down the hallway. No unnatural silence pulling him back to his parents' bedroom. No blood seeping into his socks, staining his pajamas and his favorite stuffed animal. No scream catching in his throat as he saw his father's bloody body, heard his mother's last gasp. No dogs barking or sirens wailing . . .

"I killed them." His voice was harsh, raw with hurt and the tears choking him. "It was my fault."

"What are you talking about?" Tara smoothed her hands down his shoulders, touching, soothing.

"They should have been asleep. They would have stayed asleep, if I had stayed in my room, hidden under the bed. I did not." He stared at her with eyes full of bleak despair. "I heard noises and I climbed under my bed, but I didn't stay there. I heard more noises and I went to their room even though I knew something was wrong. When I saw the men, it was too late. One of them spotted me. I closed my eyes then and called to my mother with my mind. That's the way it always was with us. She was my grandfather's daughter, born of powerful medicine. She could be far away and still hear my thoughts, feel my feelings, just as my grandfather heard her that night and felt her pain.

I woke her up. She called out to me, surprised the men and drew their attention while I ran back to my room and hid." He started shaking then, uncontrollably.

"It's all right, Zane. It's over."

"Do you not understand?" he said in a growl. "I took my mother's life, and my father's." Anguished eyes caught and held hers.

"The robbers did that, not you. You were a victim, and you survived. You should thank the Great Spirit."

He stared at her incredulously. "My parents are dead and I should be thankful?"

"Yes," she said with such conviction it made her lips tremble. "He gave you two people who loved you the way a mother and father should. At least you knew real love, even only for a little while." She swallowed against the sudden tightness in her throat. "Some people live a lifetime and never know what it feels like to be truly loved." The minute the words were out, she wanted to snatch them back, tuck them deep inside and forget she ever said them. But it was too late.

"You speak as if you know."

She managed a nod and willed her voice to continue. "I'm one of those people." She stared down at her hands and saw a small girl sitting alone in front of the television, eating dinner alone at a huge dining room table, singing herself to sleep at night because there was no one to do it for her. "Everything was always more important to my parents than I was. Everything came first. Their ambition, their passion." She closed her eyes as

293

the all-too-familiar sense of isolation stole around her and crept inside.

"Then came Merle," she went on, "and I was no better off. Still lonely, still unloved, I just didn't know it for a while. I was so hungry, and he was like a great big cheeseburger. I didn't see the health risk, I just sank my teeth in, hoping for a little taste of heaven. I was always last with everyone in my life, my parents, Merle, but you . . ."

She stared up at him, holding his hands tightly. "You were the most important thing to your mother and father, and they saved you. Don't blame yourself or block out the past because of guilt or fear. They sacrificed everything so you could live, not kill yourself with guilt. Let them rest in peace knowing their son is alive and well because of them. You're alive, Zane. *Alive.*"

He was, he realized, staring down at their clasped hands. He had remembered the past, faced all the memories he'd blocked for so long, and he was alive, his lungs pumping oxygen in and out, his heart beating against his ribs. Still, a coldness lingered inside him, his body still shook and suddenly he needed more than words to push away the lingering doubts.

He needed to *feel* alive.

He needed her.

Zane scooped her into his arms and walked out onto the porch. He sat her on the railing and stripped her jeans and panties off with eager hands before he stepped back to remove his own breechcloth. Her gaze mirrored his hunger and desperation as she watched him, waited for him, her body so lush and inviting. So welcoming.

He stepped between her legs, and her long limbs closed around him. She was warm and deliciously wet and he thrust deep into her. His hands grasped her buttocks, kneading the soft flesh as he pulled her tight against him and relished the feel of her slick passage gripping him, her frantic breath filling his ears, her heart echoing the frenzied rhythm of his own.

He pumped hard, driving into her, exorcising the last of his demons, the guilt and the fear and the rage of being a helpless child and a victim. Later, when he spilled his seed deep inside of her, all the darkest parts of his soul stepped into the light, and Zane knew what it felt like to be truly alive and thankful.

For life. For love. And for the woman in his arms.

"I think I'm getting hungry," Tara murmured as she sat on the front porch of the run-down cabin and stared at the orange brilliance sinking below the horizon. Her stomach grumbled as if in agreement, and Zane's deep laughter rumbled from behind her. With his hair-dusted thighs framing hers, she leaned back against his chest and rested her arms atop his, which folded around her to ward off the coming chill.

She felt anything but cold. Warm and safe and comfortable and sated . . . A sigh parted her lips, and her stomach grumbled again. "Forget think. I know I'm getting hungry."

"You have been busy working up an appetite." His arms tightened possessively, and she had the distinct impression he was looking forward to more "work." The hardness pressing into the small of her back supported the notion.

She smiled. "Don't you ever get tired?"

"Of you? No."

"But you would," she murmured under her breath. "Eventually."

He stiffened. "What are you talking about?"

"Nothing."

"I heard you."

"You weren't supposed to."

"I did."

She leaned away from him, bending her knees and reaching for her notebook and the shoe box of newspaper clippings she'd gathered up after they'd dressed a few moments ago. "You know it's unnerving to be around someone with such a keen sense of hearing. Do you eat some special root that promotes hearing?"

"I listen with my heart as well as my ears." His hand closed over her shoulder, pulling her back into his embrace. "And my heart says I would never grow tired of you."

Something tightened inside of her, and she took a deep breath, desperate to ignore the strange sensation. To ignore him and the things he made her feel and think. Crazy, impossible things like happily-ever-afters and babies and rocking chairs.

"What does your heart say, Tara?"

"To move on to a new subject." A safer subject. She pulled away from him and slid a blessed few inches away to sit cross-legged with the shoe box and notebook in her lap.

Surprisingly, Zane didn't pursue the subject. He gave her the space she needed to breathe and simply sat there, his back against the cabin wall, one forearm resting on a bent knee as he stared at the awesome view.

Opening the box, she retrieved a few clippings. "So your grandfather showed up the day after the murders to get you?"

"He heard my mother in here." He tapped his temple, then his chest. "He knew even before the authorities sent a message. I did not get a clear look at any of the men, no distinguishing features, so I was of no use to anyone. My grandfather brought me here to live in solitude. To get over the nightmares. He told me to forget, to shut out the past, that it was all just a bad dream. Soon I believed him. The nightmares lessened and finally went away."

"You were blocking out the past. It's a common thing for children who have endured severe trauma. I did a small piece on a shelter for abused women and children back in San Diego. That's how many of the children dealt with the abuse. They blocked it, pushed it so far back that it was like the past didn't exist for them. It's how they coped."

"It is how I coped, as well. My life before these mountains ceased to exist. No mother or father."

"Until I showed up."

"You asked a lot of questions I could not answer.

It stirred my memories, chipped away at this block you speak of."

"I'm sorry."

"Do not be. I needed to remember. To stop dying inside and start living." He flashed her a wicked smile. "You are wonderful to live with."

The thought sent a thrill of delight through her. "What I still don't understand is why your grandfather hid you away."

"I was afraid of people."

"But by hiding you, he only encouraged the fear. Why would he do that?"

"Because he was an old man as frightened as his young grandson."

The voice came from everywhere and nowhere, and Tara's head jerked up.

She saw the bird perched on the porch railing and her heart stopped. There'd been no loud flapping of wings, no frantic screech to warn her about the crazy raven's return. It was as if he'd materialized out of thin air.

"There is so much to tell you and so little time."

"This isn't happening." Tara blinked, but the bird didn't disapppear. The voice came again, echoing through her head, forcing her to believe the impossible. To believe what Zane had claimed all along. The raven was his grandfather.

"You are hurt." Zane felt the pain in his chest and he moved instinctively toward the raven—knowing even before he saw the dark blood staining the glossy black coat, that death had come to claim his grandfather for the final time. "What happened?"

"My own foolishness." The raven limped out of Zane's reach and a drop of crimson splattered the wood railing. *"She brought death, Zane. Just as I told you. But it wasn't yours; it was mine. The prophecy promised my death, not yours. She came and I fought her, and I lost. Now this spirit body is failing me. I knew she would take you away from me and I could not stand for that."*

"I would never leave you, Grandfather."

Sad laughter echoed around them. *"It is I who said those very words to you, do you remember? I promised never to leave you, and I kept that promise. My body died, but my spirit stayed here with you."*

"I needed you to survive."

"Then. You were young and frightened, but strong. You were a strong boy and now you are a strong man. You would have survived without me. Your will is strong, like your mother's. I did not stay because you could not survive on your own. I would not leave because I could not bear to let go. That is why I told you to block the past, to fight it. I did not want you to think of your mother or father, to remember them. That is why I hid the clippings. I wanted to erase your past, make it one big black void of fear so you would always stay here, with an old, lonely man who feared being alone."

More crimson dripped onto the railing and Zane's heart gave a painful thud. "Let me help you, Grandfather. Let me doctor your wound and ease your pain as you taught me."

"There is a time to die, and mine is long overdue. My spirit should have died alongside my body, but

it did not. I could not bear to let you go, so I held on to this life. But the time has come to let go."

"No." Zane's voice was gruff with the emotion rolling through him. His heart constricted and his chest tightened and he reached out.

His fingers grasped at thin air, and he blinked to see the raven a few inches beyond his grasp, as if he'd misjudged the distance. But he hadn't. The raven had been there right where his hand lay. A telltale drop of red wound around his knuckle, slid into his palm, and he closed his hand, as if he could hold on to the life slipping away right before his eyes.

"Do not grieve for me, Zane. I have wronged you."

"No! You saved me."

"I kept you alone and afraid."

"Safe," Zane said, fighting the truth, that his grandfather was partly to blame for his isolation, his loneliness. "You kept me safe."

"I trained you well. Even with the truth in front of you, echoing through your mind, you do not want to accept it. But you must. I deceived you."

"You gave me a home when I had none!"

"Here. Far away from civilization, from life, with an old man who'd already lived his. You should have been out in the world, in civilization, living, Zane. Truly living. Instead of here with me, nursing death and fear and all the things I should have protected you from. I perpetuated your fear. I robbed you of life."

Zane shook his head, but inside he feared his grandfather was right. He remembered the whispered warnings of doom, of danger that waited should he leave the mountains. And when he'd tried, when he'd run for help, his grandfather had been there to drag him deeper into the mountains, nurse him back to health and feed his fear of the outside. Of outsiders.

"What I did was wrong. I do not ask forgiveness. Only understanding. I lost my daughter not once, but twice. The first time when she left the mountains to go away to college. She always wanted to do more living than she could here, yet she learned her life's trade right in these forests, with these animals. To speak to them with her mind, nurse them with her hands. Still, she wanted more. She wanted knowledge to back up what was in her heart, so she left.

"I grieved for her as if her spirit had passed," the raven went on. *"But I did not know the true meaning of a broken heart until I lost her spirit, as well. When I heard her cry out, felt the pain in my own body, I knew she had been taken, and I could do nothing but pray for her and go to you. To claim what was left of my daughter. You, Zane. I meant only to give you a home until you grew, but then you made my days so much happier, fuller. I was selfish, but I hope you can understand. I never meant to deprive you. I just wanted you to stay here with me. To live off the land and appreciate it the way your mother never could."*

"I do. I will. Always."

"Always is a very long time. Too long for such a short, precious thing as this fleeting journey we call life. I am sorry for your fear, your pain. So sorry."

"Grandfather!" The word was a prayer on Zane's

301

lips as he watched the raven flap his wings. Feathers ruffled, beat at the air, then, in an explosion of black, the raven disappeared.

Anguish drove him to his knees. His fingers grasped at one glossy black feather that floated to the ground. Through a burning rush of tears, he stared at the offering, cradled it and touched it to his lips.

The soft contact sent a wave of peace through him, washing aside the grief and hurt, and Zane whispered, "All is forgiven."

Then he heard his grandfather's final words rumble deep inside his head, his heart.

"Thank you."

The sun dipped below the horizon.

With her newfound information, Tara wrote fast and furiously the next two days, pausing only to eat and soak her ankle in the stream. She kept her thoughts focused on her future rather than on Zane Shiloh, and grew even more determined to keep her distance. The less contact, physical or otherwise, they had while she finished her story and her ankle mended, the better.

It would be easier to say good-bye when the time came, for she still meant to say good-bye. So she kept her distance. Body and mind.

Surprisingly, Zane made the situation easy for her. He didn't press the topic. In fact, he didn't turn to her at all. No more nightmares, no need to escape.

No need for Tara.

All the better, she told herself, determined to ignore the ache in her chest. In a few more days, her ankle would be healed enough for her to walk more than a few feet without the cramping pain, or a makeshift cane, her story would be finished, and she could get out of there.

Out of danger, her heart whispered.

"I'm almost finished," she told him three days after they'd unearthed his past. "But I'd really like to go back to the cabin, to look around again and get a feel for the place that shaped those early developmental years. Would you take me?" She hated to ask, but with her ankle so close to being normal again, she didn't want to strain it. That would only prolong her time here.

He agreed and they left for the cabin the next morning. While Tara looked around, Zane sat outside on a grassy patch just beyond the porch steps. She'd seen him sit in the sun before and relish the heat, but the beauty of him, the peace in his body, had never failed to strike a chord in her.

But there was no peace now, she thought as she hobbled to the porch steps with her notebook and the shoe box and sat down. A frown twisted his features, his lips were compressed, his muscles tense. He looked worried. And tired. So very tired.

Even though the nightmares had faded, he still didn't sleep. She'd even offered him a Sleepy Time pill, but he'd refused. He had spent his nights staring at the ceiling of the cave, as if worrying over something.

Or grieving.

"You can talk about him, Zane."

"Who?" He didn't open his eyes or flinch, but she saw the instant tensing of his muscles.

"Your grandfather. The raven." She shook her head and a hysterical laugh bubbled on her lips. "I can't even believe I'm saying this. That I'm thinking it."

"But you cannot help yourself. You believe only what you see and hear, and you saw."

The laughter died. "And I heard. Why did I hear him? I'm not like you. I've never even had a Chia Pet, much less a real one. I don't have a sixth sense when it comes to animals, and I'm far from spiritual."

"That is not true. You have a strong spirit, Tara. It is just a fearful one."

"So that's why I heard your grandfather? Because my spirit is strong?"

"No. My grandfather communicated with only my spirit. You and I are one now, our bodies united, spirits linked. I heard, therefore you heard."

She ignored the strange fluttering in her stomach at his words. *Linked. United. One . . . No!*

She opened the notebook on her lap and reached for her pen. "I didn't mean to get into a spiritual discussion. I just wanted to say I'm sorry for your loss." Her fingers faltered for a moment and her voice caught. "Very sorry."

"Do not be." He sat up, one arm resting on a bent knee as he glanced at her. "You were right. I have known great love, and I am fortunate. I have my memories now, of my mother and father. I remember going to the zoo where my mother worked, petting the animals. I remember my father reading Shakespeare to me at bedtime, the rumble of his voice that tickled the insides of my ears, the warmth of his arms." He closed his eyes as if seeing the past, feeling it, and a small smile curved his lips for a sweet moment before he looked at her again. "And I remember my grandfather and all the things he taught me. Many things, about survival and respect and love. I do not deserve your sorrow."

She shrugged. "Okay, then I envy you."

His gaze locked with hers and a storm cloud passed over his face. "Do not envy me either."

Exasperated, she shrugged. "Then what should I feel?"

"Should?" His eyes darkened and locked. with hers. "That is not the question at hand. Rather, what *do* you feel?"

As always when he asked those deep, thought-provoking questions, she turned away. She nearly laughed as the irony struck her. In the course of two weeks, he'd turned the tables on her. Now he asked the questions, and she dodged them.

"Since when did you turn into a psychologist?" She opened the shoe box and started sifting through clippings, looking for one in particular that gave his birth date. She'd yet to put that detail into her story—

Her gaze snagged on the picture of him being led from the house as a small boy and she hesitated, something shifting inside her. He'd been too young, too innocent to be surrounded by so much chaos.

"I remember this." His deep voice rumbled in her ear and she realized he'd sat down on the steps beside her. "There were so many people, so many questions, and all I wanted to do was curl up and cry." A bleak look crossed his face, and she ached to reach out, to erase the past for him, but he needed to remember. To sort through the feelings, pick and choose the ones he needed to hold on to.

And she needed to keep her distance. Stay impartial.

He finally shook his head, his expression eased, and silent relief crept through her. "The past is over." He stood up and walked across the grass to retrieve some acorns that had fallen from one of the trees. "So what will you do now?"

"What do you mean?"

"You have all your answers." He indicated the shoe box in her hands. "Your story is complete, or nearly so. What will you do with it?" He turned away from her, giving her his profile as he stared at the surrounding mountainside.

"I'll finish the actual writing, then turn it into my editor at the *Sun* as a front-page feature. . . ." The words faded away as her attention snagged on the small boy in the picture. She traced his delicate features, his tightly shut eyes, and his question echoed through her mind.

What will you do?

What would she do? What could she do?

The thought shattered as branches shifted and a small squirrel skittered up to Zane. He held out the acorns in his palm and the animal took one to nibble. There was no fear in the animal's movements, not the slightest hesitation or suspicion because Zane was a man. This animal came willingly to Zane because he was more than a man.

He was a kindred spirit. Despite his earliest years in Chicago, he'd been here most of his life. This was his home. His haven.

Her story, she reminded herself, doing her best to ignore the ache in her chest; pain for a small boy who'd endured too much, sympathy for a man who'd spent his life hiding from his past, and joy for that man because he'd finally made peace with his memories.

A peace she would shatter if she gave his story to the world. Zane would turn from a man to a celebrity, and his privacy would cease to exist. His safety. His life.

So what? Think about your future. Your Pulitzer. Your story.

That's all he is. A hot topic. The story of a lifetime.

The problem was, despite Tara's best efforts, Zane had crossed the line into something more. Something personal. Something that made her rip the clippings into tiny, unreadable pieces, shred her notebook pages and forfeit her dreams in a run-down cabin bordering paradise.

As she stuffed what was left of the best story of her career back into the old shoe box, she finally admitted the awful truth to herself. There was no *falling* involved.

Tara was already in love, and she was this close to making the second-worst mistake of her entire life.

Chapter Seventeen

She was leaving.

Zane knew it the moment he touched her, swept her into his arms and then started back for the cave. The turmoil he'd sensed over the past few days raged more feverishly, filling her eyes with a sadness he couldn't begin to touch. To ease.

He was a man who had fought the most vicious enemies, who did whatever was necessary to survive, yet he was powerless to destroy whatever haunted her.

She wouldn't let him.

The realization filled him with fierce pride and an overwhelming sense of frustration. Pride because she was his equal, who could be neither bullied nor dominated. And frustration because she was his equal, who could be neither bullied nor dominated.

But she wasn't leaving. He wouldn't let her. He would make her stay, keep her in the cave, do whatever he had to to keep his mate. She was his. *Mine*, he thought, his arms tightening protectively around her as he carried her, and he wouldn't let her go.

But if he forced her to stay, she would hate him. He would hate himself—

He slammed his mind shut to the doubts and focused on the damp grass beneath his feet, the woman cradled in his arms. *His* woman. The chilly wind swirled around them. The smell of earth and darkness and her fragrant femininity filled his nostrils, and a fierce protectiveness gripped him.

"Are you okay?" Tara's soft voice pushed through the buzzing in his ears.

He stared down at her, into her, and saw her lips part on a gasp. She knew what he was thinking, knew that she was his and he meant to keep her.

"You're definitely not okay—"

A growl rumbled from his throat; then he plundered her mouth with his own, his tongue pushing past her lips to stroke and taste and conquer. She was his and he meant to have all of her. To taste every inch of her, savor her essence on his lips, make her writhe and moan until she knew without a doubt they were meant to be together, that he would never let her go, never let another touch her. Ever.

He ended the kiss and picked up his steps, climbing the steep slope to the cave in record time.

The dark interior welcomed them as he strode inside. He didn't bother lighting a fire. He was already blazing. Hot. Hungry.

Easing her to the ground, he slid her down his hard length, letting her feel every inch of how badly he wanted her. Another gasp parted her lips and he kissed her again, hard and insistent. His hands were everywhere, touching, branding, claiming what he'd already taken possession of. Her breasts plumped beneath his fingertips, her nipples hardened, and he moved lower, stroking the heat between her legs, plunging deep into her mouth with his tongue in warning of what he was going to do to her. What he ached to do. What she wanted him to do, he realized when he slipped his hands into her jeans, between her legs, and felt her woman's passage. So warm and slick and ready for him . . .

She managed to tear her lips away. "I . . . please," she gasped the minute his fingertip probed her moist entrance. "Don't . . ."

"You are mine."

"No."

"You belong to me."

"I don't belong to anyone."

"Yes," he said in a hiss as he slid his finger deep and her delicious moan filled his ears, "you do."

"No." But the word was softer, weaker.

He withdrew his finger and then once again slid it deep, relishing her quiver, feeling the trembling on her lips as he took her in another kiss that left him dizzy and shaking.

He needed her. He moved his hands to strip the jeans from her body.

Without his intimate touch, she seemed to gather some control. She grasped at his hands, which pulled frantically at her jeans. "No, please . . . *stop.*"

The word, desperate, heartfelt, pleading, touched that part of himself he'd tried so hard to block out. His humanity. While she stirred his wild heart, she also stirred his compassion, his sympathy, his conscience.

And where the wild man in him refused to hear her protests, to consider her feelings, the civilized man heard all too clearly.

"You are leaving," he said, the words raw and rough, his chest heaving frantically with each harsh breath he took.

"I was thinking tomorrow." She tugged at the button on her jeans, holding the end flaps as she gasped for every breath. "No reason to put it off. My ankle's feeling much better. I think I'm up to a few days of walking. If you could just help me back toward Marshall Peak where you found me and point me toward the nearest park ranger station, I can make the rest of the way on my own."

Please. Though she didn't speak the word, he heard it. In his head. His heart. His breaking heart . . .

"Tomorrow," he said quietly. Then he turned and left the cave, for the wildness in him wouldn't be put down for long. It rioted for control, for dominance, for her, and he didn't know how long he could resist.

If he could resist. So he turned to the night and ran, blending into the forest, becoming just another wild thing. He wanted no thoughts, no feelings, no doubts or regrets, pain or frustration.

But what he wanted and what he felt were two very different things, and while Zane could run until he collapsed from exhaustion, he couldn't escape the truth.

She was leaving, and he was going to let her.

She was leaving and he was letting her.

The knowledge festered inside her as they headed down the mountain the next day, walking a little way, then resting. They picked their way through nearly impenetrable forest and maneuvered a particularly dangerous crevice where the mountain split. The opening, craggy and uneven, was barely large enough for Zane's powerful body, and Tara marveled at how he'd managed to spirit her through the small space after he'd first found her. But then he'd been determined to take her up the mountain to safety—as determined as he now seemed to lead her down and let her go.

She marveled at the sudden change in him. Last night, after the fierce need she'd felt in his touch, his kiss, she'd thought she would have a fight on her hands.

Not that it would have been much of a fight, she thought, remembering the heat that had engulfed her body. A few more touches and she would have been begging him to continue rather than stop.

She'd sat up all night, wondering what she would do if he came back, if she could resist, if she wanted to. But he'd stayed away, leaving only the chill wind and the strange, lonely sounds of the crying night to keep her company and fuel her thoughts.

He was letting her go.

She should have been happy. He wasn't crying and begging and laying a major guilt trip on her. Or bopping her over the head with his he-man club and dragging her back to his cave. He was being agreeable, and that made ending the relationship—make that fantasy—much easier.

It was great while it lasted, but it was over. Done with. Finis. End of story. She had a life waiting in San Diego. Her own life, her hard-won independence. She had friends, an apartment, bills and responsibilities. She couldn't just chuck everything to move out here and live out some secret fantasy she'd never known existed until she'd met this real-life Tarzan.

Abandon her life for a man? She would be making the same mistake all over again, forfeiting her dreams, her future. While she'd decided not to write Zane's story, she still intended to win a Pulitzer. Someday. She loved her job, and she'd worked too hard to get where she was—granted, she was only a beat reporter for the *Sun*, but she was working her way up—to abandon it all for love.

Not that she was considering staying. She'd had enough wilderness living to last a lifetime. No electricity or plumbing or chocolate. It was a wonder she hadn't died the first day.

She hadn't, a small voice reminded her.

She'd lived and even forgotten for a little while that the situation was so terrible. The waterfall had been heavenly, the river cool, the air clean, the view brilliant. And Zane . . .

She gave herself a mental shake. Forget Zane. He hadn't even asked her to stay. Surely if he wanted her here, he would put up some sort of fight instead of just calmly walking her down the mountain?

"We must go."

"I've barely caught my breath."

"We have a great distance to cover."

She studied the surrounding landscape, which consisted of an army of surrounding trees. "Shouldn't we be getting close to Marshall Peak?"

"It is still a full day's walk away, and the nearest ranger station is another day's walk beyond that—more with your ankle still weak, unless you run into some hikers or campers." He shot her an impatient glance. "So we must keep moving."

"All right, all right. You still don't have to be in such a hurry. It's not like the ranger station's going to disappear before we get there."

Impatience gave way to annoyance, a frown wrinkling his forehead as he marched ahead of her and motioned her to follow him.

Tara started walking, but her heart wasn't in it. With each step, something inside her tightened. She found herself stopping every half hour to rest; to eat some raspberries they'd brought from the cave; to take a drink of water; to go to the bathroom; to just breathe. Her attempts to stall earned her several curious looks from Zane and a few glares.

"Even Juliet has left us behind," he snapped after she'd stopped for the third time to pick a few wildflowers.

"She's probably on another scavenging trip down the mountain."

"We will never make it by nightfall."

"So we sleep outside." She lifted one fragrant flower and took a deep breath, wishing the light smell could drown out the musky scent of wood and smoke and virile male. "What's the big deal? It's not as if you've never slept under the stars."

"I have, but you have not."

"I've been bunking in a cave for weeks. Outside is no big deal."

But it was a big deal. A huge deal. This night, tonight, would be her last night with him. The importance of it hit her like a Mack truck. She wanted one more night with him. Just one more.

Determined, she lagged behind as much as possible until the sun dipped below the horizon and she collapsed on a tree stump and groaned that she absolutely, positively could not take another step, period.

"Then we sleep here," he told her.

"Fine by me." A smile played at her lips.

"Fine," he grumbled, casting her a frown, obviously displeased at the prospect.

But Tara wasn't about to be put off. She'd forfeited what her mind and her body had wanted last night, and she wasn't about to be that stupid again. She wanted one more night to remember him by. Just one and she could walk off of this mountain with Zane off her mind and out of her system, or so she told herself.

He took a long drink from the pouch of water hanging around his neck. Trickles ran down his throat, and she licked her lips.

"There is a creek not far from here. We need fresh water, since one day's trip has turned to two."

"Sorry," she said, her smile widening. She stretched out, the grass cushioning her, and arched her back, her breasts pressing against the soft material of her shirt in silent invitation. "You run along. I think I'll do a little stargazing."

He stared at her long and hard, not missing her provocative pose, and she made a big show of sighing. The motion lifted her breasts even higher, and she could have sworn she heard the tension crackle between her and Zane. Then he growled low and deep in his throat, turned and stomped off in the opposite direction.

Hurriedly, Tara slipped off her blouse and her bra and stretched out, feeling the slick mattress of cool grass beneath her. She closed her eyes, waiting, anticipating.

Footsteps sounded and her heart accelerated.

She made another big pretense of sighing, her back arching. "I hope you brought plenty of water, because I'm really hot—"

Something cold hit her on the chest. Her eyes snapped open to see Juliet standing over her, tongue hanging out. Hot breath fanned Tara's face.

"You have rotten timing, Juliet. Get lost, would ya? Zane will be back any minute and I could care less what you scavenged this time—" Her gaze shifted down and the words tangled in her throat.

Tara took one look at the choker and its smiley face sitting atop her bare stomach and started to scream.

Dressed once again, Tara stood next to Zane and stared down at the human remains littering the bottom of the deep ravine. Juliet had led them to the body when Zane had returned.

It was in bad condition, but Tara knew it was the missing photographer. She felt desperately ill.

Help. The word she'd heard so many times whispered through her head. With a trembling hand, she retrieved the missing-person flyer from her pocket. The photographer.

The *dead* photographer.

"That makes twice you've screwed up now." *Twice* . . . Mary's words echoed in Tara's head, and dread churned in her stomach.

"His skull is cracked," Zane said, examining the body. "It looks as if he hit his head."

And someone left him for bear food.

Just as they'd intended to leave her.

"She looks dead."

Stumbling, she tried to escape, to get as far away as possible. She started to sob and shake, the reality of what had almost happened to her—what *had* happened to this unfortunate man—cementing inside of her. She remembered the flashlight blinding her, forcing her eyes closed, but not until

317

after Mary had made the comment, "She looks dead."

"That makes twice you've screwed up now."

Zane caught up and wrapped his arms around her, holding her tight until she calmed enough to tell him in a quiet monotone that belied the frantic beating of her heart that she suspected Mary and Cecil of murder.

Forget suspected. She knew. While she'd never relied on hunches before, or trusted her instincts, she did so now. Zane had taught her that. To trust her own feelings. To listen to her heart.

Murder.

She reminded him about the legend, the Beast of Bear Mountain, and how Mary and Cecil were playing off Zane's myth to make tourists think a Bigfoot inhabited the area. How Cecil had dressed up like Bigfoot to give curious reporters some hot photographs to sell to their papers. How this unfortunate photographer had probably gotten a picture of Cecil putting on his Bigfoot suit, and now he was dead.

"Twice you've screwed up now." Twice . . .

As dead as she would have been.

She clutched the missing-person flyer and paced back and forth. "I have to go to the police. Now."

"No."

She turned an incredulous gaze on him. "What do you mean, no?"

He shook his head, a frown carving his face. "You cannot go. It is too dangerous. I will not let you."

"So, now you get possessive." The worry in his eyes touched something deep in her heart, but she wouldn't let it sway her. For all her desire to fall into his arms and let him sweep her away from the death and scandal she'd stumbled upon, she couldn't. Someone was dead. Murdered.

"You will come back with me," he told her, gripping her arm.

"Forget it, Zane." She shrugged away from him. "I can't. I have to report this right away. Mary and Cecil are criminals. If that bear didn't make mincemeat of them, then they deserve to go to jail. They're *murderers*."

"No!" He grabbed her again, and this time he wouldn't be put off. Picking her up, he tossed her over his shoulder and started walking, one steely arm wrapped around her legs, the other grasping her backpack. "We are going home."

"Okay, fine," she muttered to his backside. *Fine?* What else was she supposed to say? She was in no position to argue. And arguing with Zane would have been futile.

Action was the only thing that would work in this case. She hated herself for what she was contemplating, but she really had no choice. She had to see Mary and Cecil brought to justice, regardless of Zane's concern for her safety.

She played the docile little woman for all of two hours, her eyes wide and observant, carefully scanning their surroundings, keeping track of the direction they'd come from. Then she started to cry, a soft, sad sound that made him stop and ease her down his body, into the comfort of his arms.

"I'm so tired, and so thirsty. It's been such a traumatic night." She feigned a huge sniffle, while Zane stared at her, as if he could see the wheels spinning in her head. The lie.

"Stay here, Juliet." He shot the dog a commanding look. "Watch over her." The animal whined a response and settled down a few inches away from Tara.

She leaned back against the trunk of a tree while Zane went off to find a creek.

She really was tired and thirsty. That part hadn't been a lie, she reminded herself as she plotted her next move and tried to ignore a rush of guilt. Restlessness and the fierce desire for justice made her contemplate jumping up and starting back right now, but he would catch her. He knew he could, too, otherwise he never would have left her alone while going to the creek.

Better to stick with the plan. She rummaged in her backpack, pulled out the Sleepy Time pills and put four into her pocket. She'd taken three before and gotten the best night's sleep of her life. Zane was bigger, so four should knock him out, but not hurt him. Plenty to keep him sleeping for several hours while she got a head start on the trip to the ranger station.

Zane returned and settled down beside her, handing her the pouch. After taking a healthy drink of water, she slipped the pills into the container while his back was turned, stifled her guilt and handed him the water.

"Drink up."

He drank long and deep, and she barely resisted

the urge to snatch the water from his hands. She knew she wasn't hurting him, but the deceit of it all, the lying and plotting, bothered her more than she'd anticipated. She steeled herself. She had to do this. There were two murderers running loose and she couldn't, in good conscience, hide away up in her mountain utopia with Zane while Mary and Cecil continued to run their dangerous scam. Someone else could die, and Tara would be responsible.

"I'm sorry," she whispered much later that night when Zane's deep, even breathing filled her ears. His arms were wrapped around her, and she closed her eyes for a long moment, relishing the sensation, letting the heat sink deep into her bones, to keep her warm on all the cold nights to come. Lonely nights even more desolate than those in her past, because now she knew what she was missing. The warmth and security. The love.

Summoning every ounce of strength she possessed, she quickly disengaged herself. She feathered her lips over his, thankful when he didn't so much as stir.

Eyes, look your last!
Arms, take your last embrace!
And, lips, O you the doors of breath, seal with a
righteous kiss . . .

Romeo's last lines rang through her head, her heart. She wiped away the sudden tears from her eyes, grabbed her backpack, instructed Juliet to watch over Zane, and started back down the mountain.

Dawn was just breaking when Tara walked through a gap in the trees and saw a real human being leaning over a rabbit trap—the first person she'd seen, other than Zane, in two weeks. Relief swept through her, easing away the dread that had built up when she'd again passed by the photographer's remains a good twenty minutes back.

"Hey! I need some help—"

The man turned, a dead rabbit dangling from one hand, the open door of the trap in his other. The words died in Tara's throat.

"Cecil." She gasped as Cecil Ott's disbelieving gaze met hers. So the bear hadn't gotten him. Cecil was alive and well and standing right in front of her. Talk about rotten luck. "Oh, no."

Silence hung between them for several frantic heartbeats as the man stared as if seeing a ghost. Tara's mind replayed the images of the dead photographer, his body now ravished by the weather and the local wildlife. Dead. Fear paralyzed her.

"You're dead," Cecil finally said, his incredulous voice echoing Tara's thoughts.

"You two really left me for dead! The bear didn't get you. You actually *left* me." She'd known the truth, but somehow hearing the proof drove home the magnitude of what had happened.

"We had to leave," Cecil said defensively. "That old bear was after us."

"And he almost got me."

"You were already dead. You hit your head."

"Is that what Mary told you? She lied. She saw me. I was alive. My eyes were open. I was *alive*."

He shook his head frantically. "That ain't true. You hit your head and bam, you was dead. Just like that. Mary saw you, said she checked."

"I did hit my head, but that was minor. My ankle was sprained, I was incapacitated, but your sister didn't check. He saw me and said I looked dead. But she didn't know for sure. You two abandoned me. I could have *died* out there. Just like that photographer." Tara inched backward, but she needn't have bothered. Cecil didn't so much as step toward her.

He sank to the ground, the dead rabbit gripped in his hands, despair sweeping his features.

"But it wasn't our fault. Mary said we couldn't help it. You took off running and hit your head, just like he did." He snapped his fingers as if that explained everything. "You were already dead, she said. Dead on impact, like that photographer." Wide, frightened eyes caught and held hers. "He was already dead when he hit. Mary said so. She checked."

"Like she checked me?"

"She said he wasn't breathing and we should leave him 'cause there wasn't anything we could do except bring a whole mess of trouble down on ourselves."

"You shouldn't have listened to her. You should have gone for help, Cecil. She's crazy."

"She's my sister. The only person I got."

"She almost killed me. I wasn't dead. I was alive and breathing, and the two of you left me."

"You were dead." He got to his feet, a strange light in his eyes. "*Dead*. Mary said so and she don't lie to me. Never has."

"And never will." The female voice came from behind, and Tara went deathly still, the hair on the back of her neck prickling. "You were dead, all right. You *are* dead."

The barrel of a rifle pressed into the small of her back, and fear gripped Tara, squeezing her heart and lungs until she stopped breathing altogether.

"You won't get away with this," Tara whispered.

"I already did. Once. You'll be twice."

"I wasn't alone in the woods. Somebody else saw the body. He'll tell the police."

"Who? The Beast of Bear Mountain?" Mary started to laugh, a chilling cackle that sent fear slithering down Tara's spine. "You're lying. You're all alone, Miz Martin, and you're about to die. Alone. Now tell my brother good-bye and let's you and me take a little walk."

"Cecil," Tara pleaded. "Don't let her do it. Right now you're just a victim, but if you let her kill me, you'll be an accomplice. You might as well pull the trigger yourself."

He shook his head. "But you're already dead. Mary said so. You're already dead. Ain't that right, Mary?"

"That's right." Mary nudged Tara with the rifle and forced her around. "Now walk back up the way you come, back toward that nosy photographer. He got a picture of Cecil changing into the suit, did you know that? I told that man not to wander out into the woods at night, but he wouldn't listen. You big-city types got a problem when it comes to listening, don't you? Hardheaded, know-it-all . . ." The words faded into a strained silence as Mary urged Tara forward, shoving her toward the trees. "We'll see how much you know when you wind up keeping him comp'ny from now through the hereafter."

"A scam to drum up business," Tara said. "That's all it was, wasn't it? A scam, and that photographer caught you just like I did."

"Hey, we got to eat like everybody else. When the highway come through here, it messed things up royally. Some of the folks in town picked up and moved on, but me and Cece been here our whole lives. We ain't movin' on. We're stayin' right here, like our momma and daddy, our grandmama and granddaddy. Expansion." Mary snorted. "Expansion, my foot. That's just a fancy word them government people use to justify uprooting folks and making themselves a heap of money they'll waste."

Questions raced through Tara's mind, and the burning need to know pushed aside her fear. "Was the rest of the town in on it?"

"Not directly, mind you. They're good, Godfearing people. They wouldn't be a party to anything a little underhanded."

"A little underhanded? That's an understatement, don't you think? We're talking *murder*."

"It ain't murder. It's an unfortunate accident. I ain't gonna shoot you, missy, unless you force my hand."

"Then what are you going to do?"

"Push you down that ravine and let nature take its course. You'll hit your head, and if you don't, I can crawl down there and give you a little smash to the temple. An accident, is all." She chuckled and Tara felt the first wave of cold fear wash over her. Her legs buckled and she stumbled.

"Get up." Mary grabbed Tara's arm and jerked her upright. "Yeah, the townsfolk would never be a party to this—none of 'em got the good sense I have for business—but they're reapin' the reward. They're selling a ton of goods to the folks who mosey on down here to get a look at the Beast. They're in on it, even if they don't know it."

"So this is it," Tara said when they reached the edge of the ravine. She stared down at the rocky bottom, her gaze sweeping the brush that partially concealed the photographer's remains. She closed her eyes for a long moment and tried to calm her heart. The smell of life and death mingled in her nostrils, filling her with dread, anticipation, fear and elation, a volatile mix that sent the adrenaline pumping through her, firing her senses to life.

Help. She sent her own frantic call to the mountains, begging the spirits and the beasts, and Zane, for the assistance she so desperately needed. If only she hadn't given him the sleeping pills. If only she'd listened to him in the first place, to her own heart, to that small, scared part of her that loved him so fiercely it hurt.

She swallowed and summoned her voice. "So what are you going to do now? Push me?"

"First I'm gonna give you the chance to jump." Mary poked Tara with the shotgun.

The soft crunch of grass, the swish of branches filled her ears, like thunder on a quiet day, and she turned. Her gaze shifted from Mary to the forest looming behind her. Nothing. Just the wishful, desperate hope of a woman about to meet her maker.

"Go on and jump." Mary smiled, a cold tilt to her lips that said they'd reached the end of the line. "Cooney Rainer says that old medicine man who haunts these parts can fly. Maybe he'll take a likin' to you, swoop in and save your hide. Course he might not. That Cooney ain't playin' with a full deck, you know."

"You're the one who isn't playing with a full deck. You want me dead?" Tara took on a fighting stance. "Do your own dirty work, because I'm not jumping."

Mary uppended the shotgun. Just as she pulled back to slam the butt into Tara's chest, a growl filled the still silence. A dog burst from the trees and leaped at the motel owner.

Mary went down, Juliet on top of her, growling and snarling. The gun fell from Mary's hands as she warded off the vicious snaps of Juliet's jaws, and Tara seized the moment. She snatched up the weapon and aimed.

"Thanks, Juliet," she murmured when the dog paused in her attack to lick frantically at Mary's face as if to say, "No offense." "You're a lifesaver, girl. And you," Tara said, leveling the rifle at Mary, "are a murderer." She nudged the woman with her shoe. "Now get up and start walking. I've got a hot bath and a box of cupcakes waiting for me, and I'd be willing to bet you've got a lengthy jail sentence with your name written all over it."

Chapter Eighteen

Zane burst through the break in the trees and came to a staggering halt, his head still fuzzy from just awakening. What had made him so tired? He blinked frantically as he saw a crowd of people teeming over the area where he and Tara had found the photographer's remains. All wore uniforms he vaguely remembered from his own nightmarish past. Policemen. Emergency personnel. Reporters. A roar filled his ears, and his gaze cut to several motorcycles topping the crest, carrying more of the uniformed people.

Juliet whimpered at his side, nudging him forward, but he couldn't move. He was frozen to the spot, his gaze locked on the woman he'd charged down the mountain for. To defeat her enemies and protect her. But he was still furious.

She'd tricked him, left him.

A hollowness filled him as he watched her sip steaming liquid from a small white cup and talk to one of the officers, obviously relaying the story she'd told him hours ago. She seemed completely oblivious to his presence. So absorbed. Unaware.

But he was there.

Watching. Protecting.

She was safe now. The realization swept through him like the dull edge of a blade. *Safe.* His reason for dragging her back to the cave was gone, and while he wanted nothing more than to march through the uniformed men, pick her up and throw her over his shoulder, to claim his woman, his mate, he wouldn't.

As much as he wanted her to stay, he knew she wouldn't be happy here with him. She blended too well with the outsiders, craved the world she'd left behind, the society he'd vowed never to return to. How often had she complained? Longed for things he could not give her? She would never be content with him and what he had to offer.

His body. His heart. His soul. It wasn't enough.

He swallowed against the ache gripping his chest, the ringing in his ears. Juliet whimpered again, her soulful eyes fixed on him, urging him. *Do not let her go. Take her. She's yours. Yours!*

"No." The word was little more than a raw sob.

She would be restless. Resentful. Eventually she would hate him. And while his body said it didn't matter, his heart, his human heart, said that it did.

So much that he forced himself to turn away, to walk back into the forest, lost in his own misery and heedless of the camera flashes that followed him, the sighs of disbelief, the smell of danger.

Tara was safe, and Zane was alone. Again.

"I'm in heaven." Tara sank down into a tub brimming with bubbles that evening and relaxed her sore muscles. After spending the day answering questions and giving an official statement to the Bear Creek sheriff's department, she'd taken a room at a local boardinghouse. While the accomodations were modest—a small room with a single bed and a bathroom with an ancient-looking claw-foot tub and a toilet sporting an old-fashioned flush chain—Tara felt as if she'd won the lottery.

Hot water, indoor plumbing and electricity. Heaven.

So why did she find herself thinking about the hell she'd left behind? Okay, so *hell* was too strong a word. While the past two weeks had been rough, they hadn't been totally unpleasant. The wilderness held a certain primitive charm.

When she closed her eyes, she could see the cave so clearly, the earthen floor, the bearskin rugs. She could feel the fur beneath her, soft and warm, the man on top of her, hard and relentless and so very hot. . . .

She forced her eyes open and busied herself taking a quick bath, careful not to linger too long on any oversensitive areas that might stir unwanted images of him and her, the two of them together, arms tangled and—

She refused to follow the thought and finished her bath before the water had a chance to cool. No reason to linger and soak as she'd always loved to do, not when she was so tired.

A few minutes later, she slipped into a nightgown she'd pulled from her luggage. The police had found it stashed in one of the empty motel rooms at Mary's place and returned it to her. Cecil, frightened and vulnerable without his older sister to call the shots, had given a full confession and quickly led police to the spot where he'd hidden Tara's and the photographer's personal belongings.

As Tara had deduced, Cecil and Mary had abandoned the photographer to the elements, just as they'd tried to abandon her. While Tara's fall had actually been caused by the bear, the photographer had been pushed. Mary had done the deed while Cecil watched, and all because the journalist had taken several candid pictures of Cecil right in the middle of putting on his Bigfoot suit.

A shiver rippled through her. Tara had snapped several similar photos. If the bear hadn't shown up, Mary would have undoubtedly taken matters into her own hands just as she'd done with the photographer. Tara had been in the same predicament, faced the same danger.

Yet she'd survived because of Zane.

"Forget Zane. Why does everything lead back to Zane?" She mentally shoved his image aside. She had to forget. She'd already called Fritz at the *Squealer* and given a sketchy explanation, minus any mention of Zane, about Mary and Cecil's scam, and that the Beast was and always would be merely a myth.

Tara had gone on to propose a murder in a small mountain community piece, which Fritz, only mildly interested in real news, had promised to run when he had space. Fortunately for him, Lisa's honeymoon had been cut short. It seemed Ethan had had a first wife whom he had conveniently forgotten to mention. Lisa found out minutes before she said "I do" and said "Adios" instead. She was back at work writing a front-pager about a sea monster reported in the Great Lakes area.

All was right with the world, Tara's "vacation from real news" was over, and she was flying out of Chattanooga the day after tomorrow.

And not a minute too soon, she thought, slipping between soft cotton sheets. Now this was heaven. Of course, it would have been even better if she'd had a certain someone—

No. She turned on the nightstand radio and found a Top 40 station. The radio didn't offer the comfort it used to, however, and Tara gave up the bed to spend the next three hours doing her nails and drinking coffee from her portable coffeemaker. When she'd entirely exhausted herself, she climbed back in bed, but sleep didn't come even then. She spent the rest of the night tossing and turning and trying desperately to forget the past, the present, the future and the all-consuming fact that she'd been, was, and would always be, alone.

Tara was up before daybreak, sitting in the kitchen downstairs drinking her fifth cup of coffee when Wilma, the boardinghouse's owner, came in with the morning paper.

"Lots of excitement 'round here," the woman remarked, plopping the newspaper on the table.

"First murder?" Tara raised an eyebrow.

" 'Course not. Sammy Whitehead kilt his mother-in-law and stuffed her out in the shed about five years ago. Tragedy, it was, but violence ain't new to us. Neither are crazies, and that Mary Ott was a crazy if I ever met one. But to find out there's a real Beast after all this . . ."

"What are you talking about?"

"The Beast of Bear Mountain." Wilma indicated the front page. "Darryl, one of the sheriff's deputies in charge of collecting evidence, snapped a few pictures while you all were up at the peak gathering that photographer's remains."

The question slid past Tara as she fixed her gaze on the newspaper. The headline blazed back at her. REAL-LIFE TARZAN LIVING ON BEAR MOUNTAIN: THE BEAST LIVES! Zane's face, blurred but still recognizable, stared back at her, the forest embracing him as he walked back into the trees.

Tara's heart fell to her knees and dread churned fast and furious in her stomach. She bolted from her chair, nearly spilling what was left of her coffee. "I've got to get to him."

"What, sugar?"

Frantic eyes met Wilma's. "I need to rent a car."

"Fat chance now. Sullivan's got the only spare vehicles in the city, and he had a couple of photographers pay him an arm and a leg for 'em not an hour ago. Heard him tell Mitchell when I was at the general store. Place was crowded with tourists and reporters. Even a few television people.

Mitchell was in hog heaven 'cause they was buying supplies left and right and asking him questions about any available folks who could lead 'em into the mountains. And dirt bikes. Why, every boy in the county's put his cycle up for rent, the whole lot of 'em hot to make some extra money."

"I need a way up the mountain."

"But you just came down, honey."

"And I have to go back up again," she said with a desperation that drew a sympathetic gaze from the woman. "I forgot something. Something really important."

"Well, I got a Jeep out in the garage. I'll let you borrow it if you promise to be back by sunup."

"Promise." Tara snatched the keys from the woman's outstretched hands and headed out the doors, her steps picking up when she saw a van emblazoned with a local TV station's logo pull up in front of the boardinghouse.

As Tara steered the Jeep through town, headed for the trail that would lead her up Bear Mountain, her dread turned to outright fear. Wilma hadn't been exaggerating. There were people everywhere, filling the sidewalks, packing the stores. All after one thing. The Beast.

Zane.

And Tara knew she had to find him first.

The scent carried to him on the night breeze. Strong, potent, drawing him from the icy river.

He flew on swift feet down the mountain, racing, his senses alive and raw, filled with *her*. It couldn't be, he told himself over and over, but he ran anyway. Fearful yet excited. Angry yet forgiving.

He reached a break in the trees. Moonlight spilled in a brilliant circle, and there she stood, surrounded by light, and his world was dark no more.

Her gaze locked with his and relief swept her features, eased the worry lines around her face. She flew at him, into his arms, and the anguish that had been eating him up inside eased. He knew then, as his heart thumped its next beat, that he couldn't let her go again. He wouldn't.

"You have to leave here." Her frantic words tumbled over one another in their haste to get out. "There are people in town, media, who'll be crawling all over this mountain by daybreak. Someone took a picture of you yesterday, and now everyone's after the Beast—"

"I love you."

"You have to come with me—What?"

"I love you."

"You love me?" Wide, disbelieving eyes stared up at him.

He nodded. "I love you. Did you not know?"

"How would I know? You never told me. You let me walk off this mountain," she said accusingly. "You didn't even try to stop me."

"I did, and you tricked me."

"That was after. I *had* to go to the police, and you tried to stop me."

"I wanted only to protect you. Is that not love?"

"No—yes." She shook her head. "I don't know.

I told you I'm new to this love business. I've never felt so . . . so confused."

"You want to kill me one moment, and kiss me senseless the next?"

Her gaze snapped to his. "How did you know?"

"Because it is exactly what I feel for you." His fingertip traced the curve of her cheek. "Perhaps I will kiss you first though, and save the killing for later." His lips met hers in a slow, thorough exploration that left them both breathless.

"I . . . that was some kiss."

"Yes. Perhaps we will have a few more of such kisses; then I think I shall set about killing you slowly. Sweetly." He traced the curve of her cheek, watched her lips part and felt his need for her grow. He frowned. "You tricked me."

"And you followed me." She glared. "What a stupid, stupid, *stupid* thing to do, Zane. I tore up my story to preserve your peace and solitude, so you wouldn't have to face a mob of media as fierce as the one that attacked you after your parents' deaths. And what do you do? You traipse after me, smack-dab in the middle of a crowd, and get your picture taken."

"You are angry."

"You're damned right. I gave up my Pulitzer so you could stay here, and you messed it up. The reporters who'll be crawling all over here in a matter of hours won't be half as nice and considerate as I was. You're just a story to them, Zane."

"And I'm more to you."

"Yes," she admitted.

He smiled. "So you do love me."

"I never said I didn't."

"You never said you did."

"I do," she said almost reluctantly, and his smile disappeared.

"But you do not want to." The words hung between them in the suddenly tense silence.

"Maybe I don't," she finally said, "but that's beside the point. I do, and I'm here. Speaking of which, we have to get out of here. Now."

She loved him.

While she didn't speak the words, he saw them in her eyes, in the worried crease of her forehead. The knowledge sang through his head, filling him with joy the way the sun filled him with warmth.

"Will you come with me?"

Her question doused his joy and stirred a lifetime of fear and regret. *No.* The refusal sat on the tip of his tongue. He didn't have to leave. Just run and hide as he always had. Protect himself. Survive. Push deeper into the mountains, higher until he was beyond any expedition's reach. Far away from the flash of cameras, the prying questions. Far away from her.

No! While his body might survive, he would die inside. He'd already started to wither, to shrivel up—until she'd shown up moments ago and breathed life back into him. He drank in a deep breath and relished the mingling of sunshine and ripe, sweet woman.

"Please, Zane." Her desperate gaze touched his. "Will you come with me?"

"Yes." He would leave his life, his home, to follow her to safety. To follow her, period. For he

338

could not say good-bye again. Not now. Not ever, and if that meant sacrificing everything he was, so be it. "Come along, Juliet!" he called, and the dog came, swiftly bounding from out of the brush.

He focused on the reward and not the task as he accompanied her back down the mountain and left his world of trees and solitude and friends, for concrete and noise and people.

A worthwhile trade, he told himself over and over, and when she smiled at him, he actually believed it.

He loved her.

Tara turned the knowledge over and over in her mind less than twenty-four hours later as she sprawled across the king-size bed in the penthouse suite of Chattanooga's finest downtown hotel, one of the few upscale establishments that permitted pets—after a sizable deposit and a few intimidating looks from Zane. They were now over four hours and two hundred miles from Bear Creek and danger.

Several expeditions had already started working their way up the mountain by the time she and Zane had descended around daybreak. He knew the land like no one else and had avoided society far too long to be caught so easily, however. With him leading the way, they'd slipped past a group of reporters completely undetected and reached the safety of Wilma's Jeep.

Then it was Tara's turn to lead. With Zane stowed in the backseat, she'd driven through town, Juliet beside her, retrieved her luggage from the boardinghouse and offered Wilma an extra hundred dollars to let her keep the Jeep for a few days—she'd already hired someone to drive it back to Bear Creek after renting a Blazer for use over the next few weeks until the hoopla in Bear Creek died down and Zane could go back.

He'd told her he meant to stay with her, not just until the excitement faded, but permanently. Of course, she didn't buy that. The part of her that had spent years alone, craving love that had never been given, was too gun-shy to believe him. While she might love him, she couldn't quite trust that he felt the same. Not the unconditional, without-a-doubt, you're-the-only-one-for-me kind of love.

Her gaze shifted to the bathroom door. While Zane had started his exploration of indoor plumbing, Tara had left Juliet lazing on the carpet and raided the nearest department store to buy him some clothing and personal items. She'd already been back a half hour and he was still holed up in the extra-large bathroom indulging in the sunken bathtub and whirlpool spa.

She lay back on the bed and stared at the ceiling.

He loved her.

The notion filled her with excitement and dread. Of course he *thought* he loved her; he'd yet to see another woman. But now they were in civilization, with handfuls of women who would be falling all over themselves the moment they set eyes on him.

He was a hunk straight off the cover of some romance novel, straight out of the hottest nighttime fantasy, and he, like every other male, would undoubtedly gravitate toward his equal—a fertile sex kitten named Bambi who looked like a centerfold and could give him loads of babies.

Tara blinked back a sudden burst of tears and summoned her courage. What did Zane know about love? Absolutely nothing. She was the first woman he'd slept with and so he was infatuated, but that wouldn't last long.

A few hours, tops, she told herself, eyeing the new jeans and shirt and boots she'd bought for him. Once they faced the world, Zane masquerading as an average citizen rather than the Beast, he would get an eyeful of women to choose from, and he would gladly take back those precious words.

He loved her.

She fought the sudden urge to lock the door, to hole up in this room, this moment, and hold on to whatever it was he did feel for her—gratitude, infatuation, lust, love. . . . *Not* love, at least not the permanent kind and the only kind she was interested in.

When he walked out of the bathroom, wet and gloriously nude, she wiped frantically at her tears and motioned to the clothes on the bed. "I thought we'd go out for dinner while Juliet gets acquainted with the kennel downstairs."

The moment of truth had arrived, and Tara was going to face it, to get it over with and get on with the rest of her life.

Without Zane Shiloh.

*   *   *

341

Surprisingly, Zane didn't so much as glance at any of the dozen or so women who strolled by and smiled his way as he and Tara sat in a local restaurant. His attention was riveted on the fully loaded cheeseburger and French fries sitting on the plate in front of him.

Not that she blamed him. Her mouth watered as she glanced at her own identical order. It wasn't until she'd indulged in several bites that she turned her focus to the matter at hand.

She watched as he wiped his mouth with his napkin, then returned the linen to his lap. He was trying so hard to fit in, as if he really meant to stay. He'd asked so many questions during the ride to Chattanooga—about the Jeep they drove in, the roads they navigated, the signs and houses they passed, the gas stations perched every few miles. He'd absorbed her answers like a sponge, soaking up anything and everything, so intent on surviving in her world. On surviving, period. That was Zane. A survivor, and an exceptional student. She'd given him a crash course in table etiquette before they'd left the hotel room, and so far he hadn't missed a beat, just as he'd quickly adjusted to the new clothes, to walking rather than running, to sitting in a chair rather than cross-legged on the floor.

Despite shaving and his valiant attempt to act civilized, there was something undeniably uncivilized about him. It was more an aura than anything he said or did. Other than his initial sniffing of his food, as well as every condiment on the table, he looked like any other guy having a burger.

Any other incredibly handsome, *GQ* cover model–type indulging in a little beef and potatoes.

But there was something wild about him, a feeling he stirred, an energy he emanated. A potent sexual energy that heated her cheeks and forced her take an extra sip of wine every time he glanced at her.

"I can see why you missed this so much," he said after he'd swallowed the last of his burger.

"Actually, I didn't miss the burger nearly as much as I missed this." She shoveled a forkful of "Death by Chocolate" into her mouth and let the taste sink into her tongue. Closing her eyes, she rolled the flavor around, savoring the sweetness until a groan parted her lips.

When she opened her eyes, Zane was staring at her, his eyes blazing with blue fire. A look she knew so well. His hand moved under the table, his fingers burning through her jeans to stroke the inside of her thigh, and she jumped.

"Don't."

"Why not?"

"You're not supposed to." She glanced around nervously. The patio overflowed with people, and dozens more strolled by on the sidewalk. "There are people everywhere."

"So?" He glanced around, his gaze piercing several nearby couples. "Do they not touch? Mate?"

"Not in public."

He didn't move his hand. "What is public?"

"Out in the open. Sex is something done in private."

"We mated out in the open. In the waterfall, the river, on the riverbank—"

"But there weren't other people around. Watching."

"No one is watching this." He moved his hand for emphasis, his fingertips coming within inches of the sensitive spot between her legs. "And who cares if they are. You are mine, Tara, and so you must accustom yourself to my touch. Anywhere. Everywhere." His eyes darkened and she swallowed. "You look very beautiful."

"You're finally seeing me with all my makeup, not that I wear a tremendous amount. Just a little mascara, some blush and lipstick, but even worn minimally, the stuff creates quite an illusion."

"Illusion?"

"Something that looks real, but isn't. I'm not really beautiful. Makeup does wonders; then there's my new clothes." She indicated the white poet's blouse. "This soft material minimizes a too-full bust." She touched a strand of hair. "And my blow-dryer . . . Where would I be without it? A cool setting tames my usually untamable hair and keeps me from looking like a scarecrow—"

"It is not your makeup or your blouse or that strange blowing device you tried to use on me."

She shrugged and gave him a small smile. "I didn't want you to go out with wet hair and catch a cold." It seemed silly now.

"It is you, do you not understand? *You*. Whether back in the cave without your makeup and minimizing clothing and blowing device, or here with them, you are beautiful."

Her ears played with the words, savored the sound of them the way her mouth had savored the decadent dessert. He sounded so . . . sincere.

She stiffened. "I'm not beautiful. More like average."

"You are beautiful."

She tossed her napkin to the table. "Are you blind, Zane? Look around you." She leaned closer and indicated the next table. "Take a look at that woman over there. The brunette. She's gorgeous, centerfold material all the way, and she keeps smiling at you."

"So?"

"Sooo . . ." Did she have to spell everything out? "You could probably get together with her if you wanted to." Even as the words sailed past her lips, she wanted to snatch them back.

What the hell was she saying?

The truth, she told herself, summoning her courage. *Better to face it, lay his options on the table and let him leave now, than wait until he discovers his appeal on his own and then leaves me.* Otherwise she would always wonder, worry, fear what was to come.

"Get together?" His forehead wrinkled.

She let out a frustrated sigh. "As in sex . . . *mate,*" she ground out, wishing the words didn't hurt so much to say. "She would mate with you in a second. Half the women here would. All you'd have to do is smile at her, say a few nice words." Great, she was giving him pickup advice. But she couldn't help herself. The words poured out of her mouth, pushing him away, urging him just to get it over with. "Tell her she looks pretty, stare into her eyes, and I guarantee she'll fall right into your arms. Your bed." She snapped her fingers. "Just like that."

"But I am not so sure I like the bed. I sat on it for a few moments and it felt . . . too soft. Juliet likes it, though."

"Forget the bed. You can do it anywhere. It doesn't matter. The point is, you could have her."

"But I do not want her."

"Why not? She's beautiful and sexy and . . ." *All the things I'm not.*

"She is not you, Tara. And I want you. Only you." He stared at her, his eyes blazing with such certainty, and it was then that she believed him. Trusted him.

She always had, she realized as dozens of images from their past rushed through her mind. She'd trusted him, believed him; she simply hadn't believed in herself. Hadn't thought herself worthy of the love he offered, and so she'd downplayed the gift, doubted it, for fear that if she embraced such a rare thing, it would slip through her fingers the way it always had in the past, with her parents, with Merle.

But this was Zane.

That was the trouble. He was different. Special. She'd been so fearful of not measuring up in his eyes, she'd ignored the bald truth; she didn't measure up in her own eyes. She'd never been on the receiving end of love, and despite all of her self-esteem building and her vow to defeat her insecurities, she'd never quite won the battle.

In a sparkling instant, with dozens of attractive women surrounding her, Tara felt like a star in an otherwise starless sky. Beautiful, attractive, worshiped. Loved.

Victory was, indeed, sweet, she thought as she finally said the words she'd vowed never to say to another man again. To anyone. "I love you."

Chapter Nineteen

While the media, not to mention bounty hunters, fortune seekers, tourists and a nationwide organization called the Befrienders of Bigfoot, combed Bear Mountain in search of the Beast, Tara reintroduced Zane to the high points of civilization, from pizza to ice cream, music to movies, libraries to department stores.

They shopped and talked during the day and spent their nights making love, though they didn't use the bed quite as often as she would have liked. Zane preferred the floor or the shower or anywhere but the strange softness of the down-covered mattress, while Juliet seemed in heaven sprawled across the lavender-scented pillows.

Not that Zane wouldn't have endured the bed had she asked. He would have swung from the rafters for her. He was attentive and eager to please, particularly when she caught a mild case of the flu and spent a few mornings in bed.

She'd finally found heaven. Any normal, red-blooded female would have been thrilled. So why did she feel as if something was missing?

The flu, she told herself, but then when the sickness seemed to pass and she felt better, happiness still eluded her. Oh, she had her moments. When they were laughing together, or dancing—another high point she'd taught him—or making love. But then there were other times when she felt a terrible sinking sadness, like when they visited the zoo and she saw him reach out to the animals, all of which were beyond his grasp.

Caged.

Not the animals, but Zane himself. Caged by society, by humanity.

Ridiculous, she told herself, tamping down the doubts niggling at her. Zane wasn't trapped. He was free and exactly where he wanted to be.

So why wasn't she counting her blessings?

The question eluded her until Zane turned to her one night after making slow, sweet love and murmured, "You are not one of those people."

"What people?" Her soft voice echoed in the dark silence of the room.

"One who spends a lifetime without ever knowing true love. I love you." His voice was rough and husky. "Enough to sacrifice everything so you are never alone again. Never lonely."

The declaration should have sent her spirits soaring. He offered what she'd longed for her entire life—true love. Yet it only made her want to cry, and as the days progressed and his words haunted her, she realized why.

Sacrifice.

It all came down to sacrifice. Zane would give up everything, his life, his identity, all to be with her, while she gave up nothing.

Zane gave and she took.

She was back in her relationship with Merle, only the roles were reversed. Like Merle, she was doing all the taking, thinking only of herself, while Zane gave selflessly the way she'd done for so long. Too long.

So what? You're due, a small part of her screamed, the part that feared being alone again. Lonely.

It was the part that pushed her through the next few days and urged her to ignore the restlessness that surrounded Zane. She pretended not to notice the way he paced whenever they were indoors a little too long, or his infatuation with the rain when it pelted the window, or the way he liked to slip out onto the balcony and climb up to the solitary rooftop late at night after he thought she'd fallen asleep. Instead, she concentrated on giving him all the comforts her world had to offer. New clothes, an electric razor, all the hamburgers he could eat.

But they didn't make up for the one thing he needed the most—his freedom. She'd finally admitted that to herself earlier that day when she'd paid the doctor a visit about her recent illness and received the surprise of a lifetime.

Everything was different now. Tara wasn't pretending anymore. Zane needed his freedom, and she meant to give it to him.

To both of them.

It had been nearly three weeks since they'd checked in. The hoopla in Bear Creek had died down. The pictures of the Beast had been dubbed another scam, and Zane and Tara were scheduled to fly to San Diego tomorrow. To start the rest of their civilized life together.

She watched the torn pieces of their plane tickets float to the ground at her bare feet before she stared across the rooftop to the man who'd become both her lover and her best friend.

A three-foot ledge spanned the edge of the building, and Zane stood next to it, not staring out over the city, but looking above, at the star-filled sky. He wore only a pair of blue jeans, his feet bare, his muscled torso reflecting moonlight. Wind gusted, ruffling his hair, making him look as untamed as the first time she'd seen him. Wild. Primitive.

Her heart shifted and tears blurred her eyes.

"How did you get up here?" His deep voice slid into her ears.

"Like you. I climbed the fire escape from the balcony."

"That was dangerous."

She sniffled and tried for a smile. "Danger's my middle name." Her voice grew serious. "Remember what you told me about running with the animals? That it made your insides all jumpy, snatched the breath from your lungs and made you feel alive? That's how climbing up here made me feel. Jumpy, breathless, *alive*. That's why you came up here, isn't it? To really feel alive? Free? You miss the mountains, the wide-open space, the trees, the river, the animals—everything."

Rather than deny her statement, he held out his hand. "Come here." His voice was gruff, hoarse. Blue eyes sparkled across the distance to her, gleaming with a predatory light that was unmistakable. Feral. Instinctively, she knew what he wanted.

Not the comfortable, civilized lovemaking they'd become accustomed to over the past few weeks. He wanted more from her. He wanted . . . *her*.

Now. Here. With the sky embracing them, the stars shining down, the wind caressing bare flesh. No beds or blankets, rules or restraints. Nothing but a male and a female coming together, body to body, soul to soul, mate to mate.

A moment of fear sizzled through her, feeding her excitement. She stepped toward him. Her heart pounded faster and blood rushed through her veins, warming her already dangerously warm body. Her nostrils flared, drinking in his scent— the intoxicating aroma of aroused male and barely checked lust—that carried to her on the softly gusting wind.

Five steps and his hand closed around hers. He made quick work of her nightgown, pulling it over her head and tossing it to the ground. Then he dropped to his knees and stripped her panties down her legs. He paused then, staring up at her, his gaze locked with hers.

Her skin flushed hot and cold, his warm breath brushing her nerve endings along with the whispering breeze. His lips feathered across the sensitive flesh of her belly; then he moved away from her and stepped out of his jeans.

He was beautiful in his naked glory, his tanned skin gleaming in the moonlight. Dark hair sprinkled his chest, swirling down his abdomen. His manhood, huge and hot and hungry for her, twitched beneath her stare, and an echoing tremor rippled through her.

They came together then, and there were no soft kisses or tentative touches. Just heat. A blazing heat that seared over her skin, melted into her bones to set her entire body on fire.

He turned her away from him and placed her hands on the concrete ledge. The motion bent her forward and lifted her bottom in sweet invitation. He stroked her, fingertips trailing over the wet heat between her legs, testing her, readying her. She shivered and rotated her hips, and he answered the silent plea. She felt him straining in the cleft between her buttocks before he bent his knees and plunged deeply into her, one steely arm anchoring her in place.

He took her savagely, pushing deeper with each thrust, claiming and conquering and loving her in a way that no man ever had, or would. Because he was more than a man. And less. Godlike, yet primitive. Human, yet animal. Complicated, yet simple.

"Close your eyes," he whispered. "And remember."

Kimberly Raye

And she did. The blazing lights of the city faded into pitch-black. The sound of voices and traffic drifting up from the street below faded into the croak of frogs, the chirp of crickets, the hum of cicadas. Her palms flattened, not against a concrete ledge, but the coarse bark of a towering cedar. She felt the damp dirt and slick leaves beneath her feet, smelled the musky fragrance of raw earth and hot sex.

Eyes shut, Tara felt more animal than woman, a creature of the wild. Zane pushed her harder, higher than ever before until she shattered. He climaxed seconds later, spilling himself inside, a growl rumbling long and low in his throat.

He held her then, his arms wrapped tightly around her, cradling her as their heartbeats slowed and reality dawned around them. While she unlocked the gentleness in his soul, the humanity, he twisted the latch and freed the primitive side of her, the wildness that longed for fresh air and a place untouched by society's norms.

Tara opened her eyes and turned in his arms. With a trembling fingertip, she traced the contours of his rugged face.

"You don't belong here, Zane. This is my world, not yours."

A troubled expression twisted his features. "What are you saying?"

"I want you to go back home, to the mountains, to peace."

Anger flared in his eyes. "You do not love me then? Is that what you are trying to tell me?"

"I *do* love you. That's why I can't let you do this.

354

You don't belong here, surrounded by noise and people and rules."

"I belong with you."

"I know that." A grin tugged at her lips. "That's why I've got a proposition for you."

"What is a proposition?"

"A deal. I give something, you give something. You see, I'm new to this love business, so it's taken me a little while to come around. Love is all about making propositions. It's all about give and take. Sharing. Compromising. Geez, I sound like some self-help tape."

"What is a self-help tape?"

"That's beside the point. The facts are that I love you and you love me. I belong in the city, or at least close enough to have electricity and running water, and you belong in the mountains with the animals and the trees and freedom."

"Meaning?"

She smiled and kissed his lips. "We combine the best of both worlds and make each other the two happiest people on the face of the earth. Uh, make that three."

"Three?"

"As in, there's going to be an extra mouth to feed in about seven and a half months."

"A *baby?*"

Joyful laughter bubbled on her lips. "Don't sound so shocked. You couldn't be more surprised than me."

"A baby." His words were filled with awe as his hand stroked her still-flat abdomen. "But you said . . ."

"I was wrong." She shook her head and blinked back sudden tears. "All those years, I thought it was me. Merle said the doctor gave him a clean bill of health, so when we didn't conceive, I—he was convinced it was me. But it wasn't." She smiled as the tears spilled down her cheeks. "I'm as healthy as a horse, and once the morning sickness is over, I'll be eating like one."

"A baby," he marveled, his hand making tender circles on her abdomen.

"Our baby." She grasped his hand and kissed his palm. "That's another reason I can't let you ruin both our lives by insisting on moving to San Diego with me. We just wouldn't be happy there. You're an outdoorsy guy, and I think I could get used to an outdoorsy life."

"The cave?"

"Not that outdoorsy, but close enough. You'll have your mountains and I'll have my cappuccino maker."

"Then where do you . . . *proposition*,"—he used his newfound word—"we live?"

"I'll tell you all about it later, but first things first. I expect you to make an honest woman of me, and in return I promise never, *ever* to force you to make love in a bed again."

He pulled her close for a slow, lingering kiss, before she murmured, "I should have known things would end like this. You and me, together. Tara and Zane . . . It has a nice ring to it, don't you think?"

Kimberly Raye

Epilogue

"Welcome to the Wilderness Inn." Tara stood behind the counter of the newly renovated Mary Ott Motel and greeted the group of nature enthusiasts who'd just arrived for a two-week early spring hiking expedition into the Smoky Mountains.

After Mary and Cecil's arrest, the bank had foreclosed the mortgage on the motel and put it up for auction. Zane and Tara had gotten it for a steal, fixed up the run-down cabins, installed a hot tub and recreation room, and opened for business just three short months ago.

"Your expedition leaves bright and early at six A.M.," she told a smiling man wearing a three-piece suit.

"It won't be soon enough for me. I'm an accountant and I've just finished a busy season. I need a break."

"And you'll get it," Tara promised. "All of you," Tara told the entire group. "A bon voyage breakfast will be served in the dining hall beforehand, where you'll all have a chance to meet your guide."

The guide she spoke of slipped up behind her several moments later, after the guests had left for their cabins with the drooling Jack, Jr., her newly hired bellboy, carrying their luggage.

"How are you feeling?" Zane slid a strong arm around her waist and nuzzled her ear as she leaned into his strength.

"Like I'm going to have this baby any minute now."

His hands splayed over her stomach, smoothing and caressing. "I think you are."

"I wish. My due date's not for another two weeks."

"I am sure it will be much sooner than that."

She raised an eyebrow. "How do you know?"

"I've seen many bears ready to birth their cubs."

She stiffened. "Are you calling me a bear?"

"Well," he said, drawing out the word. "You have certainly been as grouchy as one, snarling and growling every time the babe pains you." When she frowned and started to pinch his arm, he caught her hand. "But you are much, much prettier. And warmer," he murmured in that husky voice that never failed to send shivers up her spine.

"That's because there's a lot more of me to keep you warm." Her emotions shifted abruptly, anger turning to despair, and she fought back a sniffle.

"I'm huge. My hair is limp and blah, and I have elephant ankles."

"You are beautiful." He turned her in his arms. Blue eyes caught and held hers. "All of you. And soon we will have a beautiful child."

She smiled and wiped her eyes. "A little Tarzan as wild and handsome as his father." She traced a fingertip along Zane's bottom lip, down his stubbled jaw. Zane did shave occasionally, but he still hadn't grown accustomed to the habit. Not that Tara complained. She loved the raspy feel of his newly sprouting beard.

While he couldn't get used to the feel of a razor on his face, however, he had traded his loincloth for worn jeans that accented his lean hips and strong thighs. Though he still wore the loincloth on occasion, during midnight hikes and seductive swims and . . .

A shiver rippled through her as she remembered endless nights of lovemaking beneath the stars. When renovating the motel, they'd built a cabin deep in the mountains, with more privacy for Zane's peace of mind, a generator and indoor plumbing for Tara's, and a huge skylight in the bedroom.

Give and take.

"Business is good," he remarked, staring over her shoulder at the registry. "Every cabin is full."

"I told you that last article would bring tourists." Tara had traded her journalistic aspirations to write nature and travel pieces for several national magazines that not only paid well, but had a positive effect on the economy of Bear Creek. After the hoopla surrounding Zane, Tara realized she didn't have the drive to follow in her parents' footsteps. She preferred happily-ever-afters and the simple joy of living each day with the man she loved.

She touched her hand to her stomach as the baby gave a vicious kick and a telltale spasm seized her.

"Maybe I should cancel the expedition tomorrow morning," he said. "And stay with you."

"You mean *us*." She turned misty eyes on Zane. "I think this bear's ready to growl one last time," she said, and then she kissed him.

Dear Reader:

I hope you enjoyed *Something Wild.* I've always been a huge fan of the old Tarzan movies. To me, Tarzan embodies all the qualities of a real hero: honor, courage, intelligence, a touch of danger and mystery, not to mention really great pecs and a body Hercules would kill for. It's no wonder the King of the Apes lives and breathes in the fantasies of thousands of women, myself included. I am grateful I had the chance to make Tara's fantasy come true. For when one woman finds love, it gives hope to us all!

I love hearing from my readers and can be reached at P.O. Box 1584, Pasadena, TX 77501-1584. Please enclose an SASE for a reply and an autographed bookmark. I wish you many hours of happy reading and lots of sizzling nighttime fantasies!

Sincerely,
Kimberly Raye

FRANKLY, MY DEAR...

SANDRA HILL

By the Bestselling Author of *The Tarnished Lady*

Selene has three great passions: men, food, and *Gone with the Wind*. But the glamorous model always found herself starving—for both nourishment and affection. Weary of the petty world of high fashion, she heads to New Orleans for one last job before she begins a new life. Then a voodoo spell sends her back to the days of opulent balls and vixenish belles like Scarlet O'Hara.

Charmed by the Old South, Selene can't get her fill of gumbo, crayfish, beignets—or an alarmingly handsome planter. Dark and brooding, James Baptiste does not share Rhett Butler's cavalier spirit, and his bayou plantation is no Tara. But fiddle-dee-dee, Selene doesn't need her mammy to tell her the virile Creole is the only lover she ever gave a damn about. And with God as her witness, she vows never to go hungry or without the man she desires again.

_4042-5   **$5.50 US/$6.50 CAN**

Jade NORAH HESS

BESTSELLING AUTHOR OF
BLAZE

Kane Roemer heads up into the Wyoming mountains hell-bent on fulfilling his heart's desire. There the rugged horseman falls in love with a white stallion that has no equal anywhere in the West. But Kane has to use his considerable charms to gentle a beautiful spitfire who claims the animal as her own. Jade Farrow will be damned if she'll give up her beloved horse without a fight. But then a sudden blizzard traps Jade with her sworn enemy, and she discovers that the only way to true bliss is to rope, corral, and brand Kane with her unbridled passion.

___4310-6 $5.99 US/$6.99 CAN

FLAME
CONNIE MASON

"Each new Connie Mason book is a prize!"
—Heather Graham

When her brother is accused of murder, Ashley Webster heads west to clear his name. Although the proud Yankee is prepared to face any hardship on her journey to Fort Bridger, she is horrified to learn that single women aren't welcome on any wagon train. Desperate to cross the plains, Ashley decides to pay the first bachelor willing to pose as her husband. Then the fiery redhead comes across a former Johnny Reb in the St. Joe's jail, and she can't think of any man she'd rather marry in name only. But out on the rugged trail Tanner MacTavish quickly proves too intense, too virile, too dangerous for her peace of mind. And after Tanner steals a passionate kiss, Ashley knows that, even though the Civil War is over, a new battle is brewing—a battle for the heart that she may be only too happy to lose.

_4150-2 $5.99 US/$6.99 CAN